To a Fungus Unknown

Other books by William C. Tracy

The Dissolutionverse:
Novellas and Novelettes:
The Five Hive Plateau
Tuning the Symphony
Merchants and Maji
The Society of Two Houses
Journey to the Top of the Nether

The Dissolution Cycle:
The Seeds of Dissolution (Book I)
Facets of the Nether (Book II)
Fall of the Imperium (Book III)

Other Books:
Epic Fantasy:
Fruits of the Gods

Anthologies:
Distant Gardens
Farther Reefs
The World of Juno

Science Fiction
The Biomass Conflux
Of Mycelium and Men
Down Among the Mushrooms
To a Fungus Unknown

To a Fungus Unknown

BOOK 2 OF THE BIOMASS CONFLUX

William C. Tracy

Space Wizard Science Fantasy
Raleigh, NC
www.spacewizardsciencefantasy.com

Cover art by MoorBooks
Editing by Heather Tracy
Book Layout © 2015 BookDesignTemplates.com

To a Fungus Unknown/William C. Tracy.— 1st ed.
ISBN 978-1-960247-06-3

Author's website: www.williamctracy.com

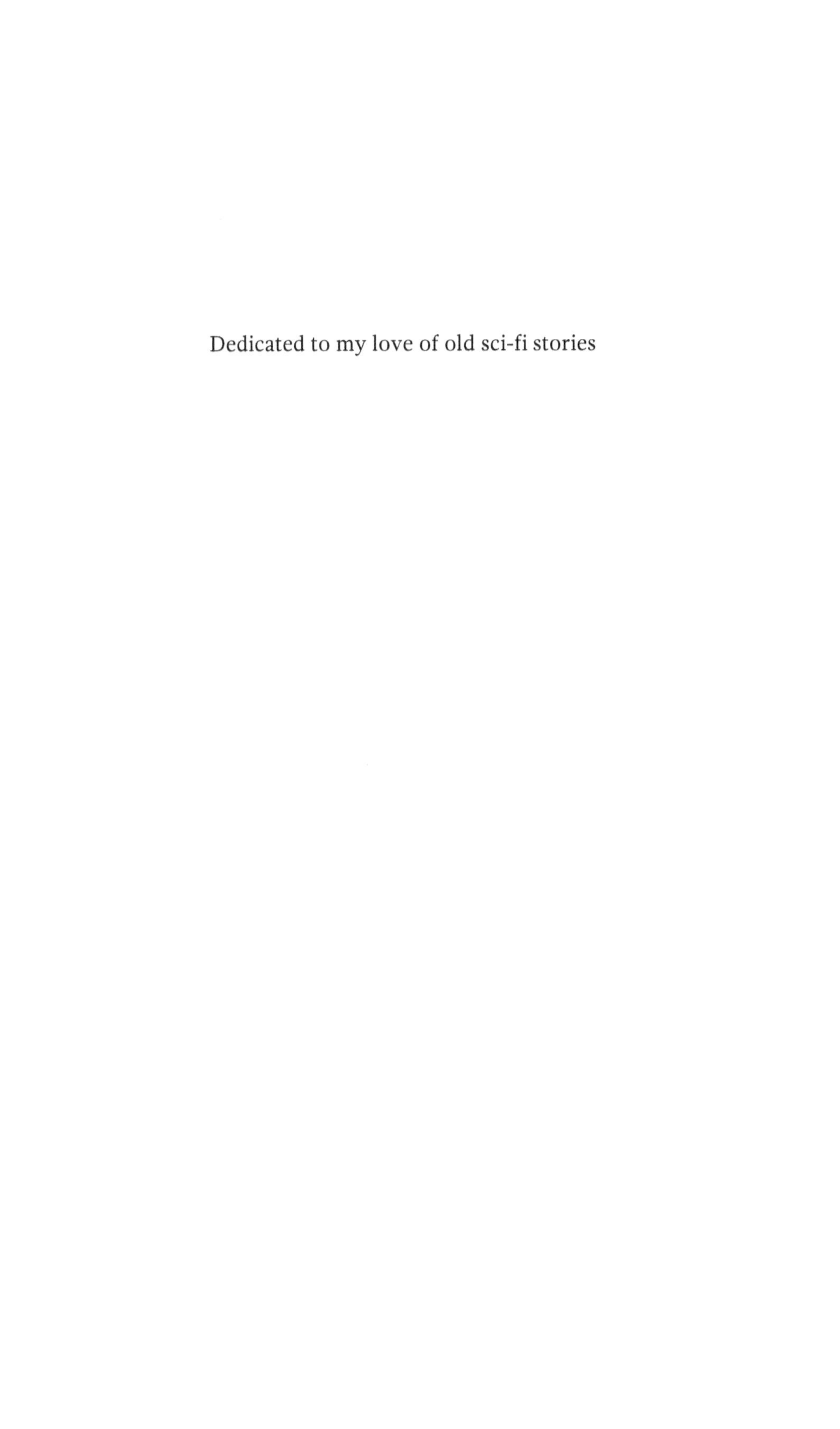

Dedicated to my love of old sci-fi stories

CONTENTS

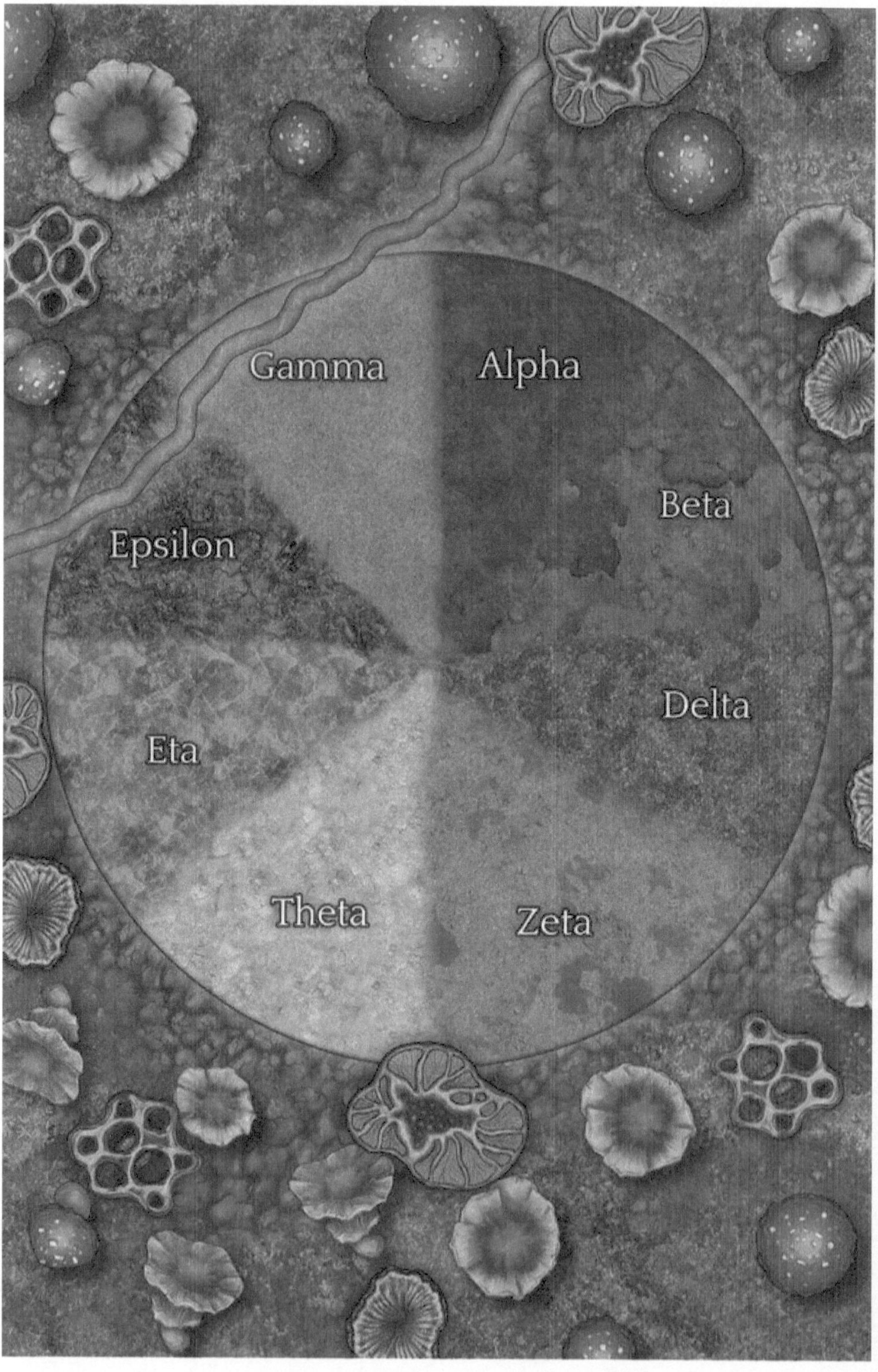

Gamma
Alpha
Beta
Epsilon
Delta
Eta
Theta
Zeta

A Timeline of Events

5.77 megaseconds (2 months, 2 weeks) before landing:

A fleet of eight generational ships from Earth arrives in their eleventh star system since beginning their journey. The system is categorized and named. The fourth planet, 11d (Lida) orbiting around 11 (Lev) is determined to be conducive to life, more than any other target so far.

The eight Admins are revived from sus-ani: Jane Brighton, Ahman Ragab, Dmitri Novikov, Xi Wenqing, Rajani Kumarisurajinder, Alessandro Giordano, Maria Gutiérrez Delgado, and Polunu Kim. They all have genemods from Earth that enable them to live for centuries.

Vagal supersoldiers re-engage the chain of command, causing conflict with the generational inhabitants of the fleet, who have been operating largely independently for four hundred years. The soldiers will live almost as long as the Admins, while the Generationals live more standard-length human lives.

There is a large amount of fungal biomass covering the planet, often to a depth of dozens of meters.

Landing to 6 weeks after landing:

The fleet glasses approximately a ten-kilometer diameter landing site near the equator of Lida. This is where they will begin constructing a city (labeled an arcopolis) from the ships of the fleet.

Meanwhile, the biomass of Lida, which is itself sentient, watches the events with curiosity. It labels the glassed area as the "Ring of Death" and the settlers as "The Children Who Ate Their Parents" (confusing the fleet ships for living beings).

Thirteen days after landing, an instability in the UGS Khonsu during deconstruction leads to a catastrophic collapse of the ship skeleton and the loss of twenty-three Vagals and fifty-eight Generationals. It also opens a crack in the ground, leading to the discovery of a cavern under the glassed site still containing biomass material. It turns out to be deadly to the Vagals who investigate. One of them, Anderson, loses a hand to fungal infection.

More caverns are discovered, and preliminary investigation into the nearby river and biomass at the edge of the glassed site leads Frank Silver, a Generational, to the revelation that the biomass covering the planet is one individual entity, with expressions of animal, plant, and fungal cell material. It is not suspected to be sentient, merely very well adapted to living on Lida.

6 weeks to 1 year after landing:

The biomass begins actively observing the humans who have landed, attempting to categorize them. Meanwhile the colonists find many of their animal species are dying from fungal infections and plant species are being changed by the biomass into unusable crops. The colonists heavily cull their agriculture to keep the most successful species alive.

The Admins try to find ways of killing the biomass, with little success. They also determine there is a severe lack of metals on Lida, likely because much of them are held within biomass structures. Admin Jane Brighton decides to use much of their remaining nanotanium metal from the fleet to start construction on a wall that will encircle the first two Radians of the colony—Alpha and Beta. This will keep out the worst invasions of the fast-growing biomass. The colony had been projected to take ten years to complete all eight radians. That timeline is now uncertain.

One of the colonists, Jiow, begins to meet a group that is unhappy about the direction Admin is taking on the colony and wants to secure more supplies for the Generationals.

Agetha Xenakis is called to where her husband, Daved Xenakis, has fallen into a deep shaft under the colony, containing one of the only sources of metal found. While he recovers, he dreams of the moss and tiny creatures he landed on at the bottom of the cave.

Seven months after landing, the decanting tubes are restarted to begin growing children for the colony. Many colonists begin families, and Agetha and Daved are given a top spot due to his injuries and his discovery of metals.

Meanwhile, the Admins plan construction of the next Radians using the new metals, but determine they must find another source of building material.

1 year to 5 years after landing:

The biomass continues to make advances against the colony, while the Generationals construct the colony and the Vagals battle against biomass incursions. Frank discovers that the biomass has already hybridized with the local honeybees. Even worse, it is already intrinsic to the colony, and the best they can do is hope to live with it.

While tensions mount between the Generationals and the Admins, Agetha and Daved welcome their new child, but their happiness is short-lived, as Daved collapses soon after. Doctors find his body has been overrun by fungal strands, and he succumbs soon after.

Jiow also has a child by herself, though with genetic material donated by Frank. As the two children grow and Agetha and Jiow help each other in child-rearing, Admin develops plans to limit the Generational's influence in the arcopolis, while developing a new building material.

Frank, along with some other scientists, develop resinplast—a byproduct of biomass material—but they have problems in turning off the biomass' rampant reproduction. After several years, they finally discover a way to suppress the viral communication in the biomass, rendering the resinplast useable.

Agetha, like most Generationals, is hard at work leading a construction crew, but this affects her ability to raise Phillipe, her child. Jiow takes up the slack with her child, Choi, but Agetha's relationship with Phillipe suffers.

Jiow takes part in raids on the colony supplies, culminating in an attempt to steal rumored nuclear weapons. The rumors are false, several Generationals are captured, and later they are forced out into the biomass—a death sentence.

Anderson discovers a full life in the arcopolis, especially in the new Beta Radian market, where he begins to write stories, prompted by a mentor.

The colony draws inward, reducing their ventures out into the biomass as Beta Radian is finally completed after five years.

5 years to 20 years after landing:

The next generation of the colony, nicknamed "Grounders," begins to grow. The Admins, led by Jane, begin to plan for when the Generationals are all gone. They look to the future, while the Generationals and Grounders are living their lives. Admin gradually forces the Generationals out into each newly completed Radian, Gamma at ten years, then Delta at fifteen, leaving the first radians for the Admins and their Vagal soldiers.

As Choi and Phillipe grow, they adapt to life in the colony. Many of the oldest Generationals are dying off, or sometimes just disappearing— as Admin secretly sends troublemakers out into the biomass.

Anderson settles down, becoming an established writer as well as leading Vagal soldiers. There have been heavy casualties, and only a fraction of their number is left.

Agetha pours herself into her work, to the point where her son leaves home as soon as he can, to join a new Grounder recruitment to shore up the number of Vagals.

Jiow avoids being captured after the attempt to steal nukes, and keeps her head low, going about her life.

Frank meanwhile keeps working on the resinplast formula. They have a building material, but it is only a matter of time until the biomass adapts to it, as it has to every other attempt to keep it out of the colony.

Finally, the biomass watches and observes. It takes in those Admin has sent out into the biomass, to try to understand how humans work. There are many failed attempts, but it learns more each time.

Almost Complete

40 years after landing

Observations on the Children Who Ate Their Parents:

These lifeforms have six main forms of presentation. The first, elite form spends most time in the shells created for protection from weather conditions. Rarely seen. Likely responsible for higher-functioning and strategy. Often has a coterie of support drones when traveling. More research is needed on this form, as even forty planetary rotations have not yielded their full purpose within the Children.

Agetha placed the last of her long-sleeved wool sweaters in the cargo crate. She'd collected them over the years from some of the best weavers at the arcopolis markets.

"Have you got all the cookware?" she called down the hall to Beth. She eyed the blue line on the wall, as if the direction indicator would answer her. They'd had to paint the lines when they moved in, as Admin certainly hadn't planned for ship-based orientation pathways in the housing on Lida.

"Almost," Beth's voice wafted back. It was a rich, firm voice. Curt when explaining, warm when speaking to a loved one. Agetha's wife was just as annoyed as she was to be moving, again, at their age. They had thought the apartment in Zeta Radian would be the last place they lived. "Just got to stack all these damn pans together. Are you certain you really need the zero-G covered pots?"

Agetha tried to answer, but her throat closed before she could get a word out. Fucking menopause. Shouldn't she be done with this by now? The zero-G pans were the only reminder she'd let herself keep of Daved, her first spouse. He'd died, a victim of the biomass that defined their life on Lida. It had been nearly forty years ago, soon after they landed. And after her child wanted to have nothing to do with her, she'd been nearly alone for the next thirty years. Until she met Beth.

"Agetha?"

"Keep them," she croaked out.

Beth's face appeared around the doorway after a few seconds, mahogany skin to Agetha's oak, braids fastened with metal bands clinking together as she moved.

"You alright, love?" She was holding one of the damnable pans—the Dutch oven, the one with the scratch by the venting spout where Daved had dropped it soon after they landed. He'd been so used to letting it hang in the air on the ship while he was cooking.

"Just...remembering."

"We'll make new memories in the apartment in Eta Radian," Beth said, but it was one of the doctor things she said. Agetha could see the anger in her face, though she tried to hide it.

"Just like we did here in Zeta, and like you and I did when we lived in Delta, and when we first landed in Alpha? How many times is Admin going to force us out? Once Theta's complete they'll force us out there, too. And then to whatever arcopolis they start building next, if we're still alive by then." She waved a hand. "Sorry. I don't mean to rehash."

Beth set the pot down on their bed. "Love, no one likes moving, and Admin's full of their own egotism. But they say it's for the good of the colony. Give the Grounders their space to grow, create, and build the next generation. We're in our sixties."

"I built this apartment *myself*," Agetha said, touching one of the resinplast walls with a fingertip. "As a place where we could grow old together, and it's only been ten years."

"Come on," Beth said, wrapping an arm around her. "You also destroyed half the block while you were building it, if I remember correctly. It's just resinplast. We'll have all our things, and Harie's coming by later to help us load up the garden pots."

Harie had been more of a son to her than her biological son, first a member of her construction crew, then her foreman, then the leader of the crew when Agetha had been forced to retire. That last had been when the biomass evolved to use plant reproduction in addition to its usual methods. They had nearly lost the city, and would have, if Beth's mycophage hadn't put a stop to the biomass' surge.

Beth's original unstable mycophage had enraged the Admins so much they banished her to a hospital in Zeta Radian, back when that had been the one under construction.

Agetha touched her wife's cheek. "I would never have met you if that seed pod hadn't shot through my hand."

Beth reached up to clasp her fingers. "This hand. Seems to be working well now, or does it need some exercise to check your dexterity?" She waggled her eyebrows.

"You're all dusty from packing," Agetha said. "I don't think much of your medical standards."

Beth kissed her palm. "Only part of me is dusty."

Agetha leaned in for a real kiss. "I guess you're right. Must be those medical standards."

Then she sighed. Beth was only working two days a week at her medical practice now, barring the random neighbor with an injury. She'd turned back to her first love—bioorganics. Beth's mycophage had suppressed the floral expressions of the biomass' DNA, at least around the city, and her solution—given anonymously to Admin—now coated the walls of the arcopolis. The years since had been quieter, with biomass incursions much rarer than they had been the previous thirty years. It had given the city a chance to develop, for good or bad.

"What is it, really?" Beth asked. "I know moving's a bitch, but we've got almost everything packed up now. Just have to get to the new apartment in Zeta."

Agetha leaned against her wife. "I know. I just...want it to stop at some point. Things are so much different than when we landed. The new buildings in Eta and Theta use those strange, twisty blueprints. Harie's more of a gardener than a builder now. The houses are all packed together. My knees won't survive more stairs."

"But most of your body parts still work decently well, as do mine," Beth said, waggling a calf back and forth. "The older Generationals are mostly in mobility devices, or prone. You wouldn't believe how many I've seen come through the office who can barely raise their heads. Bedridden and dependent on others to help them out. At least we were still pretty young when we left the ships. Try being a fifty-year-old in zero-G and *then* live in a gravity well for another forty years."

"It would be nice if more of the Grounders helped out their elders," Agetha said. "Harie comes by, but I practically raised him." Unlike her biological son. Her jaw clenched and she pushed the memory away. "Ugh. I sound like an old lady. But I haven't seen Choi or Frank for ages, not since Jiow walked out into the biomass."

"It was her choice," Beth said. "And with as far along as the cancer was, I don't entirely blame her. We can only hope the biomass ate her cancer along with her and choked on it." She opened her arms.

Agetha rubbed her face and melted into Beth's hug. "Let's finish packing," she said into her wife's shoulder. "The faster we get out of this house, the less I'll have to think about it."

* * *

40 years 2 months after landing

Juliane rubbed his nose. It had that drippy, weepy feeling that meant he was going to have another day of allergies, or some virus from the biomass. Maybe it was just a big weather change, though Admin insisted they lived in the most temperate part of Lida. Most people in the arcopolis didn't have allergies, Father Kofus had told him. Just like all the other children, he'd been genetically screened before gestating in the decanting tubes, but something had changed after he was about eight years old. His older sister and sibling didn't get sick all the time. Why did he?

He pulled out one of the alpaca-wool handkerchiefs habitually stuffed into his pockets and blew his nose, then sniffed. He'd be blowing it the whole day until his nose went red. Speaking of red. He looked down into the handkerchief, then pressed it back against his nose. Another nosebleed. That was two this week already. Father Alvin would be wringing his hands with worry the next time Juliane showed up at their house with his laundry. Maybe he'd learn how to do his own this time. Probably not.

He kept walking along the Alpha Radian streets, behind a crowd of heads covered with wool hats. Always covering one's head had become the fad lately, which was fitting at least in the rainy season. He was already late for work in the Alpha food distribution center, where he served as a recorder for their inventory management system. It was a boring job, but a cushy one. Father Alvin had pulled strings to get him something in Alpha, and far away from the biomass. His fathers had finally moved out to Delta a few years ago due to mounting pressure from Admin. They had been one of the last Generational families allowed in Alpha Radian. His sister had taken over their cozy little apartment to raise her own children with her wife. His other sibling looked to be settling down with a poly group finally, and here he was, wiping blood off his nose in the misty morning.

His hand shook as he finally took the handkerchief from his nose. Another tremor. This was a new development, and he felt like he should be more concerned about it, but...he wasn't. He had a hard time focusing on his allergies when they weren't directly affecting him. He watched his fingers spasm, almost dropping the handkerchief before compulsively gripping it, smearing fresh blood on his fingers. His left leg almost buckled under him and he leaned against the steelcrete side of one of the city center records buildings. Passersby gave him a glance, but no more. They were almost all Grounders like him, mostly first and a few of the young second generation with their parents or running errands. Here and there was an older Generational, none under fifty years old and most nearing seventy. Juliane caught sight of a handsome young Vagal with a mechanical hand trailing three grounders. A true Vagal was a rare sight, though more common in Alpha than the other radians. They were easy to identify because of their youthful appearance, even forty years after landing, and because of their confident swagger. He'd seen this Vagal several times before, on his way out to Beta Radian. Most of the defensive core that kept biomass from entering the arcopolis was now first-generation Grounders, with the remaining Vagals all in positions of leadership.

He sighed and tried to push away from the wall. His feet refused to budge and Juliane almost toppled over, just managing to catch his balance and hide his surprise. The twitches had never been this bad before.

He looked up and over the towering nanotanium wall separating Alpha Radian from the crawling vines and mycelial mats of the biomass. He could just see the tips of the tallest fungal towers, standing a hundred meters high or more, out past the wall. Out there, chaotic creatures roamed over the mossy mat at ground level, the mobile creations of mushrooms that acted as defense systems of the biomass. All children took at least one field trip into the terrifying jungle of fleshy growth outside the wall. There was a relatively defanged section near one of the doors in the Alpha wall. Juliane had taken his one trip and promised never to go out there again, which Father Alvin had firmly agreed with.

He thought Father Kofus might have disapproved, but he never said a contradictory word in front of Father Alvin.

His entry to the inventory recording warehouse was getting later by the second.

"Come on," he muttered to his feet, as if they would hear him and obey. They did not.

He was pressed to the wall as if loitering there, but his legs refused to walk the extra block to his office. He should have been petrified, but he'd had a few twitches like this over the last few weeks. They were just temporary. Just an effect of his allergies. He strained again to come off the wall, like he was fighting against someone holding his legs. Juliane gritted his teeth and clenched his abdomen.

"Get. Off. This. Wall." He forced every word through his teeth, but was rewarded only with a fit of coughing. He pressed the handkerchief back to his mouth and nose, trying not to spray Grounders with mucus and blood.

It was a full two minutes before he collapsed back, panting, his legs still locked in place. He pressed a hand to his chest, and his fingers traced a hard lump under his skin. A spasming muscle? Had he coughed a rib out of place?

His gaze wandered to the place he worked, counting the seconds he was already late. What had he been thinking about?

His hand was still on his chest. Funny that. There was a—

He really must get to work or Janut, his supervisor, would have words for him.

Juliane nearly collapsed as his legs loosened, doing a little waltz to keep him steady. His hand stuffed the abused handkerchief into his pocket almost of its own volition. He jerked forward, as if on strings, trotting the wrong way along the nanotanium street, nearly colliding with a person riding a motorized bicycle.

"The other way." He'd felt this strange loss of control one other time he'd had these twitches, almost like someone else was driving his body. But that was ridiculous. It was just allergies. He turned his feet back the correct direction with a sigh, only ten minutes late to work this morning.

He felt like he should have been more concerned with his allergies, his twitches, his nosebleeds. But he simply couldn't focus on them most of the time. They faded into the background so quickly when they weren't right in front of his face, like he just couldn't keep them in his head. They must not be such a problem if that was the case. He hadn't even bothered to tell a doctor. Only allergies, really.

Juliane continued his walk to work.

* * *

40 years 3 months after landing

Choi pulled their goggles down to peer into the resinplast circuits in the printer.

"Frank? Did you get this latest readout?" They looked up when their uncle didn't immediately answer. The older man was staring at nothing, likely doing something on his HUD. The devices were few and far between these days, heavily repaired and modified. Frank was working on a replacement using resinplast parts, but wouldn't let Choi help with the project, saying they had too much to do with the programmable resinplast project to also work with the HUDs.

"Uncle Frank." The older man shook himself and focused on Choi.

"The what now?"

"The readout I sent you from the printer. It keeps throwing an error when printing the latest seed design. Admin's breathing down my neck to get more programmable resinplast out the building sites. We're never going to complete the latest updates to the building models if the printer doesn't do what it's supposed to."

Frank's eyes went distant again and he leaned back in his chair. Choi stretched and cracked their neck, blinking in the harsh light reflecting off the nanotanium walls. They were more used to the rare alloy than the steelcrete and resinplast of the other radians, after twelve years of working full time with their uncle. The two of them were the main research team on developing new resinplast solutions, and Choi wouldn't trade it for anything.

"Hm. The chemical receptors aren't responding to the new viral commands," Frank said. "Something's interfering with the co-opted reproduction commands, which means the new form we want the resinplast to take isn't happening."

"That's the same problem I fixed last time," Choi answered. "It's like the feed material isn't receiving our hijacked viruses anymore. Like it's reverting back to the original biomass' growth instructions."

"The resinplast has been stable since Dr. Harley's mycophage barrier was perfected," Frank countered. "If the biomass finally evolved around it, that's bigger news than we want. The new growth in Eta and Theta could be compromised."

Choi let their arms dangle by their sides, deflating. "If the structure has evolved past the latest stopgaps, that's at least another year of research before we're back on task. Eta Radian's taken almost ten years to grow, and Theta is just getting started. We still have over half the buildings to print seeds for. Admin won't wait much longer. They only barely agreed to the new growth timeframe because we *promised* nothing would go wrong with this method."

"Shortsighted of us, wasn't it," Frank said. He cut Choi's next words off before they formed. "Almost like one of us was desperate to get this thing into production because of the potential benefits."

"I was ready to take another year for development," Choi protested.

"I didn't say it was you," Frank chuckled. Then he sighed. "Programmable biomass. Now the one ore vein under the city is exhausted, it's the holy grail on a planet with no nearby sources of metal in the crust—at least not close enough for us to get them without getting eaten by the biomass."

"Well, this holy grail needs some adjustment, and I'm not sure where. Whatever is interfering with the viral commands is sneaky," Choi said. "I'll keep tracking down the source. If I can determine how the biomass is working around the co-opted signals, it could save us years of setbacks."

"Good luck. The original resinplast took five years to get right, and then we had to keep adjusting it. You've only been at this programmable stuff for four."

Choi tapped the air in front of their HUD. "There are a finite number of ways for the biomass to interfere in the process. It's not like it has purposeful direction. I'll find the cause soon enough, or Admin will have our heads." They bent back to their work.

* * *

40 years 3 months 3 days after landing

Over the next three days, Choi tried every workaround they could find to make the printer spit out the correct seed template. They were working on a new residential section for Theta, and needed a new row of apartments. Frank offered suggestions, but was largely tied up in the final revisions to the new HUDs, which were slated to go to Admin and the Vagals next week.

"It's not even printing the test seed any longer," Choi said, holding out a misshapen mess to Frank. When first creating the resinplast, their uncle had discovered how to co-opt the viral information the biomass used to communicate between the animal, plant, and fungal sections of its DNA. For the programmable seeds, Choi had added new commands to the viruses rather than just stop their communication.

Programmable biomass had such utility that they could hijack the original viral propagation methods in order to propagate forms they preferred over the chaos of the biomass. There were so many patterns encoded into the biomass DNA, Choi had their pick of structural elements and supports, many coming from the fungal towers. It all hinged on their discovery of a "control" virus that directed where and how the other viruses traveled. They were the basis of communication in the biomass DNA, like cell-surface receptors were in humans. Except there were *also* cell-surface receptors in the plant, animal, and fungal cell-types contained in the biomass. It was another layer of complexity tying the complex organism together.

The biomass was *one* organism, spanning the entire planet. The theory was that it had subsumed many other species that once existed here, and the final product expressed features from many of those now-dead species. It was what made the biomass so deadly, but also so useful.

Thankfully, while it had taken some plant and animal genes into it, humans seemed resilient, which Frank insisted stemmed from their extra-solar ancestry, and the genetic drift humans had accumulated on their four-hundred-year voyage to Lida. The Admins and Vagals were unchanged as well, but that was likely due to the genemods they'd received before leaving old Earth.

"Have you changed out the processing board? They get old after a while," Frank suggested, still staring off into space, testing the new HUD.

"Twice," Choi answered. "From unrelated stock. The second time I ran an extra purification and cell burn cycle, and didn't even load more than the test program. It's still reverting back to...this." They hefted the mass of hyphal strands and chaotic mycelium clusters. It looked like a dug-up mushroom bed.

Frank's gaze shifted from his HUD to what Choi was holding. He sat up suddenly. "That looks like a native biomass node."

"Could be?" Choi hadn't seen virgin biomass in a few years. Not many had. Admin Kumarisurajinder had samples brought in on a bi-annual basis, to make sure there were no more unprecedented evolutions like the Flowering episode that happened ten years ago. But most of those samples went to the pure science and biology departments, not to the practical section where they and Frank worked.

"Bring the damn thing here." Frank pushed his HUD back and gestured. When Choi put the misshapen seed on the desk, Frank bent his head until his nose almost touched the thing. Choi waited, frowning.

"Don't like it," Frank finally said. "Throw it in the incubator, and see what it grows, if anything. Meanwhile, I want a full reconstruction of the printer. Use one of the prototypes in storage and bring it up to current specs."

Choi raised their eyebrows. "That will take—"

"I know how long it'll take," Frank snapped. "Just get the fucking prototype."

Choi nodded and scurried to the storage room. Something was worrying their uncle a lot—enough to throw a two-week delay into their schedule on a hunch.

A printed seed could be placed in the right foundation and grow into an apartment, a wall segment, a depot, a warehouse, or anything in between. But they had only programmed a small selection of buildings so far into the viral code. Half of Theta was still incomplete.

If Choi could just get the resinplast to cooperate, large-scale building techniques could be applied to small-scale tools. Putting together a forklift from parts was tedious. Growing the entire chassis from a custom printed seed was the goal. As long as the biomass didn't evolve out from under them.

If this affected the rest of Theta, the last section of the arcopolis, or even delayed the opening of Eta Radian again, Admin was going to blow a collective fuse. The whole city had been scheduled for completion in ten years after landing, when Choi would have been eight and a half. They were nearing forty, and only seven of the eight pie pieces were near completion.

* * *

40 years 4 months after landing

Jane Brighton accepted the report her secretary Christiaan flipped to her HUD. Ahman Ragab—the Administrator for transportation, R&D, and their school system—had recently taken on the role of mapping new portions of the biomass with recent additions to their drone fleet. Their R&D department had some creative uses for the resinplast they were forced to use instead of metals. For the first time in over forty years, not all of their resources were turned to construction of the arcopolis. Soon Eta Radian would be complete, and the rest of Theta would be well underway. They could begin turning their attentions outside of the arcopolis.

"Thank you, dear," she told her secretary. "By the way, Yana said she isn't coming to eat tonight, but Ivan is. Something about a big project for the food science sector." Christiaan would have to leave soon to pick up their latest set of twins, Besh and Ovia, from the care center, while their middle set—the twelve-year-olds, Micai and Flalia—were staying with Dmitri Novikov's kids tonight in the power management and tech Admin's house.

She looked through a screen of dense information. "Now, what is this report?"

"Ahman has several square kilometers mapped out on all sides of the city, Jane," Christiaan replied. "And Ivan already told me what his sister was doing. I've updated the dinner menu." It had taken twenty years of sleeping together and their first set of children before they dropped the 'ma'am' every time they spoke to her. It was mildly infuriating that they'd only replaced it with her name. It made them sound overly concerned.

She flipped through the report, stopping twice in the middle to tap her HUD, getting it to reconnect to the network. She couldn't wait until the new versions were ready. Her HUD had been replaced so many times it was just a collection of bandages.

Aha. She narrowed in on survey results in the middle of the report. That was why Christiaan was hovering like a nervous hen.

"The shallowest biomass is on the other side of arcopolis, is it?" The reverse had been true when they landed, but it was unsurprising, given how fast the tangle of fungus grew. "This will restrict our options for the proposed road to the site of the next arcopolis, wherever that may be."

They hadn't picked a final placement, but it wasn't like they were running out of time. She, Christiaan, Ahman, Dmitri, and all the other Admins with genemods from back on Earth would live another three hundred years or more. The Vagals who had survived would live nearly as long. It was the blessing that allowed them to direct the long-term survival of the colony, until they could replicate the same sort of life-extension technology that would enable their tiny settlement to truly take over Lida and make it theirs. Jane could remember the towering buildings of New York, at least before tidal waves had taken many of them out. No problem with that here, though such buildings might be overrun with biomass if they weren't careful.

"It means any commerce must go through Eta and Theta, artificially bolstering that side of the arcopolis, Jane. I've run analyses on moving the Admin buildings to another—"

Jane waved them away. "We're not moving out of these buildings. By the time we have a big enough second city to contribute to commerce, the Generationals will be long gone, as will the first generation of Grounders." The Generational population was down more than fifty percent from the original landing contingent, but replaced twice over by Grounders. "If you're assuming there will be a power struggle, don't worry your pretty head. You and I are staying firmly at the top, as are the children."

They had a plan, after all. Two children every ten years. And because Jane had chosen to partner with one who also had the Admin genemods, time was barely a factor. Not like poor Ahman. They were devoted to their wife, but she was nearing ninety. Fortunately, the decanting tubes they used to gestate meant there were no body issues with pregnancy such as menopause, or not having a uterus in the first place. Jane could better direct her energies to making the colony succeed, and Ahman could continue to make children with their wife's DNA after she was gone, if they chose. It wasn't often practiced, but the two were devoted to each other.

Christiaan only nodded, though the glint in their eye meant their train of thought paralleled hers. They were the best secretary or subordinate she could have asked for, but they were also conniving, manipulative, and self-serving. It was why they got along so well together.

Jane turned back to the report, skimming over more subs-sections and a few of the summaries. The thing was over three hundred pages long. The drones had classified several new subspecies in the biomass, some mobile and some not, many displaying characteristics of the plants and animals they had brought from Earth. There were several new and disturbing types of traps and dangers too, from pools of acid, to elaborate vices that slowly constricted around prey, spines digging deeper into the victim as it struggled. If they had this information when they landed, they could have saved hundreds of Vagal lives. Or at least some of them.

Ahman had been busy the last few years. She hadn't actually talked to them since the yearly Admin meeting, four months ago.

"How is the mineral reclamation program going?" she asked Christiaan.

"Well enough." They sighed to let her know "well enough" wasn't up to their standards. "We've found no other significant veins of ore in this area past the one we found right after landing." The one that had been revealed by the Khonsu accident that killed twenty-three Vagals and somewhere over twice that amount of Generationals.

"Naturally the easy option isn't the one available," Jane said. "And collections from the biomass? Surely we have some stored up by now."

They'd discovered over the years that the biomass was the likely culprit for the lack of minerals close to the surface of Lida. The fungal towers that reached hundreds of meters in the air had structural elements of iron, aluminum, and copper. There was some sort of natural refining going on in the extremely advanced evolution of the biomass.

"We've managed to gather several hundred kilograms of iron from the fungal pulp used for printing, Jane," Christiaan said. "The issue is that it's contaminated with particles of the biomass and burning the impurities out creates too high of a carbon concentration. The copper reserves are better, which is helping to replace some of our electronic components, but getting enough material for structural elements is on a completely different scale. We barely have enough to add to large-scale resinplast prints like new digging equipment."

"Which we need if we want to create a road through this goddamned thicket surrounding us," Jane finished for them. "Fuck me if I don't want to just burn the entire planet down to the ground some days. I'd do it, too, if I thought the fungus would stay lit long enough for the fire to catch. Give me a strong enough torch and I'll fix all our problems."

"While I agree in principle, Jane, collecting base metals is our best option, unless there is some new development," Christiaan said. "At current estimates, we can build the core building of a new city out of biomass-resistant metals in another ten years, at the current rate."

"That should give us long enough to figure out how to get there," Jane sighed. That was the next hurdle. Once the city was complete, they'd have to engage with the biomass directly, something they hadn't done since landing.

"Tell Ahman to keep mapping," she said. "We should decide the direction of the second arcopolis at the next yearly meeting."

Christiaan nodded, and left Jane to her thoughts.

* * *

40 years 5 months after landing

"What do you think of that one?" Harie asked his new intern Clarine, a tanned and lanky second-generation with the robust melanin distribution favored by many Grounders when selecting traits for their children. The sun was a constant presence in the equatorial regions of Lida, though it rained enough to keep drought from affecting the gardens too much.

"Looks fun!" Clarine said. She ducked her head to peer through one of the low windows, covered with a transparent membrane. "See how that stair twists all the way around the perimeter?"

Harie routinely noted places in the Eta Radian where errant fungal branches needed to be trimmed from the new self-growing construction. The house he pointed to was growing in the wrong direction. He'd been planning to assign it to be torn out and started again, which meant it wouldn't be ready for the opening ceremonies. Instead, he made a note on his tablet to ask if any Grounders wanted to live in an experimental house that twisted through two hundred degrees of rotation between the first and second stories. This was one of the older seeds, close to four years into its growth, and the first generation was prone to errors. The later ones were much more regular, but his last shipment had been delayed by two months already.

"Hm." Harie made another note to try the house on Grounder families with young children. Clarine was all of fifteen, if not younger. Harie's poly group was debating over three or four children in total—six parents was more than enough to let Harie focus on his work while they were growing. He still wasn't sold on his role as a new father, but three of the group had already moved work schedules around. Plenty of time to get in practice with Clarine.

He pointed to another row of apartments, growing above a bank of storefronts. The second story had been started directly on the first, and the overlap between the two seeds had produced some unwanted transition elements. "What about that one?"

Now Clarine frowned. "How deep does that fissure go, there?" She pointed a thin brown finger at a deep crack between the lower and upper stories.

"Good catch," Harie said. "Though it's not as bad as it looks. Throw some filler in the hole, and as long as it doesn't buckle the ceiling or floor too much, no one will notice. The mesh is surprisingly stable." He pointed a little farther down the transition. "This is what you have to look out for."

"That little bump?" Clarine wrinkled her nose in an endearing way and Harie smiled.

"Yep. Sometimes those bumps hide voids that can be as big as a meter across. The programmable biomass is far from perfect, but it does save a lot of construction time. I used to lead five teams of twenty. Now there are less than twenty people looking after all of Eta. We're more sculptors than a construction crew."

"Are the rest working on Theta?" Clarine asked.

"Not as many as you'd think." Harie kept walking, his eye roving over the apartment. He'd learned to recognize common problems in the four years as the back half of Eta was grown from woody seeds bigger than his two fists together. Agetha had turned her nose up at them when he showed her the first one, but her wife Beth had asked him questions about it for half an hour.

"Most of the old construction crews have been finding new jobs in repair or reconstruction in the finished radians, and there are only a couple crews' worth planting the first seeds in Theta. We're still waiting on some promised construction forms to implement the center radian administrative complex. Those are the only ones still to use metal construction."

"And Theta will take another *ten* years to finish? Admin is okay with that?"

Harie tried to think in years like Clarine would. It was a good portion of her life. No telling what position she'd be in when the radian was finished. "Once the scientists demonstrated the stability of the structures, especially to biomass incursions, they leapt on the idea. I don't think an extra five, or even ten years, really meant that much to them, or the Vagals."

"Have you seen one of *them* before?" Clarine's green eyes were wide-eyed in awe. Harie chuckled.

"I have. I've even spoken to Admins Ragab and Kumarisurajinder a few times." He didn't think Clarine's eyes could get any bigger. "Of course, that was when I was young, before they started staying in the center Alpha complex all the time."

"Do you think they really watch us, like the other kids say?"

It was a popular theory, even with some adults, that the Admins sat in their administrative tower, twenty stories high, and peered through drones or telescopes at the citizens of the arcopolis. Almost all interactions over the last twenty years had been through children of the Admins, many of whom were older than Harie, but still looked like they were in their early twenties. Even most of the Vagal patrols were teams of trained Grounders.

"They only watch kids who get reported by their team leaders," Harie said, then made a very obvious note on his tablet. He heard Clarine's gasp before he looked up with a smile.

"Don't *do* that!"

Harie laughed. "I'm sure they won't look too closely at your test scores. Now, tell me what you can see in this next row of houses."

While Clarine rattled off what she saw, Harie glanced to the wall separating this radian from the biomass. It was still growing, only as high as his chest, and didn't obscure the writhing mass of growth, five or six times taller than he was. It was closer to the wall near Eta, more wild and untamed than the sections by Alpha and Beta. Back when he was leading a team under Agetha, they didn't go anywhere near the new biomass growth. One false step and your leg was being chewed off by a mushroom with teeth, or a woody projectile was shot through your head, or you started dissolving in acid.

These days, the biomass seemed quiescent, like it had determined they weren't a threat. Clarine and her peers had it easy. The second generation of Grounders didn't have to deal with nearly as many lost parents and workplace accidents as when the first half of the arcopolis was still being built. Ever since the programmable biomass had been introduced, incursions around the Eta wall dropped off. It made Harie uneasy, but at least it gave him more freedom to tend the new houses. Just two more years and the first of the seeds would near completion. His job would change to interior finishing to get them ready for habitation. If all went well and the delay got sorted out, they would plant the rest of the building in Theta over the next year, and in another eight or ten, this arcopolis would be complete. Harie would have a chance to take it easy with his family.

* * *

40 years 5 months 2 weeks after landing

Observations on the Children Who Ate Their Parents were continually collected. With over forty rotations of the planet on record, more patterns were emerging in how the different forms interacted with each other. The mobile signal carriers who had agreed to communications were an excellent source of information about the Children.

Even without full communications established with the Children, the newcomers had begun to copy local architecture and add pragmatic upgrades to benefit their continued existence. Memory nodes compared the new data to subsummations in the past. No others had shown the level of persistence and evolution as the Children. They would be a fascinating resource for further creation.

When experiments with communication had first yielded results, it was assumed total subsummation would soon take place. Yet then the Children had resisted the first attempts with the sixth forms to create a new union. More observation was advised.

Now, a new method had been determined. The Children had co-opted communication methods for their own, and that development could be replicated. Such ways had been discarded in the past in favor of more data in case of unforeseen contagions, but no longer. Efforts of communication would finally be realized, or else, the Children's incursion would be rendered for the last surprises it contained. There was reluctance as that objective was settled, yet unless changes propagated in the near future, it was certain that was the correct course of action.

Taking a Walk

40 years, 6 months after landing

Observations on the Children Who Ate Their Parents:

The second form of presentation seems to be a protective form. Perhaps due to lack of resources, this form is dwindling in numbers, and though members of the fourth form are attempting to recreate their aptitudes, the forced evolutionary convergence is faulty. The converted members do not share many of the pheromonal communication strategies or the deductive functioning of the original second form. There is potential for weakness in this transition which can be easily exploited.

Juliane clocked out of his job early in the afternoon, leaving a pile of reports as yet unprocessed in the food distribution inventory management system. It was the fourth time this month he'd clocked out early with no explanation. One more and his time credit ratio would be permanently docked.

Yet Juliane left. He knew there were consequences, yet it was also hard to care. The consequences went to the back of his mind, and from there, were forgotten. For the past several months he'd been constantly sick, dribbly and congested with some new allergy. He'd asked around to see if a new plant stock had been introduced from the old ship genebank, but nothing new had been introduced in years, out of fear of how the biomass would contaminate the stock. There weren't many seeds left in the bank by now. Most everything that would fail had done so spectacularly in the first few years of the colony, before he'd been born. The plant varieties introduced after that point had their genome checked against the common ways the biomass co-opted them.

Maybe the biomass had found another way to alter one of the crops. It happened from time to time, but unless they turned into an aggressive form of flora, they were cleared for use. He'd heard the Vagals torched the entire crop of plantains, five years back, after the fruits started crawling out of the ripe peels and sucking people's blood.

Rather than going back to his own home, his feet turned to his parents' house. It was in Delta, quite a walk from where he worked in Alpha. But he'd left work early, hadn't he? He had some time to visit his fathers.

It was nearly an hour later when Father Alvin opened the door of their apartment.

"What a surprise! But Julie, you haven't walked all the way out here, have you? With your constitution?"

"I'm perfectly fine Dad," Juliane said, remembering why he didn't visit that often. "Just the normal allergies." And the bloody mucus and twitches, but he didn't mention those. He felt oddly present, for the first time in weeks. "Is Father around?"

"He's reading in the other room. Come say hello." Father Alvin led Juliane deeper into the apartment.

"Our errant son has deigned to visit." Alvin pecked his husband on the cheek as Father Kofus took off his HUD. "Didn't even bring his laundry this time."

"How's things, Jules?" Father Kofus enveloped him in a hug, and just for a moment, Juliane felt an *urge* to reach out...but then it was gone.

"I thought I'd drop by. No real reason, as it were. It's been simply ages since I visited, and I clocked off a little early today."

"Everything's going well at the inventory processing site though, isn't it? Had to pull a few strings to get you in there," Father Alvin said.

"Oh, just fine. Don't you worry. Maria says to say hello." That pacified the two, as he'd known it would. Maria was an old colleague of Father Alvin from the fleet days.

He stayed for a few minutes, idly chatting with his fathers about this and that, but he kept brushing that annoying feeling away. As if one motion would solve everything. Just one action.

But not to his fathers.

He left them debating whether to eat at a local Ship food restaurant or cook in that night, and continued walking. Juliane soon reached the edge of Delta, with no goal in sight. He simply wanted to go for a walk. Did he have enough time credits available to get all the way to Zeta? And why there? The thought tickled his brain, as if someone else was thinking it for him. Likely just an effect of the allergy. This was a strange one.

He scratched at his chest, at that strange lump which...

What was it, exactly, that made them all keep to their radians? The sections of the arcopolis had segregated over the years. Alpha Radian was for administrative buildings and the Vagal barracks, Beta was the entertainment and culture hub, Delta was for schooling, Gamma was industrial, and Epsilon through the forming Theta were for residential and families, along with a sprinkling of local shops and markets. Most of the remaining Generationals were out in Zeta and Eta, but each radian boasted their own market, with a collection of regional oddities.

Juliane's feet stepped around the nanotanium hub that marked the center of the circular city, where all radians touched. Vague surprise flashed through his thoughts that he was here already. How long had he been walking? A spike of pain shot through his left foot, and he doubled over...

At the center of all eight radians, there was a memorial in steelcrete to those who had died in the great Khonsu crash, just after landing. He stopped to gaze at it. He hadn't seen the monument in several years. Then he looked down with annoyance. Why did his foot hurt? Best to walk it out. It was getting late.

Since he was out, maybe he would go to Epsilon. The market there had a great selection of spices made from certain types of fungal tower fronds and one of the lichens that grew on their trunks.

But his feet turned toward Zeta. He scratched at his neck, suddenly itchy. There was a spot his fingers touched, raised and scaly, like...

When he looked at his arm, there were hives popping up along his skin, red against his olive tan skin. He should find a blocker to treat that. The hospital in Zeta was supposed to be quite good. Good thing that was the direction he was going.

But he didn't. The thought faded, like honey dissolving in water. The market. An *urge* to go there coursed through him, strong in his mind, though he hadn't the capacity to question it. One foot in front of the other, he passed along the kilometers of the arcopolis, feet sending spears of pain up his legs which he ignored, the sun slowly sinking in the sky. This near the equator of the planet, the days were roughly equal, though it was technically approaching winter. The Admins and Vagals thought that was a significant time of year, though crops could be planted here year-round. He didn't see the reason behind the mid-winter celebration.

The market would be open until late in any case. He *needed* to go there. But why? Really, now he thought of it, what reason could there be for him risking his job, his time credits, just to gallivant out to...

The fear and urgency faded from his mind. He still had those thoughts, but they just weren't that important. They passed through his mind, swimming under the imperative to get to the market. Some part of him, deep inside, was banging against a wall where answers were just out of reach on the other side.

And then...

That feeling, too, faded. Juliane felt at peace.

The market was bustling, even at this time of evening. His right hand was trembling, twitching uncontrollably, and he used his left to still it. Each step was an effort, as if a weight dragged him back, like someone *didn't* want him to be here. But why not? It was a beautiful evening, there was a wind coming over the wall bearing the fruity, musty scent of the biomass, and he could see an array of beautiful art made by the residents of Zeta Radian. A perfect day to be out.

He turned away from that table, the art no longer interesting him as he saw a booth filled with large, fresh, healthy-looking vegetables. But those too dropped out of his thoughts as his eyes met those of the Generational behind the table. There was no doubt she was one who had come with the fleet, her dark skin holding lines around her eyes, and white encroaching into the thick braids bound with metal ringlets.

Juliane's hand trembled again, epileptic, and he seized it with his other, forcing it to stop. Her eyes flashed down and she frowned, perhaps about to offer assistance, but he pressed both hands against the booth, hidden beneath the bounty of vegetables. He smiled.

"Amazing produce you have," he said.

"Thanks," the woman said. "I've worked on all these hybrids myself. They're the most resistant to biomass infection you'll find in the city."

"Exquisite," Juliane said, though he didn't mean it. His brain was pushing all the buttons for small talk, he realized, as he asked what exactly the Generational had done to make the produce more resistant. The realization was like a wind sifting through leaves—there, then gone. As she spoke, he inched closer, his legs moving with no thought from him, as if someone pushed each muscle individually, causing him to sidle around the booth.

He surprised himself by asking for more clarification on the protein molecules that went into the biological resistance. He'd heard those terms before, but didn't know what they meant. It was like his brain found terms in his memory and put them together without him having to do anything. It was almost pleasant.

As if in a fog, his body rounded the side of the booth. His left hand trembled whenever he removed his right from clamping it down, but that was acceptable. A newness was coming. A birth. A transfer. A decision.

He was finally close enough, though someone screamed deep in his mind where he couldn't hear, as his right hand pointed to a particularly large carrot, asking about the purple striated coloration. As the woman bent down to see where he pointed, his trembling, palsied, left hand came up and gently placed itself over the back of her neck.

The Generational jumped, then held strangely still for the assault. Juliane would have asked questions if he was capable.

After, there were no apologies. No excuses. No suspicions. They nodded to each other and there were no words, but a feeling of *complete* between them. The woman *felt* to him, like he heard the metallic braids in her hair clacking together, though they weren't moving.

Juliane turned away and walked out of the market, both hands steady at his sides.

* * *

40 years 6 months after landing

Lieutenant Anderson watched Grounders and the occasional Generational move past Sona V. Gore's booth at the Beta market. Anderson had published books under that name for over twenty years now, and he still thought of the booth as belonging to the old Generational. He'd never found out the man's real name, or what he did for the colony besides write. Some days he regretted that, but most of the time he didn't. The mystery sparked him to write, to discover the unknown.

Anderson kept Gore's last letter in a drawer of the little table in his booth. The old man—though Anderson was older now than he had been when he left—had disappeared one day, with only the note to show he existed. Well, that and his many books. Now everyone thought those books had been written by Anderson.

Gore could have been one of the many who walked out into the biomass, never to be seen again. He could have died of a sudden illness, or simply decided he didn't want to be Sona V. Gore anymore. But his note echoed the whisperings floating through the Generational community at the time. The Admins had too much power. They should not be the only ones to direct the colony. And the Admins had solidified their power soon after. Anderson watched the crowds pass, happy, fed, and looking for ways to pass the time. Had those just been the observations of a person coming from a long line of those used to fending for their community, with no leadership, grown over hundreds of years as the fleet reached Lida?

They could be. But the note still rested at the bottom of the drawer, with its direction to keep learning and observing. Whatever the reason, Anderson had stepped into Gore's shoes almost without meaning to, and here he was, twenty-two years later, with a row of smutty romances printed on thin resinplast sheets.

Anderson watched the latest customer approach. Cora had alerted him to her several seconds ago, when she was still across the courtyard. Over the years, structures had been built up around the market, to keep the rain out. He no longer had to cover everything to keep his books dry when it rained.

"The new King's Manservant is out?" the young woman crooned as she bent over the table. Her hands were already reaching for it, and Anderson picked up a copy for her. She hugged it to her chest. "Will you sign it, Mr. Gore? I'm your biggest fan! The way King Dominic pines for Laurence is *sooo* romantic. I could never write anything so steamy!"

Anderson thanked the young woman, signed her book with his prosthetic right hand—they always loved that—and took the few time credits he charged for each copy. Honestly, he didn't need them, being a Vagal. If he could have given them away for free just so people read them, he would have. But there was a strange value people put on something they had to sacrifice for. It made the object dearer.

There wasn't much call for Vagals these days. There were only about five hundred of them left, nearly all promoted to officer positions. Noce was a captain, and Anderson himself was a second lieutenant, only because he'd spent so much time at this table instead of leading teams. After the concoction someone invented ten years ago—and anonymously sent to Admin—that kept the biomass from eating the resinplast walls, the emergency calls to root out invasive hyphal strands had dried up. All well and good. Anderson hoped he would never have to lose another team member, even if most of the defensive force was now made up of first and second-generation Grounders. They were good kids, though some were nearing forty.

Anderson let his eyes unfocus and scan the crowd. It was something he did while at the table, and why Vagal command let him sit out here. He kept an eye on the population of the arcopolis and reported any potential disturbances. He'd so far prevented five homicides, thirty-eight thefts, two kidnappings, and one bomb threat while sitting at a table, and that wasn't even counting the petty squabbles and fights he'd broken up. He kept a tally in his personal files. His HUD was nearly worn out, but still received calls, most of the time. And it was a good place to jot down story ideas stemming from watching a mass of people move. It was a surprisingly fertile ground from which new ideas sprang. New ideas to challenge people, as Gore had written in his last letter.

Many observations were due to Cora—his implant and the thing that made a Vagal what they were. It had access to his full nervous system, and did something to his aging process as well, making him nearly as long-lived as an Admin. There were gray-haired Generationals using walkers who were younger than him.

The implant also made Vagals the fighting force that could handle biomass incursions and the tricks the fungus developed, like acid traps, hair-trigger spines, and deadly gas. Anderson tapped his nanotanium hand on the table. It was far from the closest call he'd had with the biomass—only a few weeks after they landed—but it was a part of him now. He oiled and adjusted it as easily as he washed and cared for his flesh hand.

Both hands clenched as his heartrate increased. Anderson's eyes snapped into focus, scanning the crowd. The subconscious deduction from Cora often alerted him to problems before he knew they were happening. He was itchy, like he needed to jump up and run a few kilometers. But where was the disturbance? Something in the market? Overhead? In the biomass? He looked to the sky, the ground, among the crowds of people. What had Cora found? He'd come to trust her innately over the years. She'd saved his life more times than he could count.

Anderson stood up, looming over the table. A few people looked his way, then back to what they were doing. There was no pattern in the crowd—nothing encroaching. Had Cora been wrong for the first time? Maybe they were only planned to last for forty or fifty years.

He waited for his heart to slow, but it didn't. He tapped nanotanium fingers against the table, shifted from foot to foot, his head panning right and left across the crowd. It had to be there. The sky was empty, and no one was screaming about homicidal mushrooms.

A shot of adrenaline made him twitch as he looked to the left side of the open market, past Jerrif and Stan, who sold art, and Mushi, who sculpted pots. A thief? If so, they were a good one. Tracking pickpockets was hard. He looked for anyone moving erratically, or against the crowd.

There.

He saw a young woman out of place, though he couldn't quite figure out how. She was wearing a hat low over her head and non-descript clothes, probably a second-generation Grounder. He watched her for a full minute, tracking her patterns. She wasn't a pickpocket, even though she did brush against two, three, four people while he watched. What *was* she doing?

Then he saw it. As she touched a fifth person, fingertips to back of the neck, as if by accident, there was a pause, like both knew it was happening. The participants stopped for a heartbeat, then continued their motion as if nothing had occurred. Anderson's eyes narrowed and he scanned back across the crowd, trying to see where the other people she touched went. One was a large person in a wide-brimmed hat. They were still here, perusing Jerrif's art, as if nothing had happened.

Back to the girl. She was in a relative clearing in the busy market morning crowd, and as her hand twitched, he watched to see if she'd squirreled away a personal item. But no, she simply made an odd looping gesture with that hand, one knuckle out.

A signal. But to whom?

He followed the path of her gesture across the market square. Another hat, this one made of straw with a brim to keep off the rain. As he turned on his HUD's recording feature, the person below the hat was just finishing the same gesture and angled to meet the girl. Anderson watched their paths intersect and the two turned toward the theater district, passing out of the market. He marked their faces, committing each one to memory along with their clothing. He stopped the recording. He wasn't sure what he'd just witnessed, but it was something the participants wanted to keep hidden, and that meant he had to find out what it was. Learn. Observe. Write. Grow. Gore's parting words burned in his mind.

Anderson sat back down on the little chair behind the table, which creaked in protest. He tapped his HUD to make sure the connection was clear.

"Noce?" he asked once the connection cleared.

"Yes, Lieutenant," his commanding officer said, always present, thought they might well be at home with their family.

"Something weird just happened here. I'm sending a small clip through." The network was sluggish on a good day, unless you were inside the Vagal barracks or the Admin building.

"Received," Noce said after a moment. Another beat, then, "What am I seeing here?"

"Not entirely certain, Captain," Anderson said. "But Cora went wild as it happened. Could we have a secret society on our hands? A rebellion?"

"You trust your implant too much, Lieutenant. Possible, but unlikely," Noce answered. "It's only supposed to help you in a fight. You act like it's a little mechanical prophet in your head. I don't see anything overtly suspicious. Likely some new hand gestures the new generation have made up. Us old fogeys are being left behind."

"Understood, muux," Anderson said, adding the term of respect only partially sarcastically. "Permission to follow up?"

"Granted," Noce said, without hesitation. "It's not like we're doing anything else at the moment, and it's always better to be sure, even if we're just cracking down on the local kids' secret sign language. Let me know what you find."

Anderson sat behind his table, scanning the crowd.

* * *

40 years 6 months after landing

"Frank? Did you see this?" Choi called across the lab as they lifted the newest printed...object from its cradle. It wasn't the test seed. It wasn't even anything they'd printed before. It was a seed-type shape, with some logic behind it, but each seed had very tiny contours contained within them. It was possible to see which of the building types each was, with enough investigation. This seed was none of the ones Choi had programmed.

"Print finished?" Frank called back. Choi's uncle sauntered from the break room in the back, occupied by various squirreled-away snacks and other foods, along with broken equipment. He brushed crumbs from the silver beard he'd kept the last few years.

"It's finished," Choi said, "but I'm not certain *what* it finished. Did you schedule a new type of test print?" They held out the thing—all angles, and hollows. There were flat sides and curved, but the way they blended together made Choi's eyes twitch as they tried to follow the shape. It looked like a three-dimensional representation of the complex geometric solids the theoretical mathematicians played with.

"I—what the hell is that?" Frank said, stopping a meter away to glare.

"It's what I programmed the printer to print. Or rather, it's not. I *wanted* a new test seed to check the resinplast board I'd installed, but I got this."

Frank gingerly took the print from Choi's grasp. Resinplast was neither colder nor warmer than the surrounding air, though it had the strength of metal. He tapped on it, then looked through one of the many insets in the surface. Some went through the entire object, and others seemed to link to different holes. He rolled it around in one hand, and it moved strangely, as if its center was off like a weighted ball.

"It doesn't have any similarity with the test seed," he finally said. "But it's also not a mess. It's been designed."

"Not by me," Choi said. "We've only coded a few building designs into the programmable virus strains. This looks like it could grow into a completely different object."

"Let's take a sample," Frank said.

Several hours later, Choi looked up from their microscope. "It's not using the viruses we've programmed. In fact, the viruses are completely new ones. It's an original construct."

Frank was fiddling with the now-removed resinplast board. The flat squares contained specially treated sections of biomass containing many of the different cell types and communication viruses they'd discovered over the past forty years. He'd been the one to adapt them over the last decade to grow into a number of useful building types. "This board has new sample sections on it. Did you add any?"

"No. That's a new board," Choi said. "In fact, it's supposed to be completely nominal—no deviation from our designs last year."

They looked at each other for a moment.

"Did...you add anything?" Choi asked. Frank shook his head.

"We're the only ones with access to this lab. I know the folks in genetics like to play pranks, but they wouldn't mess with the programmable resinplast—it's too expensive to make."

"That came from the box with the other nominal printer boards," Choi said.

"Hmm." Frank pushed to his feet.

Several more hours later they reached the conclusion that *all* of the nominal boards in that case had the same, new sample reservoirs the first board did.

"I called the genetics team," Choi said. "They swear they didn't prank us this time."

"Well, someone did," Frank answered. "I'm tempted to send a request all the way up to Admin Kumarisurajinder. Is Admin putting their fingers where they don't belong again? *Someone* had to authorize this change."

Choi stared at their uncle. "Or some*thing*." They had seen weird things come from resinplast during their time researching it. New growth in prints that had been stable the day before, odd additions and errors in a few of the printed parts, and once even a whole housing module that had changed the direction it faced overnight. Nothing like this, though. No changes so consistent. All the previous odd sightings had been shrugged off as weird errors and permutations of the biomass. But always in the back of Choi's mind, there had been a growing catalog of irregularities.

"Don't get paranoid," Frank said. "Strange shit happens all the time."

"There are no other causes here," Choi answered. "No one else has access. I checked those printer boards when they arrived. They were standard boards." They took in the entire lab with a glance. "This time, the changes seem like a directed effort rather than a one-off error."

Frank was already shaking his head. "No. No. We went through this before you were born, kid. We mapped the movements of the animal-like creatures in the biomass, how its communication worked, reaction times, and anything else we could think of. There's no way." His denial was almost too quick, as if he'd been expecting the suggestion. He'd studied the biomass for nearly fifteen years before Choi began to work with him. What else had he seen in that time?

"We've seen unexplained connections in fungal extrusions kilometers apart from each other," Choi said. "Seasonal variation, adaptation to our presence—"

"All from environmental pressures, *not* from intent," Frank said. "It has unusually fast responses because the whole fucking surface is one single organism. But it's still subject to normal biological pressures."

Choi held up the printed shape. It had several gouges from the samples they'd taken. "What if those normal biological pressures are a part of the organism? This is a *design*. Not an accident. Not an environmental response. This is co-opting the equipment you developed to program the resinplast. This is *planned*."

"Then why haven't we discovered this yet, huh?" Frank growled. "We've been on this rock over twelve hundred megaseconds—forty years to you Grounders—so shouldn't there have been *any* sign before now?"

"Unless you dismissed it as natural variation. We've also been restricted to the city," Choi suggested. "We haven't scouted even a fraction of this planet. Maybe we missed a first contact situation, or it's been staring us in the face. There are things out there..." They waved a hand to the distance, past the nanotanium wall dividing Alpha Radian from the rest of Lida.

"Watch where that line of reasoning goes," Frank said, one hand up as if to restrain the conversation from going any farther. "You won't like it."

"You mean if the biomass is..." Choi looked around as if the Admins might pop from behind a crate to accuse them of heresy. They lowered their voice to a whisper. "*Sentient?*"

"Nuh huh. Not gonna fucking happen," Frank said. "Because if that's the case, then where does it stop? The biomass is all connected. Every part of this planet. It is *one* organism, split into billions of different expressions, from tiny moss and flying bugs to the giraffe-crabs and fungal towers. Hyphal roots to mycelial extrusions. The thing is an entire kingdom in itself, or more—as if we tied all our plants, and animals and ship technology, Admins, Vagals, Generationals, and Grounders, all together into one being. *What* is sentient? What *is* it? And can we harvest resinplast from it, or are we committing genocide? What did we do when we glassed the area under the arcopolis with the ships? *Have* we made first contact? Can we? Are we at war, from all the people who have died? Or has it even noticed us? Believe me, these questions have been asked."

"Not in my lifetime," Choi said. There were always murmurs from the scientists about how creepy the biomass was, especially the older ones who'd actually gone out *into* it, but no one ever crossed the line into assuming it might be sentient. Was that because the scientists and engineers had already thoroughly discounted it? Frank had obviously done some theorizing before.

Frank shook his head like he was trying to dislodge a fly. "The Admins would throw us out into the fungal forest if they thought we were talking about this again. There were discussions on top of discussions after we landed. I sympathize, really. I used to say the same things as you, but every test always ended up with the same answer. So, it *can't* be...what you said. Find out *who* is fucking with us, or leave it. If we have to abandon the project, we will."

Choi's hand with the strange print had sagged during their uncle's tirade. Why not make it very clear they'd done this research before, instead of refusing to talk about it? If that was the case, then they wouldn't have to repeat this discussion with each generation.

However, to suggest abandoning programmable biomass was unheard of. Admin had made it their priority soon after Choi had presented their idea, backed by Frank, so for Frank to suggest simply walking away showed how scared he was.

Frank had prepared them for this job from when they were a child, just because he had been friends with Choi's mother, before she walked into the biomass. They suppressed a pang of loss at the thought. He had been there Choi's entire life, the father they didn't have. Authority, supervisor, and family all in one.

"I'll put the equipment away," they said. Frank nodded once and went to the door.

"I'm going for a walk," he said, and left.

Choi stared after him. They had never seen Frank so upset. Their uncle was not one to abandon a project because of one setback.

They looked down at the object in their hand. They also didn't abandon projects. Despite how sure Frank was, Choi would do their own research. The Generationals might have had more technology and resources in the first few years, but Choi had *lived* here all their life. They *knew* the biomass. There was no way they were letting this go.

* * *

40 years 6 months after landing

Jane frowned at the latest report. There were too many people calling out sick lately. Was there some new virus going around? Fortunately, the genemods the Admins and Vagals got before leaving Earth prevented more viruses from taking hold, and absolutely obliterated bacterial infections, but that meant Jane didn't have a good way to gauge what was going around. She had to depend on reports from Generationals and Grounders.

She hated depending on reports from outside the Admin building. They were never focused on the real goals of the colony—finishing the arcopolis and starting on a new one. She'd envisioned three or four cities by this point after landing, but no, they had to pick the one god-forsaken dirtball inhabited entirely by belligerent fungus.

She sent a message through her HUD to Christiaan to cross-check reports from the schooling, R&D, and industrial sectors. Was everyone getting sick?

"Dammit!" she cursed as the message bounced. Her HUD was fritzing again. She sent the message again, and again. On the fourth time it went through.

Is there a reason for four copies of the same message? came Christiaan's reply a moment later.

Jane restrained herself from throwing the fucking HUD against the wall. They were precious enough as it was, at least until the new resinplast ones were ready, but that was delayed too. Everything was delayed, or falling apart, or diseased.

Just get in here. Now it sent on the first try.

Christiaan appeared a few seconds later. "Yes, Jane? I've got to pick up Micai and Flalia from school in a few minutes. There's some bug going around and three of the teachers are out."

"Good. Check on the levels of infection while you're there," Jane answered. "Or, not good, but you know what I mean. Has the medical division identified any cause yet? Are they working on a vaccine or antibiotics?"

Christiaan shook their head. "Not yet, Jane. It seems to knock Grounders out for a couple days, and then they're back at work. Generationals are taking up to two weeks to recuperate, but most of them are redundant in the workforce at this point. My analysis indicates we'll likely see a decrease in productivity over the next few weeks, and then get back to normal. It could be a new virus from some complication with the biomass, but we haven't had a large-vector infection for fifteen years."

Jane wrinkled her nose. "Fine. Get Rajani to alert us the minute she's got a cure, or the infection wears itself out. It's not a terrible time for this to happen, with the delays in the new seeds for Theta. Maybe all the delays will happen together, so the schedule isn't pushed out even farther."

"A good wish," Christiaan said diplomatically.

"Yes, I know. When has anything gone to schedule?" She sighed and rubbed her face. "Anything new from the programmable resinplast seeds? The grounder construction crews are cranky they don't have any new construction to tend."

Christiaan stared into the distance, airtyping. "They are still chasing production problems with the latest updates. Reading between the lines, they seem not to have any idea why the latest seeds aren't functioning correctly. Do you want me to—"

Jane waved a hand. "The less we bother them, the faster they'll figure it out." She thought. "Unless this goes on another six months. Then I'm going to personally stake them out in the biomass."

"Understood, Jane." Christiaan left to pick up the kids.

* * *

40 years 6 months 1 day after landing

Agetha started as the front door wheezed open, then closed. She peeked out of the kitchen, but it was Beth, as usual, home from the market.

"Everything alright?" she called. Beth usually flew through the door when she got home, made a stop at the restroom, and was into another project before Agetha could think. Today she was still standing by the front door as if she'd forgotten something. Agetha frowned and went to her wife.

"What is it, honey?" she asked, touching Beth's arm. Beth started, then smiled at Agetha.

"Must be something going around," she said. "Feels like I got hit by a falling slab of resinplast." She enfolded Agetha in a hug.

Agetha touched her forehead. "You're burning up. Let's get you some tea and a blanket." She pecked Beth on the cheek—probably best not to exchange too many fluids if Beth was sick—and led her wife into the kitchen.

"Thank you, dear," Beth said, and put one hand on Agetha's neck as they walked. It was a strange gesture, not one Beth made often, but Agetha put it down to her wife being sick.

Things slowed.

For an instant, it was as if Agetha stared out of Beth's eyes too. Her body was rigid, and a scream built up in her at the loss of control. There was nothing she could do, like connections from her brain weren't getting to the rest of her body. She wasn't even breathing. She wasn't *breathing*. Pain built up in her chest, a pressure threatening to burst out of her...

Fifteen minutes later, Agetha had Beth settled with tea and an alpaca-wool blanket, tucked into one of the resinplast chairs. She scratched at her neck, right where Beth had touched her. She must have messed up the tiny hairs that grew there. Sometimes that was all it took to make her itchy all day. That wasn't her favorite part of growing older—the hair.

After dinner, they watched one of the new entertainment feeds from Beta Radian. It was another epic about community and building something bigger than the people involved—fairly standard philosophy for the colony. Agetha missed the old star horrors the ships produced before they landed. It was a recurring theme among the Generationals, to search for mystery and the unknown lurking between star systems. But down on Lida, almost none of that genre was produced. The Grounders kept their eyes down, and never looked to the stars.

Agetha shivered. Beth was asleep, her head resting on Agetha's arm. She pulled the blanket closer, turned off the feed, and snuggled into her wife.

The next morning both of them had fevers. They stayed home from the market, as they had enough time credits saved up to skip some days here and there. Agetha sent a message to Gearge—who ran a table nearby—that they would be out. He replied that several others were out too, and to get better. There was something going around.

"Guh. Haven't had something this bad for years," Beth said, and sniffed back something juicy. The metal bands in her braids clacked as she wrinkled her face, and Agetha wriggled a finger in one ear. Her equilibrium was messed up. It was like she'd heard an echo of Beth's braids clacking *inside* her head.

"I'm going downstairs. If I'm producing horrible stuff from my nose, I'm at least going to analyze it to see what I've got."

Agetha didn't complain. If her wife could whip up something to combat the illness, all the better. They didn't get sick often—no one in the colony did. It was a relic of traveling through space in a bubble for hundreds of years. They'd left most illnesses back on old Earth, but occasionally one of the colonist's immune systems crossed something from the biomass and soon everyone had a runny nose, or a fever, or a dry cough. It would usually blow through the arcopolis in a week or two and disappear. She hoped this would be the same.

She took the day slow, starting a few new root stock hybrids Beth had cooked up, in hopes the new generation would resist fungal infection better than the last. It was a slow process, but their plants—the ones that had survived, at least—were getting more resilient against the biomass. Beth had been working on a pineapple varietal for the last ten years with little luck. They had gotten exactly two fruits out of the project, both underdeveloped and bitter.

Harie dropped by later, though Agetha wouldn't let him in the door. She'd sent him a message about being sick, and he'd offered to drop by with soup he'd made earlier that week from his squash crop.

"Thanks a bunch, Harie," she said through a crack in the door. Harie handed a resinplast container over, then stepped far enough back not to catch anything. He looked tired, but good. He was a rock and had been by her side for going on fifteen years. "How are the checks in Eta going?"

"Going well, for the most part," he answered. He had gray in his dark hair now, and a few wrinkles on his brow. "Got a new intern, Clarine, who's very...excitable."

"I remember when you were that excitable," Agetha laughed, then coughed into her elbow. Harie looked concerned, but she waved him off. "Just a cold."

"It was easier to be excited when we were actually *building* something, and organizing the crews," he answered. "Now I'm more of a sculptor than anything else. Or maybe a pruner. Trim a branch there, sand down a lump here, and hope everything grows like it should."

"Still an important position, and they gave it to the best candidate," Agetha insisted. "I want to come out and see the latest crop, after I get over this damn cold. Has me knocked out like the morning after a bad fungal whiskey."

Harie's face tightened in concern. "You let me know if you need anything else. More food, cleaning up, whatever."

"We'll be fine. I've got Beth and the two of us can get through anything."

She closed the door after a few more goodbyes and went to put the soup away.

Not five minutes later, there was a thump and the *clack* of breaking glass downstairs. Agetha hustled down into the little laboratory they'd hewn from the dirt beneath their apartment. Most occupants had done the same with their residences.

Beth was on the floor, bleeding from a cut on her hand, vials smashed around her.

"Honey? You alright?" Agetha rushed to her wife, who wasn't answering. There was spittle on her mouth, and the hand that was cut was twitching. A seizure? Agetha had learned a little medicine through osmosis, living with a doctor.

"Come on now, wake up." Agetha patted Beth's check, trying to keep the growing fear from pushing up through her throat and out her mouth. She checked her wife's mouth with a finger to clear it. "I can't carry you up the stairs—damn my knees—so you've got to wake up, Beth."

She didn't know if there was enough time to contact the emergency medical services in Eta. They were stretched thin, this far from the center of the arcopolis. Harie had been gone long enough that it wasn't worth chasing after him either. She looked around the lab. Adrenaline? Would that help, or kill her wife? She didn't know if Beth kept any anti-seizing medicine down here. Beth's hand was still trembling, and her eyes were rolled back.

"Damn it, Beth, *wake up!*" she shouted.

No response. Agetha clenched her fists and headed to the medicine cabinet. It was the adrenaline or hope someone got here in time. She couldn't wait.

She had the needle raised above her wife's leg when Beth's eyes fluttered and focused.

"Oh, thank all the stars," Agetha breathed, putting the needle down. "Come on, let's get you up."

Beth made sounds of agreement, though nothing intelligible, and both of them, leaning on each other, limped up the stairs to collapse on the couch by the door. Agetha lay by her wife, breathing heavily, for a long moment.

"How you doing?" she finally said.

"Feel like my brain got tenderized with a mallet," Beth said, slurring her words. "But I think it's over."

"You have any anti-seizure medicine down there if this happens again?" Agetha asked.

Beth told her a few drugs that might help, and Agetha wrote them down on a resinplast sheet. She'd have to remember to call and have

Beth checked out. Her stubborn wife wouldn't do it on her own. Hopefully there wouldn't be a next time.

"Just sit here. I'll make you some soup. Harie came by."

She messaged Harie, too, to tell him what happened, and that they were alright. He still insisted on coming by the next morning to check on them, but he'd been swamped with Theta Radian lately. One quick thought of her biological son flew through her head, tempered by twenty-three years of distance. She didn't even know if Phillipe was still alive. It was strange to lose track of someone in a population of thirty thousand, but he'd been clear he never wanted to speak with her again. Agetha pulled her thoughts back to the life she had now. Best not to think of Phillipe, or Daved, or Jiow, or any of the others who had exited her life.

Later, when Agetha tucked Beth in bed, she had to put one hand over the other to stop it trembling. This was going to be one hell of a cold.

PART THREE

Connections

40 years, 6 months, 2 weeks after landing

Observations on the Children Who Ate Their Parents:

The third form of presentation is even more endangered than the second form, though much more numerous. This form is severely maladjusted for upright locomotion under their own power. They arrived from the original parents, and it is theorized they may have been better adjusted for movement in a light gravity environment as hypothetically occurs away from a planet's surface. In addition, this form, as well as all lesser forms, break down on the genetic level far quicker than the first or second forms. It is theorized they may be a worker caste specifically bred to produce the shelters the first form resides in, then are cast aside, as they are of no further use to the Children. Observations so far confirm this.

Choi wandered around the lab, accomplishing less than they wanted. Frank had steadfastly refused to have any more discussion on the subject of sentience, and left Choi to work out the issues with the programmable resinplast on their own. They hadn't had such a harsh rebuke from their uncle since they accidently killed a queen during a beehive inspection when they were twelve.

They had put their energy into finding something to prove out their suspicions. Along with creating the original seed growth profiles, they'd also developed a program to predict and confirm the genetics of the programmed seed designs, as well as the buildings they would grow into. There were six residence floorplans, with customization for each one in terms of entrances, windows, and bonus rooms. There were also three industrial center floorplans and two shop designs. If they took a sample of the genome and viral triggers contained in a seed and fed it into the predictive algorithm they'd written, it could create a model of the growth cycle to show what the building would eventually look like.

Over the last two weeks, Choi had tested all the recently printed seeds in their virtual program, watching the seeds blossom into what should have been buildings, over years of sped-up time. But none followed the programmed function. Instead of growing into buildings, the first ones he tested unfolded in chaotic conglomerations, as if a child had stepped on a dollhouse. It was probably the fault of the program they had written, failing to understand what the building was for now it had been changed, but the seeds were completely unacceptable for planting in Theta Radian. Each completed seed building would be finalized with select finishing work—sanding down walls, reinforcing floors, and adding little decorative touches. If these seeds got out, the construction teams working on Theta Radian would have to completely reconstruct the results. It would be slower than simply building the Radian from scratch. Admin would come breathing down their neck for the delivery soon enough, and Choi had little idea of how to fix their issue.

Even more telling were the printed designs from last week. They were evolving, and these the program could predict more accurately. While the first seeds from the corrupted boards looked like collapsed houses, the later ones still looked smushed, but also *different*. There were alternate entrances, and one had an elegant spiral stairway that went nowhere. Choi was reminded of Frank telling them about experiments in AI-generated art in the fleet. They had been intriguing, but seemingly without purpose. These were much the same.

Something—or someone—was interfering with the printer boards and continuing to interfere. The more Choi thought of the confluence of factors to create the strangely designed seeds, the more their mind kept coming back to *sentience* rather than a practical joke or even sabotage.

Could this be the solution, when Frank insisted all evidence had already been explored and dismissed? Perhaps sentience hadn't been recognized because any intelligence or motivation the biomass had would necessarily be far removed from what humans experienced, if it truly embodied an entire planet. Was it a group mind? How many individuals made it up? Was all of the biomass sentient, or just a select portion? Most importantly, what was it learning about *them*?

The concept gnawed at their mind. The easiest way to be certain was to try to communicate with it, but that scared Choi even more than the biomass being sentient in the first place. They understood now why Frank had been jumping at shadows.

What did that mean for the Generationals who had walked out into the biomass? Were they entering a sentient creature? What about Choi's own mother, Jiow? The biomass killed indiscriminately. Were they training it to hate humans?

"How are the new HUDs coming?" they asked Frank one day, merely to hear about *something* that was progressing.

"Almost finished. I have a few more aspects to program, but the new interface is working well. Should be able to send the first prototypes to Admin and the Vagal command in a few weeks."

"Good, good," Choi said. They stared at their uncle for a few moments until Frank raised an eyebrow at them. "Well, I'll get back to bug hunting on the printer boards then. I'm sure I can find a way to remove the...errors...eventually." They opened their mouth to explain about the iterative design they'd seen in later seeds, then...didn't.

"You do that," Frank grunted, and returned to his soldering on a HUD, deliberately breaking eye contact.

Choi was halfway through a dissection on the latest iteration of the programmable printer blocks, when they realized they hadn't been paying attention to any of the results for the last hour. They sighed and rubbed the bridge of their nose.

"Maybe it's time for a break," Frank's voice said from behind their back, and Choi jumped. "When was the last time you went out to a show in Beta Radian, or got a drink, or a good meal? You don't need to spend all your time with an old fart like me."

Choi turned to find Frank with the almost complete HUD dangling from one hand. "You know I don't like...lots of people," they said.

Frank snorted. "Yeah, you like 'em about as much as I do, which is to say not at all. Still, you're over twelve hundred megaseconds old. Maybe it's time to find a group to share resources with? Maybe start up a kid?"

Choi squinted as they converted the ship-based time Frank still defaulted to. Close enough to thirty-nine years. Frank was in his mid-sixties and had never had a relationship, from what Choi knew.

"So not like you, then," Choi suggested.

Frank waved a hand. "Yeah, yeah, so maybe like your mother. She at least looked for someone to settle down with, even if she never did. Or what about your uncle Zhu? I hear he has thirteen grandchildren and a great-grandchild on the way."

"Enough to cover for me, then," Choi said, swallowing a lump at the mention of their mother. Frank didn't mention her often. "I don't have to get involved with all that...squishy stuff."

"After my own heart," Frank said, one hand to his chest. "Still, it wouldn't hurt to try out a relationship with one or two people. I did, even if it only firmed my aspiration to be a crotchety old bastard. Just food for thought. And speaking of food, I'm going out to Mickei's Ship Food down the street, if you want to come."

"No, you go ahead," Choi said. "I want to try working on this some more." They pointed down to the resinplast printer board, filled with cuts and slices, and sectioned into three pieces.

Once Frank was gone, Choi tried to concentrate on the board in front of them. Was the subversion in the viral communication vectors? Those had taken an expert team of bioorganicists, geneticists, and xenobiologists years to perfect. Choi had made some changes themself over the years, especially when creating the viral instructions for programming buildings, but large parts of the genetic code were too complex for one person to understand. Biomass DNA was only about sixty percent decoded after forty years.

The first changes they'd found in the seeds looked like genetic drift, but they'd gotten more deliberate over time. The board should function as intended, and create seeds, with only minor variation, that would grow into new buildings. But the seeds they'd printed today looked different than the ones yesterday. Rather than the flower-like enfolding that would grow into a building, the seeds were almost geometrical in shape.

The program they'd had running in the back of their HUD display pinged for attention.

Error: No compatibility, the program griped.

Choi frowned and glanced to where the row of strange shapes sat on a ledge. They were currently running the latest "test" seeds—that were nowhere near the test parameters.

Expand results, they requested.

Residential floorplans 1-6 match: 2%.

Industrial floorplans 1-3 match: 1%

Commercial floorplans 1-2 match: 4%

It couldn't find a match for any of the building blueprints. The classification program they had written to identify the seed shapes they had created had...failed. The virtual environment they'd designed wouldn't even try to display what these seeds would turn into.

They clenched a hand in frustration. How could they work when nothing about these seeds cooperated?

Display plan viability, they typed. Their original seeds had a viability upward of ninety percent, while the co-opted seed only had viability of forty to sixty percent. Most of them would propagate too many errors during growth. The end result would either be unstable, or unusable.

Seed plan viability at 93-97%

Choi blinked. That was better than their designs.

"What are you?" they whispered to one seed, whose shape reminded them of the designs cut into drymelons, popular at the Landing Day celebrations. Without a virtual way to see the results of the seed's growth, Choi couldn't risk sending them out to Theta. They could try to grow one in the lab, but it would take years—time they didn't have.

Not only that, but the conditions were exact. Each structure was programmed specifically for soil densities and makeup, the time of year, and water and nutrient guidelines. They would have to prepare a piece of ground, in the arcopolis, where a potentially three-story building covering a whole block might grow. It could be anything. And there was no way to hide it. Every meter of the arcopolis was accounted for in the Admin's design. If the conditions weren't correct, the seed might not grow at all.

Which meant if they wanted to see what the intelligence behind this was trying to communicate, and didn't want to randomly plant one somewhere and hope it grew, they needed official help to see it. Frank had forbidden that line of inquiry with Admin.

Meaning he didn't want Admin to take notice of them. A good caution, but what if they didn't know who it was from? What if they received an anonymous seed with instructions on how to provide the best possible conditions to grow it? Maybe a note saying it was found in the biomass, so they wouldn't come looking at this lab.

It was a stupid idea. Admin would put Frank and them under a microscope.

But if Frank didn't know about it, he was stubborn enough to deny everything and prove he was right. Choi had worked with their uncle long enough to point him toward conflicting evidence. *Could* they pull this off? Was it worth it to see what the seed might grow? But how to deliver it anonymously?

Choi swiveled their chair the other way, where their old HUD was resting—a patchwork of wires and resinplast upgrades. Their mind wheeled at the thoughts tumbling through it. It still worked well enough to make a call. Would that contact number still work? Did they even remember it correctly?

Only one way to find out.

It was possible he wasn't even alive anymore. Choi hadn't spoken to him in over twelve years. They'd tried to keep a line of contact open, but the Vagal barracks had become ever more separated from the rest of the colony, along with the Admins. The Grounders who trained with the supersoldiers rarely interacted with their non-military counterparts, and many of them died during contact with the biomass, though that was becoming rarer.

Choi spent twenty minutes piecing their old HUD back together well enough to send a signal on the wireless.

Phillipe's deep voice answered on the fifth buzzing tone.

"Well, hello to you too, Choi. Been a while."

Choi exhaled. "Over twelve years. How—how are you, Phillipe?"

"Working my way up to Corporal," Phillipe said. "And speaking of which, I have a mess of new recruits to break in this afternoon, but I answered the call when I saw the ID."

The right side of Choi's mouth pulled up in something that wasn't a smile as they remembered the squabbles the two of them had as children.

"You've probably guessed I need something."

Phillipe chuckled. "That much was clear from the call out of the blue."

"I have...information," Choi said. "Of the sensitive type. It's something Admin would be interested in." Mentioning the seed was too specific for what Choi was willing to tell Phillipe.

There was silence for a few seconds. "And I'm guessing this isn't something Frank wants you to give to them, assuming the old curmudgeon is still around."

"Right." Phillipe had always been smart, even if he had been something of a bully.

"Can you tell me?" Phillipe asked.

"Ah. No. I was wondering if you could set up a way to get information to Admin indirectly?"

"Hm. Possibly," Phillipe said. "Is this in the best interests of the colony, Choi?"

Choi had to think about that. Phillipe had a different view on the colony than he did. He'd been immersed in the Vagal culture for years, close to Admin and their ultimate plans for the arcopolis. Choi had been stuck in a lab with their uncle and had, basically, no friends. Frank received direction from Admin Kumarisurajinder, who was in charge of the science, medical, and biological divisions, but the two of them largely worked independently, occasionally interfacing with some of the other biologists, geologists, and geneticists in the colony.

"Choi?" There was a snap in Phillipe's voice.

"I...yes, I think it is in the best interests of the colony," Choi answered truthfully. They hadn't been this hesitant in years. Phillipe always brought that out in them.

"I trust you, my sibling," Phillipe said, and Choi winced, glad Phillipe couldn't see them. "I think I would have been more concerned if you didn't go silent. This is something important. I'll see what I can set up and let you know."

"Thanks. Um. Have you...have you talked to—"

"Don't say her name," Phillipe broke in, his voice like a whipcrack.

"She's still alive," Choi offered. They were planning to visit with Frank soon. She and Beth had both had nasty colds the last week or so.

"I don't need to know." Then Phillipe's voice softened. "But, ah, tell Mother Jiow hello for me."

"I...I will," Choi said. They couldn't bring themself to say what really happened. That their mother, and Phillipe's adoptive mother, had walked out into the biomass four years ago. That she had insisted on doing it on her own, while she was still able to walk unaided. Before the cancer ravaged her body any further. She'd decided not to wait on a cure, even though Choi, Agetha, and Frank had all begged her to.

The white noise on the other end of the connection turned into actual silence. Phillipe had cut the call.

* * *

40 years 6 months 2 weeks 3 days after landing

Anderson admired Noce's new office.

"Getting fancy, Captain," he said. "But the new title fits well on you." Some other things didn't fit quite as well, like the shirt around Noce's expanding gut, but he didn't mention that.

"How are the books coming along?" Noce asked. They were endlessly fascinated that Anderson had taken up writing as a hobby. All the remaining Vagals had come to terms with their awareness-heightening implants in different ways. Many of them competed in martial arts, played sports, or acted as policing and investigating forces for colony disputes, but only a few turned to the media and arts. A couple Vagals had made careers of starring in the Grounder entertainments that regularly came out. It was getting harder to place them against Grounder leads, as they were all over sixty, acting alongside twenty-somethings, even though they looked the same age.

"Another two books out this year," Anderson said. "I'm trying to bring an end to the King's Manservant series, but people just want another one. There's only so many ways King Dominic can pine for Laurence."

Noce laughed, their belly jiggling as they did. "Just have them finally fuck and tell everyone it's over. I mean, the last three books really strung out that side journey to Ibernia."

Anderson narrowed his eyes at Noce. "Do you...read my books, muux?"

"Every single damn one of them," Noce said. "Can't stop. Four of my spouses read them too."

"Is that the current group you're with, or another?" Ever since the Vagals had stopped having daily briefings a couple years ago, Anderson hadn't had a chance to catch up with Noce. With the risk of biomass incursions lessening due to the almost completed wall and the inhibitor mycophage coating the outside of the arcopolis, the Vagals mostly let the new Grounder recruits do the work of keeping the fungus out.

"A little of this, a little of that," Noce said. "I've got a new group since we last talked. Beautiful older Generational man, two Grounders, and another Vagal. But I make sure each group I'm with knows about your books. What about you? Any flings or are you still married to writing?"

Anderson shrugged. "A couple nights with someone here and there, but I've never really settled down."

"Not hanging out with your fans, are you, Sona V. Gore?" Noce wagged a finger at him.

"No, and not for lack of asking." Anderson routinely had to turn down young men, women, and enbies who wanted to get cozy with the author of their favorite series. "I turned down an entire group of Grounder kids last week, probably a quarter of my age." He stared at Noce for a moment. "That's more your thing, I think."

Noce gave a half-smile. "I wouldn't turn down some of those young ones. Just have to check that none of them are my kids. You have any yet?"

Anderson shook his head. "No, and I don't intend to. I'll let the Grounders take care of that for me."

Noce sighed and made a gesture. Their HUD, hooked over one ear, lit up in response, and Anderson stood straighter. Small talk time was over.

"Got a new HUD from the science division, finally. I have your new one around here somewhere. Sounds like Admin Kumarisurajinder has her scientists using part of the biomass communication network to bolster the wireless signal. I don't know how, but I'm not going to question it. These should be able to transmit full video real-time, finally."

"Is that why you called me in, muux?" Anderson asked.

"Partially." Noce rooted around in their desk drawer and finally produced another HUD with a grunt of triumph. "I've sent a link to your account. Get signed in with this one and see if it works. There's a video I want you to see. We should be able to watch in tandem."

Anderson got the new HUD working with some fiddling and logged into his account. The interface screen the HUD projected in front of his eye was clearer than anything he'd seen in a while and responded to eyeblinks with more precision. Almost like being back on the ship, right before landing.

He watched the video with Noce, making notations about eyelines and movement paths as they went along. It was a video from the Zeta market, similar to what he'd recorded in Beta. There was another person, this one wearing a large hat woven from bamboo stalks, who moved through the crowd like a pickpocket, except they touched people's necks. There was the same hesitation when it happened, like both parties froze for a moment.

"There!" Anderson caught the same hand signal he'd seen and marked it in the video, he followed the line of sight. "Dammit. The recipient is out of frame."

"This is the same interaction you saw?" Noce asked. When Anderson agreed, they continued. "This came crashing down on my feed from somewhere higher up in Vagal command. Probably from Admin. There's something going on, and they don't like it. Another rebellion like the fuck-up with the nukes? Secret society? A Grounder prank? We need to find out what it is."

"Agreed," Anderson said. "Though I haven't seen any sign of unrest anywhere else. It's a lot of effort to pull off a prank like this. Do you think with the construction winding down, the Grounders are getting bored? Getting up to mischief? Developing new ways of communicating?"

Noce circled an individual on as paused frame of the video. "Maybe the younger ones, but I'd guess this individual is mid-thirties. First gen Grounder. They should be settled down and past this nonsense if it's a prank."

"You have a plan?" Anderson asked.

Noce gave a bark of a laugh. "I have you. Get a team of Grounders together and check this out. I want you leading it, though. I have Admin Wenqing himself on my ass about it, and the sooner it gets resolved, the better."

"Understood, muux," Anderson said, and turned to leave.

"Oh, and Lieutenant?"

"Yes, muux?" Anderson asked.

"Don't leave me hanging with King Dominic and Laurence."

* * *

40 years 6 months 2 weeks 5 days after landing

Agetha blinked bleary eyes as she made the third round of tea for that day. It had been almost three weeks since Beth came home with her sickness, and the two of them were finally getting over the effects. Harie had been a constant comfort over that time, keeping them stocked with food, and Frank had dropped by once with Choi as well, but Agetha had kept them all on the front porch to talk, and worn a mask. This cold was bad enough that she didn't want to risk sharing it with anyone.

"I'm going downstairs again. Bring my tea down?" Beth called, her voice still nasal and stuffy, and Agetha grunted in response. Beth had run test after test, as soon as she was out of bed, and while what they had was definitely inspired or crossbred with biomass samples, it was hard to figure out what it was specifically. They'd taken all the normal anti-fungals, and the sniffing and mucus had finally gone away, leaving them shaky and weak.

Agetha's hand shook until she grasped the handle of her mug firmly. There had been another thought in her head until a moment ago. Something about the tests Beth ran? It seemed like she was forgetting something, but then, they were both in their sixties. They forgot things all the time.

She took the two mugs downstairs to find Beth with her eyes pressed to the microscope. It was originally from the ships, and Beth had saved it from one of the hospitals she'd worked at, before they were replaced with the new resinplast versions.

"How's your tea?" she asked as her wife took a sip.

"Just right. Thanks, dear. You won't believe what I just found. This is amazing!" Beth pointed to the eyepiece. "I've found hyphal mats in the samples I took today. They've managed to parasitize part of my oxygen system. It's not hurting me, but it lets the roots live in anerobic areas where they couldn't otherwise. These roots are growing into a mycelial node. They should be taking over our bodies at this rate. I've treated the slide with the anti-fungal we took, and it did nothing."

"Then are we infected? How did we get over it?" Agetha asked. She'd picked up enough jargon from Beth over the years to follow mycological analyses at least partially. She wondered why her wife wasn't more concerned by the diagnosis. Her words sounded almost rote.

"We haven't." Beth looked up with worry in her dark eyes. Agetha proffered the tea and Beth took hers.

"We should go to the Zeta hospital. There must be other people infected. They have more equipment than you do down here."

"That's a good idea," Beth said. Then she frowned. "In fact, it's the first thing I should have thought of. Why did we not do that a week ago, as soon as I started running samples? Why have I been sitting around here staring at hyphal strands grow? These things are *in* us." Her voice rose in pitch.

Beth grasped her tea and took a sip, not getting up. There was a reason for that, wasn't there? Agetha paused, thinking. There had been something important she was going to do, just a moment ago.

"Do you remember—" she started just as Beth said. "I feel like I—"

They laughed together.

"Worst thing about getting old is the forgetfulness," Agetha said. She leaned down to Beth for a kiss. "How's your tea?"

"Just right. Thanks, dear." Her eyes shifted down. "Your hand's shaking."

Agetha watched the mug tremble in her hand. "It's been doing that, I think. I wonder if it's connected to our sickness."

"But if so, I would have researched it." Beth pressed a hand to her head. "I feel like things have been escaping me lately. I feel like I've done this analysis before. Are we just getting old?"

"Must be." Agetha ran a hand across her wife's cheek, pushing the black braids back. Her fingers touched Beth's neck, and she thought she felt—

"You know, I need to clear my head, and I think I'm strong enough," she told Beth. "I'm going to go for a walk. Want to join me?"

"No, I have a few more tests to run," Beth said, taking the slide out of the microscope and replacing it with a new one. "You have fun."

Agetha got a light alpaca wool jacket from by the door. It was cool out, but it never got that cold, this near the equator. She'd been colder ever since she and Beth got sick, though. And as she'd aged, her fingers and toes got cold quickly. She wondered what she would have been like, over sixty and living in the fleet.

Well-prepared, she ventured out of their apartment in Eta Radian. At first, she enjoyed the simple sensation of her legs moving back and forth, eating up the resinplast sidewalk. They had an apartment about a third of the way out from the center of the arcopolis, an effect of moving out here before some of the other Generationals. The houses here were still constructed by hand, built when work started on Eta, before the programmable seeds made an appearance. Their apartment had been built by Harie's crew—Agetha had made sure of that.

One of the trams that crossed the city—more a collection of bicycles welded together and motorized—pulled to a stop near her, as if she had walked to just this spot, at just this time, to catch it. She really didn't have the time credits to spare, but she suddenly needed to *see* Theta radian. The last one to be built—or grown, really. She had done so much to build Alpha through Zeta radians. She'd led teams, bled and cried and raged over this city. Shouldn't she see how the newest one was progressing? It would be so much more real than hearing Harie talk about the new construction when he came to visit.

Agetha tapped her wrist comp on the receiver by the tram and pulled herself up the three steps to get to the main platform, sitting beside a Grounder couple with children and across from three more Grounders who looked like they were dressed to travel into Beta for a night on the town. She was the only Generational here.

The tram would head toward the center of the city before heading out into Theta. She crossed several kilometers of Eta, got to the central hub—where the Grounders got off—then headed back out the short distance the tram ran into the new radian. Why was she wasting time credits on this again?

But she watched the city pass by through the resinplast dome of the tram, silently sitting still. She felt like a passenger in her own head, looking out and commenting on her decisions, but having no real say. She should be worried about that. She should be trying to find out what was wrong, but she just...didn't care.

Agetha departed the tram at its last stop in Theta before it reversed inward again to where all eight radians met. This was the only track, mostly used by those involved in construction, and she'd been the only one on the tram since the city center. The very tip of Theta was occupied, and had been for many years, but out here, past the end of the tram line, there were only half-grown buildings and the occasional Grounder tending them. It was a departure from even the scarce population of Zeta. Alpha and Beta were busy, but the rest of the arcopolis had not yet filled up with people. That was good, as the city had to be self-sufficient, with crops and animals contained within the radians as well as people. They were constrained by the press of the biomass surrounding them. The documents about cities on old Earth always mentioned agriculture as located outside city centers, something foreign to people who'd lived in self-contained ships their entire early lives. By the time they got to the point the arcopolis was crowded with people, they would have already needed to expand across the planet.

There was a bicycle stop at the tram station, and Agetha took one, pedaling out along the main path through the radian. It was several kilometers to the wall, and that, she found, was where she was going.

She must have been nearly over the strange sickness she and Beth contracted—no wonder Beth hadn't found anything yet. Riding the bicycle felt easier than it had in years, and it took her less time than she thought to reach the edge of the radian. As she rested the bike against a thigh-high mound of resinplast, destined one day to be a building, Agetha looked out past the growing retaining wall. It was protected by Beth's mycophage formula, too. The biomass was a thriving, meters-tall forest outside the city, constantly in motion, with a hundred small and medium creatures frolicking and running through its depths. It was impossible to see definition from here, but she could make out several giant fungal towers poking up twice the height of the surrounding mass of fleshy fungal matter. They moved as if in a breeze, but the air was still today. Multi-legged figures climbed up and down the trunks, on incomprehensible errands. The Vagal teams were supposed to remove towers that grew too close to the wall, but they were lax in this radian, the last to be completed. There were caves and imperfections in that bramble, and those who had gone out and returned with recordings showed marvelously beautiful mossy patches, with little bioluminescent stalks, and mobile fungal creatures whose job seemed to be to take care of them. It reminded her of the dreams Daved talked about, in the months before he died.

Agetha's gaze left the biomass, fixing on the nearest growing house, all curves and swooping elements, produced directly from programmable resinplast matter. Frank had tried to explain the theory when he and Choi last visited, along with something about strange errors cropping up, but she had been deep in the throes of her cold and hadn't completely understood it. Even Beth seemed impressed. This might be some sort of shop, but it only came up to her knee. She bent over to peek inside a tiny window. Everything was small and indistinct, as if made for the gremlins her grandmother told her chewed wires, back on the Abeona. A stair, little more than a ramp, wound its way up the wall, but terminated in a bud from which petals flared into steps. What would be the front door was curved and bent in on itself, like a leaf waiting to unfold.

She passed more buildings, some coming up to her thigh, some to her knee or ankle, and as she reached the edge of the radian, they got smaller. The ones here were little more than bulbs of tightly wound material, no bigger than her head.

She kept moving, drawn as if by a string to some point she couldn't identify. Her hand was twitching by her side, but she couldn't bring herself to care. Ahead, she saw one complete building, right up against the growing radian wall, and she wondered who would live out here, so near the biomass. Why had this house been started so much earlier than the others? The ones in Eta weren't even complete. The garden was an odd combination of plant and fungus. Many of the original crops they'd planted had been changed despite their attempts to stop the biomass. Beside a patch of healthy-looking tomatoes were mounds that at first glance looked like an upside-down fish, all silvery scales around a bulbous body. Then she realized this was one of the permutations of asparagus stalks. It had been changed by the biomass into a fat, toadstool-like growth with the little scaly leaves usually found on asparagus stems covering the entire mound.

The house was a tidy cottage, big enough only for a couple or maybe a small family, with tightly bound filaments winding over each other in approximation of a sort of paneling. It reminded her of the idyllic paintings that used to grace some of the meeting rooms on the Abeona. A sense of peace washed through her.

Before she knew it, she found herself at the door. Had she presumed to walk up someone else's front walk? She couldn't remember how she got here. The resinplast path was behind her, wending between plots of beans, squash, and potatoes. The door, all of one slab like the folded one on the shop, was before her.

Why was she here? Why this house? She reached up to scratch at her neck in confusion, and found—

Her right hand, still trembling, was rising. Agetha consciously tried to push it back down. It wasn't responding, as if a string was tied to some hidden lever working her like a puppet.

"Stop!" she gritted through clenched teeth, talking to her hand. It did not answer.

One finger, thickened with age, pressed against the announcer plate by the door as Agetha raged at her hand.

"What the fuck are you doing? What is going on?" She couldn't turn her head to look away.

Footsteps approached, and Agetha tried to step backward. Her legs were unresponsive. Her neck didn't turn. But her body felt loose, relaxed.

The door opened to reveal a woman about her age, browner than Beth, but from a genetically wide ancestry. She must have been a Generational, and likely from the Hina.

"Hello?" the woman said. Her voice was clear and high. "Can I help you?"

"I'm here because—" Agetha started, then stopped. There *was* a reason she was here, but she didn't know it. She blinked, probably gaping like a fish.

"Were you sent here, dear?" the woman asked. "Sometimes it's hard to answer. Don't fight."

"Fight against wh—" her lips wouldn't finish the word. "Fight how?" She substituted.

The woman chuckled—a warm, knowing laugh. "There are suggestions sometimes, almost like urges. You're familiar?"

"I'm sorry." Agetha's head was whirling. "What's happening? Why are we—" Her words cut off again.

"Not so direct. Try another way." The woman raised one hand and made a looping gesture with it, one knuckle out. When Agetha didn't respond, she looked down to her hand and up to Agetha, very obviously.

Agetha felt the question die on her lips before it even started. So. Less direct. She was a quick learner.

"Hi. I'm Agetha," she said. "I went for a walk."

"Nice to meet you, Agetha. I'm Phyllis. I love taking walks, much like you." She made the looping gesture as she said this. "Are you new?"

Agetha considered the question, taking in the woman in her entirety. There was no knowing what she'd done back in the fleet, and she wasn't familiar to Agetha. That wasn't hard, as there had originally been around twenty thousand Generationals when they landed. But there was much more hidden here than could be articulated in a few sentences.

"You know, I think I am new."

"That's perfect. Why don't you come inside, and we'll talk about walks and words over some tea?"

* * *

40 years 7 months 1 week after landing

Agetha spent the next few weeks traveling between her house and Phyllis'. The first time Agetha broached the subject of...being new with her they both ended up speechless and trembling at each other, until Agetha copied the odd, looping gesture. She had learned, indirectly, a few more signs from Phyllis. They seemed to substitute for things they couldn't say. The looping gesture was a sign of recognition, while two fingers wiggling substituted for the trembling hands, the forgetting, and the other symptoms. There were others, and as Agetha fell into using them with Beth as well, their communication became easier. Phyllis must have been involved in construction for many years, just like Agetha, as many of her handsigns shared elements with the ones that had been used early in the colony, adapted from the original fleet signage.

At home, she and Beth both should have been frustrated, scared, or angry, but those emotions didn't come. Then, they should have been concerned that they weren't able to express themselves, but they weren't. If Agetha even thought too hard about what was happening, she found herself derailed to a different subject. She could think *around* the issue, but facing the odd occurrences head-on meant she blanked. That was like a reset button. Agetha would find herself in a room, with no knowledge of how she got there, or in the middle of a conversation. They all tried to avoid blanking.

Beth refused to take a walk, however, and she didn't seem pressed to do so. The question of *by whom* was not one that could be thought of. Beth didn't want to meet Agetha's new friend. She wanted to run tests.

There were a lot of blanks, and most of the time she forgot to record the results, but there was a purpose that drove her. She wanted to learn, though what she was learning was uncertain.

Phyllis talked about others who also liked to take walks. Some of them were new, too. Over time, Agetha learned what she couldn't talk about and what she could. It was easiest when they were both engaged in a spirited discussion. Then sometimes, if her concentration was fully on what they were talking about, she or Phyllis could slip in a few words before they blanked.

One of their favorite topics was the markets, now almost the only place Generationals worked, save for the few deemed necessary to the colony with unique skills, like Frank and some of the other biologists who knew fungi, and a few engineers who were still training Grounders to take over some of the advanced control systems keeping the power regulation and water purification running.

"It's so nice to see everyone at the market," Agetha said. "It reminds me of the ships in some ways, where people would meet for walks near the hydroponics and share food while watching the stars." While she talked, she flashed the looping gesture—the start of every coded discussion, as well as signs for the people who take walks, and for communication between people, and for the issues with forgetting they had. The gestures didn't have exact meanings. To define them was to think of them, and thinking of what they meant and why they were having a secret conversation underneath their other one led to a blank while the conversation shifted in a different direction. They had lost too many afternoons that way already.

"That sort of connection will be just as strong down here eventually," Phyllis answered. "It's up to us Generationals to create the culture we want to continue in our children and in this colony." She made other gestures in response, which Agetha let flow over her from the corner of her eye, just on the edge of her consciousness. They were ones for creating something, and for the ones who were new, and a closed fist opening which Agetha interpreted as "building." "You have a family, correct?" Phyllis asked. "How many children?"

Agetha paused at that, blinking. It was almost a relief to feel such a strong sense of grief. That emotion was not controlled or stifled, as it had nothing to do with—

"I don't have any children," Agetha said. "Not anymore."

"I'm so sorry," Phyllis said. "Sometimes the ghosts of those we are no longer with ride along with us." There was a new gesture accompanying this. Phyllis ran a finger around one ear, stopping just before she touched the back of her neck. Agetha's grief dissipated as she sat forward.

"Yes, I often feel past acquaintances riding along with me," she said, copying the gesture. She waited for the blankness, the loss of interest in the topic, but it didn't come. "Those feelings create a connection, a bridge between us." She let her fingers weave together, just for a moment.

Phyllis' eyes widened just slightly. "That's an excellent way of putting it. In fact, I might just have to use that metaphor when I speak with others."

"Good idea. Maybe my wife, Beth, will appreciate it, too," Agetha said. She stared at Phyllis, who stared back. She dared not let her thoughts run down that rabbit hole lest they disappear.

She got to her feet, pushing an empty teacup a few centimeters across the resinplast table. "It's been lovely talking with you, Phyllis, as always. You give me such interesting things to think about." She made the new gesture, two fingers running behind her ear as if pushing long hair back, but stopping before they reached the back of her neck. She made the looping gesture to end their sub-conversation as well.

"Make sure to come back soon," Phyllis said. "I could invite some others over for tea, if you want." She made the gesture for those who take walks, and the looping gesture.

"I think I'd like that," Agetha said.

As she made her way back across the budding buildings of Theta Radian, a word played through her mind, carefully disconnected from any sort of meaning or association.

Rider.

* * *

40 years 7 months 2 weeks after landing

"Why are so many goddamn people still sick, Christiaan?" Jane asked. She didn't like asking that question. "Didn't we clean the genepool when we left Earth? There shouldn't be so much as a rhinovirus left. This thing has people skipping out on work like they think the biomass is a great place for a picnic."

Her spouse shifted, standing in front of her desk. Besh and Ovia, their youngest, were playing quietly in a corner of her office. "My information indicates most Grounders are back to work, Jane, save those that need time to care for elderly Generational parents. They were hit much harder by this sickness, and many are reporting forgetful or dementia-like behavior. Admin Kumarisurajinder believes it may have an element that affects the human nervous system. Her scientists haven't found a cure yet, but she sends assurances our operations will be back to standard in another two to three weeks."

"Fine, then if everything is going so well, how are Ahman's surveys going? Can we loop a road entirely around the arcopolis wall? Then it won't matter where the next arcopolis sits. We can add a branching road at any point."

Christiaan airtyped. "The programmable biomass is the still best option for road material, through the concern Admin Wenqing brings up is that there will be a constant source of contact between the road surface and potential biomass overgrowth. Not only will this potentially block access to the road, the biomass may disrupt the resinplast makeup sooner."

"We have to get to the new city's site—wherever it will be—somehow. Unless you've got more raw materials stuffed up your sleeve than you told me about, we don't have the ability to build roads that are *not* resinplast." Jane drummed fingers on her desk, and Besh looked up at the noise, toddling toward her. Jane frowned back at her child, but Christiaan scooped them up, cradling them on one hip while they gestured with the other hand.

"Can we have Vagals escort people using roads? Attach flamethrowers to the front of the vehicles?" One of the advantages of not meeting with the other Admins save once a year was that each sent ideas to the main forum, where they could be voted on anonymously. She could throw out ideas like that without Dimitri laughing in her face, or Polunu absently explaining why it was impossible.

"Similar ideas have been discussed," Christiaan said. "Though more pertinent to my mind is where the second city will be placed, and how far away it is. That will determine how much needs to be dedicated in terms of transportation resources."

"Tell that to Ahman and his surveys," Jane answered. "We need accurate land measurements for twenty kilometers out in all directions. I'm not placing a new city on top of a sinkhole, or a giant Venus flytrap, or some other horrible surprise the biomass has in store."

"Perhaps the Grounders who have been sighted outside the walls will survey for us," Christiaan said. They pushed up their glasses, then jiggled Besh on their hip. Ovia had taken over all the blocks and was making an immense pile.

"Outside the walls? Are you saying they *do* think the biomass is a good place for a picnic?" Jane sorted through the report Christiaan sent to her. "Maybe that's where this damned sickness came from. Send a notice out to all employment sectors, telling them vacation days are officially used up as of now. I don't want Grounders outside the city until we have a plan for the second arcopolis."

* * *

40 years 7 months 3 weeks after landing

Results were already being processed on the new development with the Children. Subsummation was beginning in the third and fourth forms, though all attempts to similarly connect with the rarer first and protective second forms had been met with failure. Others, far in the past, had taken many hundreds of planetary rotations to find the best mix of attributes to achieve their highest potential.

The shells of Children from the earliest attempts at communication had been placed near the Ring of Death to help with early contact. Though the shells were not completely operational, and many required excess attention to retain mobility, it was known that similar appearances were often integral to subsummation.

Fortunately, the first forms' later gifts of third forms—perhaps because they were beginning to deteriorate—provided observation for the less-functioning forms. These had higher-functioning capabilities similar to large nodes, and were proving quite a boon.

The increase in processing interior to the Ring of Death additionally augmented signaling systems already in place, including the small mobile signal carriers, and one of quadrupedal types of fifth forms which acted as waste filtering.

Observations in the Ring of Death were increasing despite the dead collections of material, for the first time in over ten planetary rotations. Of special interest was the new, variable communication matrix. The Children had combined aspects of their original parents as well as existing algorithms. The result was a powerful new vector. It was deserving of much study as subsummation continued.

The Market

40 years, 8 months, 3 days after landing

Observations on the Children Who Ate Their Parents:

The fourth form of presentation is a newer and more evolved form of the children. They are mixed in purpose and derive characteristics from all forms coming before them, with some containing the longevity of the first form or strength and protectiveness of the second form, or even, strangely, all the weaknesses inherent in the third form. They will be the most prevalent form of the six very soon, and perhaps this is their true purpose, to explore and fill those niches the Children have not yet inhabited.

"Going to Zeta, are we?" Juliane had taken to talking to himself over the months, narrating as he rarely had anyone else to talk to. Those who didn't think like him were hard to talk to. They found the wrong things interesting.

His feet took him toward the Zeta market. He felt the need to be there today. He'd found many different needs, over the past months. He thought he should care, but then, he also didn't care. The relationship with—

The relationship was an interesting one, he'd learned. There were ways he could push and ways he couldn't. If he resisted his urges too much, sometimes his body did things on its own. As if—

But that was the way of bodies, right? There were voluntary and involuntary processes. Some of his involuntary processes simply involved going on long walks and meeting odd people. He'd picked up a few hand gestures along the way, but it was better not to think about what exactly those meant. In fact, he often couldn't. They were just another way to talk. He liked to talk. To friends, strangers, and to himself.

"Nice day for it. Clear sky, calm. I see the wheat in the Zeta crop sector is about ready for harvest." He didn't really care about the wheat, or about much of anything these days. It was simply a way to pass the time. There was a lot of time to pass. He spent much of each day moving around. Occasionally he realized he hadn't combed his hair in days, or forgotten to use the toilet and had wet his pants, or had fallen over from thirst or hunger, but those were rare. Usually, he remembered. Usually.

He didn't work at the inventory recording warehouse any longer. Late too many times, but really, his basic needs were met, and he couldn't bring himself to care. His allergies had cleared up too, for the first time in a long time. They had plagued him for years, until he finally learned to let go, to stop fighting himself. Then they cleared up. He was free to just be, to explore the colony and see everything he could.

"I didn't want to work there anymore, not really."

Yes. That was the reason. He waited a moment for the blank, but it didn't come.

He'd been planning to go to the theater in Beta Radian today, to see the few friends he'd met over the last few months who thought like him, but that plan seemed to have changed. Turns out he and his friends were needed in other places. There was a lot to do, just now. Like listening to his body and his urges, he had to listen for the other thoughts. The ones that—

"No rest for the weary. I should be angry about missing the very first exhibition of *The Khonsu Crash* remake. This one has more sensory effects than last time. Oh well, that's how it goes." He addressed the air, tipping his hat to the wheat. He placed it back in place firmly. It had a wide brim which covered his neck. He'd learned a long time ago not to go exploring around his cranium either mentally or physically. He'd just end up forgetting things.

"Perhaps the market will have interesting items to peruse." Not that he had any time credits to spare, but the right gesture to the right person opened many doors. "I wonder what my friends need me to do." He talked about *his friends* a lot these days, even though the real friend was—

"What was I thinking? No matter. Must not have been important." There were more people around here, and several glanced his way. He was used to it. He winked and waved, but none of them waved back. He hadn't felt the need to touch anyone recently either. It was an easy way to make friends.

Then his fingers twitched, and grasped at empty air, as if picking something up. Maybe it was one of the new handsigns.

As the Zeta Market came into view, connections formed. They were tentative things, feelings and urges from different directions. It was not a completely new sensation—he'd encountered others starting two months back when he—well, he couldn't remember what it was.

"New friends, again? I'm very interested to meet them. Even more interested to find out what—"

Worth a try. Or was it? He couldn't remember. He paused by the first few booths, including a line of resinplast printers, simple tool repair, and places to post lost and found items. No urges here. Whatever he was looking for must be further in.

He stopped short at a booth selling hats woven from bamboo. His feet seemed rooted to the ground.

"A new hat? But this old one was just getting worn in. Looking to cover up something..."

There were other sensations in his head now, and he found he *could* think about these. They were not quite scents, not quite feelings. They were separate, whole, sensations. One was the feel of dirt rubbing against fingers. Another was metallic objects clicking together, and the third was the smell of good soup, almost done cooking. His nose twitched.

His fingers moved of their own accord toward a hat. Juliane had long ago found resisting took too much effort and was a losing battle anyway. But this time felt more...deliberate. The three sensations had burrowed into his mind. They were—arguing? His hand passed from a high fez-like hat to a broad-brimmed conical one, to one that looked like a helmet. The sensation of fingers rubbing dirt grew stronger and his hand clasped on the wide-brimmed hat.

"This one, then? Interesting choice." His other hand took off his current hat—a shapeless and beaten-up wool thing, though with a brim, and he put the new one on.

"That one's thirty time credits," the booth's owner said. It was more than Juliane had to his name at the moment. More than he'd had in a while.

"Maybe I'll just put it back then," he said, his hand gripping the brim. It didn't move.

For the first time in weeks, a spot of panic rose in him. These connections were new, not his old friend. Who else had a hand in—

No. No blanking. He had to figure out who...

His other hand dropped the wool hat on the table and for the first time, Juliane's tongue refused to obey him.

"Take thissss one." His voice slurred. "Exchannngshe."

The booth owner looked skeptical. "I'll give you two time credits for the wool hat."

Juliane's empty hand came up, making a swooping, curving gesture with one knuckle farther out than the rest. The booth owner's smile dropped for a moment, then came back.

"Or a full trade, for a special customer."

"Thankssssh."

Juliane pivoted, feet finding a path on their own, bamboo hat on his head, something screaming deep inside his mind.

Just another day at the market.

* * *

40 years 8 months 3 days after landing

Choi wasn't panicking. It was only, today was the day Phillipe had specified in his cryptic message. He'd given coordinates and said the information should be left in hardcopy. Except Choi hadn't said they were delivering information about biomass sentience and a mysterious seed to go along with it. Dealing in secrets was restrictive for a person who craved exactness.

That was all they had. Just a place for a drop off. No instructions on who would pick it up, or how Choi was supposed to put information about the sentience of a fungal superorganism into a physical format. The seed was transportable, but what about the instructions? Choi hadn't used paper for anything since making crafts for school. They had to print out resinplast paper sheets—fortunately that printing process was still working.

Then what? Write things on a sticky note? A signed document? Print a research paper? In the end, Choi had copied a good section of the report they were planning to show to Frank—at some point—as well as other pictures and information they had collected over the years, stripping out any identifying information. It would be obvious it was from someone with a scientific background, but that couldn't be helped.

In print form, the resinplast pages made a substantial pile, and Choi printed a resinplast case to keep them in so they wouldn't blow away. They added a hollowed-out section sized exactly for the seed they'd chosen to give to Admin. After more thought, they'd also printed a new eReader and uploaded the information. Who knew what format the Vagals would want this in?

Choi stared at the empty place on the wall where the seed had been. They'd printed out so many lately, Frank probably wouldn't notice. There was an inventory, but Choi had been the one in charge of the programmable resinplast program. Frank hadn't even checked the list, as far as Choi knew.

"Just going out to the market today as it's been a while since I've been there, and I thought I'd just check on what produce was available," Choi told Frank's back, as he worked on upgrades to the new HUDs.

"Get me a bag of bean crisps while you're out," Frank said, waving one hand over his head.

"Will do." Choi tried to keep more words from coming out of their mouth but they were too nervous. "Just—it may be a while. See, I had a thought to go see the Zeta market because I was thinking they might have some fresher vegetables at that market because there's more Generationals farther out in the radians. And Mother Agetha has a booth out there you know, so..." They forced their mouth closed to stop rambling.

"Seems weird to waste the time credits, but they're your credits," Frank said. "See if they have any other kinds of veggie crisps while you're out." He still didn't turn around and Choi breathed a silent sigh of relief.

"Well, I'll be back in a while. Don't, er, wait up. Heh." They scuttled out of the lab before their mouth could betray them further, snatching the case from where they'd stashed it behind a crate of raw resinplast material—basically ground up biomass.

The tram took longer than Choi wanted, and they were tapping a foot before it arrived. They must look incredibly conspicuous, carrying this case around. Who carried a case in the colony? Everything was electronic. Did people think they were saving vegetables or sides of bacon in a custom-printed resinplast hard case? They watched colonists going about their business, a man with two kids here, a couple there, a trio getting a meal over there—without *trying* to look like they were staring. No one was staring back. Or so they thought. The heft of the seed—a dense, melon-like weight—made the weight of the case uneven. The handle dug into one side of their hand.

The tram finally came, and Choi hustled on board, tucking the case under their seat while eyeing the two people staring over their head and out into the city.

The trip from Alpha to Zeta was long, but this tram was a direct one, and cut off several stops. Choi saw a woman who boarded later eye the case under their seat. Was she working for the Vagals? Admin? They should have stuck with just the files on the eReader. They could have left directions and hidden the seed somewhere. That would have looked much less conspicuous, and they could pretend they were reading the eReader. Too late now. They averted their eyes.

The tram deposited Choi outside the Zeta market, and they checked their HUD to find the exact coordinates. It was a busy day here—the end of the week—and the market was crowded. The drop point looked like it was somewhere in the center, naturally. More people to see them carrying the briefcase.

Choi made their way into the mass of people, trying not to make contact with anyone or bang a leg with their case. At least it was easier to blend in here. They went around a person in a large wicker hat, trying to get to their coordinates. A troop of Vagals, mostly Grounders, but led by the real thing—a man with a prosthetic hand, smoking a VaporLite— swooped in from another market entrance and Choi swerved to a nearby drymelon merchant. The soldiers couldn't see them. This drop was supposed to be anonymous. That was the whole point, or else they could have gone straight to Admin with the evidence. Frank would murder them in their sleep if he found out.

In fact, they couldn't even visit Mother Agetha while they were here. It had been a while since they had dropped in on her and Beth, and they felt bad about it. They had been remiss in seeing their family since Mother Jiow had gone. But not today. Today was too important.

They absently poked the melon rind while trying to look both ways at once. Drymelons used to be watermelons, but the fungus had changed the plant. This fruit was filled with a sweet, dry, foam rather than the heavy water-filled original. This merchant had at least known enough to keep from overwatering it while she was growing it.

Choi kept the Vagals in sight out of the corner of their eye at the same time. They tried to look casual by first standing straighter, then slumping to fit in with everyone else.

When the soldiers passed, Choi breathed a sigh of relief, and turned to find the merchant eyeing them with one eyebrow raised. They had been fondling the melon for several minutes. They sighed.

"I'll get this one." Their own patch of melons looked better than this and were nearly ripe.

"Twenty minutes for one."

Choi barely kept from laughing. They could buy enough garden time to grow a whole patch of drymelons for that much.

They almost argued, but saw the same wicker hat appear from around a corner. Were they being suspicious, or was that hat following them? Maybe someone working for the Vagals to track down the anonymous source.

"Fine. Here." They put out their hand and the merchant scanned their link, then handed them the melon. Choi stared back.

"Do you have a bag or anything?"

The merchant shrugged.

Choi went the other direction from Wicker Hat, coming at the drop point from the other direction, case under one arm and the melon under the other. Mother Agetha had her booth around here somewhere with Beth. They deliberately moved over several aisles, not wanting to have to explain what they were doing here today. They almost ran over a melon-shaped Generational lady when they did so, who only laughed at him as they did a quick dance to see who would pass on which side.

Finally clear, they powered toward the drop point, between two stalls selling tools carved of the dense fungal tower material, and bags of wool. No sign of Wicker Hat or the Vagals, and Choi scooted sideways, setting the case down to pick up a hammer carved of the mineral-reinforced tower pith. The owner must have a rare nanotanium tool left from the ships to carve these. They hefted the hammer.

"Guaranteed not to break," the booth owner said. "Stronger than resinplast and can drive a nanotanium nail through steelcrete."

"It's very well carved," Choi said, for something to say. Their nose wrinkled at the stink of a VaporLite and their head whipped around. The squad of Vagals was entering this section of the market. Fortunately, the wind was blowing at their backs and toward Choi.

"I have to get back to work now, though. Maybe another time." Choi set the hammer down and tried not to glance at the case they'd left on the ground. Seed and information. They were five meters away before the booth's owner called after them.

"Muux! I think you dropped—"

Choi walked faster. The Vagals were looking around at the raised voice and Choi ducked under a stall and around a wall, cradling their drymelon.

"You alright there?"

"Oh! Stars above!" Choi jumped at the voice and turned to see Beth, her braids swinging as she stopped next to them.

"What are you doing out in Zeta?" she asked them. So much for avoiding her.

Choi stared blankly for a moment before hefting the melon. "Heard the produce out here was really good," they said.

"I see. Well, I'm sure Agetha would love to—"

Choi shook their head. "Sorry, can't today. I've got to run. Frank's on me about the new HUDs so I've got to go. Tell Mother Agetha hello, though. I promise I'll stop by in a few days."

"I'll make sure she knows," Beth said, the wrinkles at the corner of her eyes crinkling in amusement.

Choi made for the market exit as fast as they could, wondering at the strange smile that had been on Beth's face. No. They were jumping at shadows. This wasn't a conspiracy. Just handing off information—anonymously—for Admin to make a decision Choi couldn't.

* * *

40 years 8 months 3 days after landing

Agetha watched the *friend* enter the market from behind her table. Except "watched" wasn't the right word. A connection formed, and for the first time she realized she had been feeling them already. It was like another sense she had never used before. The *friend* felt like cloves and cinnamon in her brain, but she could detect a direction, and a sort of confused geniality. Yet she had been hearing Beth's metallic braid clink together in her head for weeks, and every time she visited Phyllis, she smelled a fresh pot of soup cooking, even when it wasn't. She had assumed her house always smelled like that.

"You feel that?" she asked Beth.

"Strange. I wonder what—"

Beth still hadn't learned when to stop pushing. Agetha was better at sectioning off a part of her mind, aware of it, but not poking at it like her wife did. One of Beth's eyes blinked slowly as she gave a little shiver.

Agetha made the gesture that seemed to mean a connection between Others Who Liked to Walk. Phyllis had made it a few times, but Agetha hadn't had a chance to do so yet.

"Seems like there's something else to do today besides selling vegetables," she said.

"I like selling vegetables," Beth grumbled, but made one of the gestures she knew—brushing hair back behind her ear, but not touching her neck. *Rider.*

Agetha knew better than to try to touch the back of her neck. Something always—

The connection with Phyllis grew, from a distance Agetha hadn't felt before. She closed her eyes, and the *friend* was in the middle of them. Phyllis was on the other side of the market, and Beth sitting here beside her.

No, Beth was getting up. Going for a walk. The net of perception branched away from Agetha as she moved further away. Agetha sat back, eyes closed, feeling the triangle forming around the *friend*. They had influence over this person. She poked Cloves and Cinnamon. He moved in the direction Agetha wished. Uncertainty roiled in Agetha's stomach at controlling another person's movement, even with the—

She poked again, and Cloves and Cinnamon turned down a different alley of the market. She felt Phyllis, then Beth take a turn at control, directing the person with a mental push.

Phyllis could see him now, and Agetha got a sense of frustration from her. He was easy to miss, nondescript in a crumpled wool hat with a floppy brim. Cloves and Cinnamon turned toward a booth selling bamboo hats, which hardly anyone bought. Agetha didn't know how the owner made a living.

There was a moment of contention between her and Phyllis, then her and Beth, as they each picked a hat they thought would be easy to see.

But Agetha won. Cloves and Cinnamon...didn't have any time credits. She didn't know how she knew that. She...*reached*...and told Cloves and Cinnamon to ask for an exchange. No go? She made his hand form the gesture of connection. There was a good chance the booth owner had also—

There was a response, a transaction. Hat for hat. Agetha pushed again, to make Cloves and Cinnamon give thanks.

A push from Beth. Ah. There was a reason for today's walk. Choi had come to visit Zeta Market, but why? Coming to see her? They had been scarce since Jiow walked out into the biomass. Her and Daved, Frank and Jiow. They had been close for so many years, but then Daved died, and now Jiow. She really should see Frank again soon. Right now, there were other priorities.

Intentions swirled beneath her consciousness. There were other plans in motion she wasn't privy to. There was a sense of movement, like a great river shifting course, and then—

Choi entered the triangle made of Agetha, Beth, and Phyllis' perceptions, moving erratically. They veered away from a squad of Vagal Grounders, led by a real Vagal, Anderson—the one with the prosthetic hand. Agetha had seen him many times, and even knew he sold books in Beta Market under the name "Sona V. Gore." Good books. She'd read a couple. Anderson had been the one to rescue Daved from the pit he fell into, so many years ago.

So why was Choi afraid of the Vagals? Agetha would have liked to catch up with them, if she hadn't been so busy with—

A nudge from Beth, braids clinking to draw attention. An extra shape, Choi carrying something? Intent to trade? Agetha couldn't quite make it out, but thought maybe they had something wanted by the—

Best not to worry about it. There was a need, which she was filling. It was good to be needed.

Agetha shook her head, clearing it, then opened her eyes. She didn't like that feeling, and it came more often recently. She pushed back against the—

People jumped in her field of view. A few seconds lost to the—

A few more seconds lost, but she felt reverberations from Phyllis and Beth at the same time, and Cloves and Cinnamon had stopped walking. There was a limit.

Cloves and Cinnamon started up again, veering away from the Vagals, but staying close by. He didn't want to be seen either. What were they doing that they needed to avoid Vagals? Was there something—

No. She wouldn't be put off this time. She felt the resolve from Beth, too, pushing then halting, as she lost time. Phyllis was slower, but followed their lead, pushing back against the—

Against the *Rider.*

Agetha blinked and when she focused again people had moved further than in the last time skip. Cloves and Cinnamon was shaking, and Beth was leaning against a wall. Phyllis slumped in a seat where she had been talking with another vendor.

Cloves and Cinnamon still wasn't moving. Agetha could sense the Vagal team turning toward him, wondering. She poked, and the bamboo hat shuddered forward, though she could sense Cloves and Cinnamon wasn't fully conscious. His movements were jerky and artificial. The idea of *controlling* another human made her stomach turn. Why was she helping to—

Just needed to get him out of view of the Vagals. Turn *there.* Beth picked up his control and walked him farther, until he rested against a wall behind another booth. Had they killed him? Had Agetha pushed too hard? And what had she pushed agai—

There was something terribly wrong with her. With all of them. There were many of Those Who Liked to Walk. How far had—

Choi had taken advantage of the Vagal's interest in Cloves and Cinnamon to drop the box they had been carrying. It was Of Interest, but she didn't know why. Phyllis poked Cloves and Cinnamon back toward the case, despite Vagals still looking his way. They needed it.

What did they need? And who were *they*—

Agetha took control from Beth, who had taken control from Phyllis. Cloves and Cinnamon veered this way and that, avoiding obstacles he couldn't have seen as he weaved toward the case.

The Vagals were fanning out, surrounding Cloves and Cinnamon. They'd pick him up soon. Agetha had seen their efficiency, fighting against the biomass. They were just as efficient with domestic disputes in the city. There'd been an abusive spouse in the apartment next to Beth and Agetha two years ago. They'd been interviewed by a Vagal—a true Vagal, not the Grounder replacements—and moved to a place in Delta Radian. The arcopolis didn't have a prison, and neither had the ships. The Generationals were too focused on their task to be disruptive, and unruly drunks, abusers, or violents were dealt with by their community.

That gave Agetha an idea, and she sent an impulse to the sense of good food, almost ready, some part of her mind marveling that she had adjusted to this strange method of communication with such ease. As if—

Phyllis sent back an agreement, striding toward her, one corner of the triangle of their awareness folding in. Beth was still far enough away to keep Cloves and Cinnamon under observation.

"Can I buy this?" There was already a note of disgruntlement in the voice.

Agetha realized her eyes had been closed again—when had she done that? She opened them to find Phyllis holding a crookneck squash in one large hand. "Of course. Five time credits."

"That's far too much," Phyllis said.

"Sorry, that's what we charge. It's based on the time we put into engineering the resistant strains."

"Resistant, is it?" Phyllis raised her voice. "Is it resistant to me dropping it and stamping on it?"

"I'd like to see you try, honey!" Agetha matched her tone. Heads turned toward them.

"You think you can corner the market on fungus-resistant veggies? Well, I have news for you, sister!" Phyllis stepped close enough Agetha could smell her scent—sweet, like apples, but mixed with sweat.

"Just try me!" Agetha shouted back. She was trying not to smile. This was the most fun she'd had in years.

* * *

40 years 8 months 3 days after landing

Anderson led his team of Grounders into Zeta market. The anonymous report of an information pickup had ruffled feathers all up and down the chain of command. Some Generational or Grounder was trying to tell them something important, and with the disturbing report

Anderson had gone over with Noce a few weeks ago, it warranted a full Vagal taking this on.

He scanned the group of seven he led. All young enough to be his children. Though they trained hard, they'd never have the same reactions he did. But they all had the new HUDs, and Anderson had programmed his to show any movements matching the ones he and Noce had reviewed. There'd been more sightings, but no Vagal or trained Grounder was ever close enough to apprehend them. It was as if the malcontents could sense where they were. The ranks of the Vagals were growing again, but they weren't supposed to be a police force. They were supposed to defend against the biomass. The Generationals were well versed in policing themselves, but their children were changing society.

"Four of you that way," he said, pointing to the left. "The other three with me." He went right. "We'll meet in the central section in fifteen minutes. Look for anything out of the ordinary."

There was a chorus of "yes sirs" and Anderson stalked through the booths, letting his HUD target anything suspicious. It didn't.

That was a problem, because Cora had been making him jumpy and nervous since he set foot in the market, and he couldn't determine why. She had served him well for forty years, after he'd gotten used to the different ways she alerted him. She had saved his life countless times, and now she was telling him there was a problem in this market. That meant there *was* a problem.

His heartbeat jumped higher, and he scanned the row he was in.

"See anything?"

"No sir," came three responses. Anderson pressed his lips together.

Anderson's HUD wasn't picking anything up either, but Cora insisted something was worth his notice. There were few buyers in this section, and only a few booths. Several had art, and one with a wide Generational with obvious Polynesian heritage selling clay pottery.

"I don't like this," he muttered. A shiver down his spine, like someone had been watching him, made him turn the other direction, though there was still nothing. Cora hadn't gone off this much since the giant cavern they'd uncovered under Epsilon where he'd lost eight Vagals—real Vagals. There should not be nearly this much tension from an information exchange.

He led his Grounders down another row and Cora quieted, though that didn't make him less nervous. More, in fact, because it meant he had missed something. He reviewed footage from his HUD to see if anything was tagged, but there was nothing. The colony had been quieter the last ten years, but he suspected that was about to change.

"Check your HUDs," he called back. "Let me know what you find."

"Nothing, sir," one of the Grounders answered, a large coppery-skinned man who called himself Mason. That wasn't the name his parents had given him. All the Grounders trained as Vagals adopted single names like the original Vagals as an homage, though everyone from General Smith down had told them they didn't need to.

I have coordinates for the drop. Noce's text interrupted Anderson's thoughts.

Moving to intercept now, Muux, Anderson texted back.

"Instructions received," he told his three. "Let's meet up with the others and see what they found."

Three rows down, Anderson slowed at a line of books, some romance. The drop wouldn't be for another quarter of an hour, and he had time. He recognized a few of the authors and traded a few words about what they were writing and how sales were going. Nothing like his in the Beta Market, but that was in the entertainment district. One of the authors here was quite competent. Anderson had enjoyed several of their books. He refused an invitation to get dinner later, though. Best not to get involved with anyone. Noce's relationships notwithstanding, partnerships between Admins or Vagals on one side, and Generationals or Grounders on the other were frowned upon. It made the differences in aging far too obvious. Admin Ragab had taken a Generational spouse soon after the colony started, and she hadn't been seen publicly with the Admin for fifteen years now. The age difference would be too noticeable. Admin Ragab still looked as they had when they landed, but their children likely looked the same age as their parent now. Ragab's descendants would live long—maybe even as long as Anderson, but each generation would be shorter-lived.

Anderson met with the rest of his team in the central round of the market. None of them had seen anything, but Cora had gone off three more times on the way. He worked the joints of his prosthetic, both keeping it lubricated and working off tension. His Grounders were shifting, picking up on his discomfort.

There it was again. Cora sent a tingle into his perception. Anderson craned his neck, looking for the disturbance, and this time he found it.

He was struck first by the bamboo hat—the same as on the video Noce had showed him. But they were not that uncommon. Then he realized the person was moving strangely, jerkily, as if they were in the midst of a seizure.

Anderson motioned for his team to spread out and come in from the sides to contain the person. If they needed medical help, they might collapse. They still had a few minutes until the drop.

But as the team began to move in, the person in the bamboo hat stopped completely. Shivering, though upright.

"No! I won't!" they called out, and Anderson strode toward them, ready to restrain or give medical assistance as needed. Then the person took off, jerking, and shaking, legs moving as if they had just learned to walk, and disappeared around a corner.

"What the hell is happening here?" Anderson muttered. But by the time he reached the corner, the person had vanished into the market. He flipped between recordings in his HUD, trying to determine when the seizures had started, but the HUD hadn't recorded any info on the person. There was just a blur of corrupted video where they had been.

"How?" He turned back to his men. "Send me the last fifty-two seconds of recording," he said, and blinked at the onslaught of information.

None of the HUDS had tagged the shaking person. In fact, they just...weren't there in the recording. It looked like a spot of corrupt data or a glitch in the recording, both of which were common enough. He would have missed it if he hadn't specifically been looking for the person the corruption was hiding. Was something wrong with the new HUDs? Were they tampered with?

There was no time to find the answer now.

Anderson blinked the interface away. "Guess we'll do this the old-fashioned way." He raised his voice. "Vagals—don't depend on your HUDs. Keep an eye out for suspicious behavior. I have our target, with two minutes until the meeting time."

He gave the hand signals for his team to split and comb through the next few rows. This could be the person making the drop, after all. They fit the profile of the strange occurrences in several ways.

Raised voices caught his attention.

"You think you can corner the market on fungus-resistant veggies? Well, I have news for you, sister!"

"Just try me!"

Had the person gone this way? Anderson signaled for his soldiers to converge, but only found two older Generational women in some sort of spat over vegetables. One of them seemed familiar, but all of the Generationals looked old to him now. Sometimes he would see a face that would trigger a memory from thirty or forty years before.

He shook off the feeling. The two were nearly at blows and Anderson rushed in to split them up.

A timer binged in the corner of his HUD.

"Dammit." He turned to the nearest soldier. "Mason, take care of these two."

He left Mason and two others physically holding the two older women apart and rushed back to the drop point. Cora was going crazy, making haloes in his perception, and dumping adrenaline and other chemicals into his system. His vision narrowed to a tunnel. He had the booth in his sight, his eyes zipping from the vendor with a display of fungal core tools yelling that someone had left something, to the empty space where he pointed, to the few marketgoers, all looking in his direction.

Where was the drop? *What* was the drop?

"Did someone leave something here? Sir, what was left here?"

"A case, a case, but the other person picked it up," the booth owner said.

Anderson looked left and right, seeing nothing but a person carrying a drymelon in one direction, and to the other...

A hint of a bamboo hat disappeared out of sight, ten rows down.

"Fuck!" Anderson pounded his prosthetic hand on the table, making a large mallet shake. The booth owner shut up, eyes wide.

"Who was here?" he asked.

"A person who had bought a drymelon stopped to look at my tools," the man said. Anderson's head swiveled to where the first person had disappeared.

"But when I called that he'd left his case, another man in a large hat picked it up. He went that way. I think he stole it!"

Anderson's head swiveled the other way. What had been in that drop? There were now at least two other factions in play, and Anderson didn't know either of them. Who had called with the tip? What was it? And who had intercepted the pickup? Finally, how had they *known*?

Muux, urgent information to report, Anderson texted. He was in for a good old reaming.

* * *

40 years 8 months 3 days after landing

Juliane came back to himself for the first time in—how long? He'd done things, acted in an organized manner, and the three connections— Soup, Metal, and Dirt—had taken over. But now two of them were arguing, and Metal wasn't strong enough to overpower him. It felt like they were trying to talk about their *friends,* but that was never a good idea. Too many blanks.

He'd been following another person. A squirrely scientist type, a Grounder who looked almost twice his age, who was terrible at hiding that he was up to something suspicious. The scientist wasn't a *friend.* Juliane had only had contact with *friends* in the past few months, because he'd been so deep under the control of—

He realized he was holding something. A resinplast briefcase. Who carried around a briefcase? What could possibly be inside?

The market was too busy a place to find out, even if he wanted to. This wasn't anything to do with him. He'd been co-opted, and not by—

There were too many people around anyway. He started walking, of his own volition this time, picking a direction at random. His head was clear. He headed back toward Alpha, as far away from the Zeta market as he could get. What had happened to his job? Had he quit? He had to tell Father Kofus and Father Alvin what happened.

Metal was pulling at his mind, but without the attention of both Soup and Dirt—the last was the hardest to avoid—Metal couldn't control him. That voice didn't have the same pull as—

He raised his free hand to his neck, checking for—

"No. I don't want to do this anymore," he said. Several passersby watched him warily. Talking to oneself was never regarded well out in public. Well, what did he care?

Juliane kept walking, and the farther he got from the three horrible presences, the weaker they became. There was no obvious pull from—

He was free, for the moment.

"Time to take a walk, then," he said. There were fewer people at the edge of the market, and he spoke softer, so no one could hear him. "This is my chance. Get away from everything. Maybe I can start over in a different part of the city." Never mind that it hadn't worked until now. He had to break the habit of talking to himself.

"But first." He walked to one of the shrubby trees that fought back against the biomass' influence through the city. This one had branches that drooped as if they were made of stiff rubber instead of wood, but they had pretty red flowers in the spring that the bees loved. When no one was looking, he set the briefcase down, slanted against the trunk. The brown of the resinplast was nearly invisible against the tree's bark.

Juliane turned away, feeling the urge to whistle. It had been a strange day so far, and he was looking forward to—

He frowned. What had he forgotten? He patted his pockets, his arms. On his chest, his fingers encountered a strange lump—

"No, not missing anything. What *am* I forgetting?"

He snapped his fingers, or tried to. His hand was shaking so much it took three tries.

"That's what I came out here for and I just set it down." He laughed. "Lose my head if it wasn't attached."

Juliane turned, walked to a nearby tree, and picked up his briefcase. Wouldn't do to lose that.

Aftermath

40 years, 9 months 1 week after landing

Observations on the Children Who Ate Their Parents:

The fifth form of presentation has been in evidence since the Children arrived. It is comprised of a wide variety of phenotypes, each vastly different to the first four forms. Where those are generally in the same configuration, the fifth form serves many functions, from protein storage and energy retention, to pruning of the sixth form, to communications drones. The fifth form is a boon to research, having so many easily accessible traits ready for subsummation. It has proved a ready test ground as well for the hive-based mobile signal carriers, which were the first step to discovering a more complex communication process with the third and fourth forms.

Processes were moving more efficiently than since the Children Who Ate Their Parents first created the Ring of Death in which to settle. Many planetary rotations had been devoted to researching their phenotypes, how they were different from any native material, and why they constructed so many barriers to communication.

While the first experiments had been failures, higher-functioning nodes quickly deduced that the fifth and sixth forms of presentation for the Children were the ones to which more study should be devoted.

The Ring of Death could have been recolonized in the first few rotations after creation, but compared to the total surface area, it was a tiny area, much better as a research subject, similar to a formerly troublesome area near the equator had been, before it was fully subsumed.

In later rotations, the Children had developed surprising resistance to communication and subsummation. Fifth and sixth forms which had been in the process of subsummation were destroyed before full results could be seen. Did the Children not value development and improvement?

It was only the experiments with the mobile signal carriers which had gone unnoticed long enough to provide workable results for further iterations in communication methods. The signal carriers also provided a strong interface between the clumsy propagation methods used by the sixth forms. The methods were easily interruptible, thus able to be subsumed with little effort and used as eyes and ears inside the Ring of Death. By now, they had been totally subsumed, acting as one of the main methods to collect information on the Children.

It had been many rotations before similar experimentation on the third form was to bear fruit, aided by watching the Children's processes evolve on their own.

The Children, left to their own devices, isolated themselves. Only with the decision for certain Children, usually of the third form, to leave the protection of the Ring of Death, was further research allowed to proceed. Though there were many setbacks, eventually communication was made with those of both the third and fourth forms. No Children of the first form had ever been close enough for accurate experimentation, but the second, protective form seemed much more resistant to communication, to the point where the individual forms broke down before any communication was allowed. Integrated vectors protected the shells from outside interference, a commendable addition to a form devoted to protection. Yet it was hypothesized that if open to communication, the vectors would act as a powerful interface for future connections.

An entire stretch of experimentation using the sixth form's propagation methods as a new communication axis again proved a failure and in response, the Children deployed even greater measures to balk communication, breaking down any form that attempted contact within moments. The protective shell around the Ring of Death had been infected with a phagic element inimical to contact. Many higher-functioning processes had been devoted to philosophizing on why this barrier to communication would be used, with little result. The end result, though selfish, was an admirable puzzle to solve—one which was only now being unraveled.

That of course, could not have been attempted without the generous gifts from the first forms: shells of the third and fourth forms. They had bestowed many as they left the Ring of Death in greater numbers, challenging the assumption that they did not wish to communicate. The Children were full of such paradoxes.

Now, it was little matter to spread the information to others of the Children. There had been many cycles of debate over whether to subsume the Children wholesale or not. It had finally been decided to only allow the vector nodes. Too much of potential use might be lost if the Children were brought into the whole as they were far different to any native forms.

The decision had been proved correct several times over in the past cycles. The Children had created processes for subsummation in reverse, including a propagation method using dead material for the nonliving shells they utilized for habitation, inscribing complex communication patterns into customized forms. Finally, a communication vector was offered, and quickly taken advantage of.

It was hoped those who assisted in the recent acquisition of material about the communication vectors might offer more direct communication, but that topic led to great debate. Total subsummation would lead to immediate understanding, but it was feared some styles of communication might be lost. Indeed, the new vector nodes used a new signaling system, parallel to lines of communication and only noticed during brief losses of control. It was therefore nearly impossible to decipher, and fascinating. It was hoped these many developments could be brought to full fruit.

Once again, the slower route was accepted as the correct one. Though fundamentally flawed, the third and fourth forms of the Children held nearly unbounded potential.

* * *

40 years 9 months 3 weeks after landing

"It's been over a month, muux," Anderson said to Noce, chewing on the end of a VaporLite. He'd been running through more than his usual, the past few weeks. He'd also had more briefs than he wanted, trying to explain what he'd seen—and not seen—in the market. Most of the other remaining Vagals were shut up in the Admin complex and barracks, anyway, teaching new Grounder recruits how to patrol the arcopolis for incursions—not that there were any—with the mycophage on the wall keeping the biomass out.

"Admin still hasn't found any evidence of conspiracy, and you know they're all over that like shit on a goat pen. Your team's lack of video evidence doesn't help. If there was anything there, they would have found the connection by now." Noce lit their own VaporLite and sat back, their increasing waistline straining the chair. They hadn't been out on a patrol in years. "If we'd received the drop as planned, we'd know more."

"I still think whatever we lost is second place to what I saw. There were clear indications of clandestine communication, and our HUDs were definitely malfunctioning." Anderson had been watching the markets as he ran his stall, but a few days after the frustrating exchange in Zeta market, most of the strange interactions had disappeared. With them went the warnings from Cora.

"HUDs have been fully cleared, twice." Noce shook their head, their VaporLite trailing a puff of smoke. "No evidence of tampering."

"I saw—"

Noce held up a hand. "I believe you, Lieutenant. Admin is having trouble ignoring the word of a Vagal as well, even if they aren't considering the reports of your Grounder team as closely. Thus, the two tests on the HUDs. All of them. They're clean, so whatever you saw must have been an illusion of some sort."

"My HUD *refused* to register an individual in its field of view. I find that very suspect."

"And you described them as wearing a broad hat. It was known even back on Earth that specific headwear messes with facial recognition. Given the evidence, we must assume that's the reason. Probably why they were wearing the thing, in fact."

A muscle jumped in Anderson's jaw as he clenched his teeth. Noce was likely right. He just wished he could repeat the error. But he changed the subject.

"Admin's still putting troublesome Generationals out to pasture, aren't they?" The euphemism was a badly kept secret among the Vagals. For over twenty years, since Admin Brighton first proposed the idea, the Admins targeted the worst offenders to the status quo, and "invited" them to walk out into the biomass.

Anderson sent several complaints up the chain of command when he found out, until Noce finally told him they were deleting the requests as they came in. One of the Vagals had been "invited" as well after criticizing Admin Brighton's penal system. Eventually, the practice became a sort of tradition among the Generationals and Grounders as the best option for anyone with a terminal disease, or contemplating removing themself from the colony. Anderson wondered what they would have done if anyone had told them the real beginnings of the ritual. He still hadn't worked up the courage to let any of his Generational acquaintances know. The resulting backlash might destroy the colony.

Noce nodded at his question. "The number of requests for 'extradition,' as those asshats call it, has trailed off significantly after they found the last of the group who was involved with the nuke scare— no matter that Admin Xi didn't actually have any. Why do you ask?"

Anderson frowned. "Just wondering about this group. Cora seemed convinced there was more unrest coming, by the warnings I kept getting, and I've learned to trust her. But I only saw a few more of those interactions, and only for a few days afterward. It's like they did what they meant to, then dispersed back into the colony. But *what* were they doing? I was wondering if Admin took care of them and left me without an explanation."

Noce sat forward again. "An interesting thought, but no. There aren't enough true Vagals left to mount any coordinated action without letting us all know. If there was a new 'extradition' push, I would have heard of it."

"And told me?" Anderson prompted. Noce grinned around their VaporLite, not answering. Anderson knew them well enough to ignore the taunt. "Of course you would have told me. Who else would you send?"

"Head getting too big for your station, Lieutenant?" Noce growled, though Anderson could tell their heart wasn't in it. Then they sighed. "You trust your implant too much. This whole thing might just be a fluke, a prank maybe. Something the Grounder kids are doing. A couple recruits got bored with Vagal training maybe, and decided to prank all of us, with that call to deliver 'important' information. It certainly got Admin all in a tizzy, and though I enjoy tweaking the smug bastards' noses as much as the next person, it's time to let it go."

Anderson removed his VaporLite, letting it dangle between two fingers. "Is that an order, muux?" He stood straight, eyes forward. Cora tingled in the back of his head. If Noce made him drop it, he would, but he thought...

Noce rolled their eyes. "It is *not*, Lieutenant. Do what you see fit. Just don't rile up the natives. And don't keep me waiting on your next book."

Anderson let his shoulders relax, though his stomach was still knotted. "Will do, muux." There was something going on. Cora was certain of it, and he was convinced. No other Vagal trusted their implant as much as he trusted Cora. More than he trusted the HUDs, especially the new ones. He didn't think it a coincidence that he had been one of the lowest-ranking soldiers when they landed, and now was one of the few surviving. He turned to leave.

"Anderson, let me know if you find anything," Noce called as he left.

* * *

40 years 11 months 1 week after landing

Agetha had grown better at compartmentalizing over the past five months. Ever since that day at the market, more *friends* had shown up at Phyllis' house. Every time Agetha visited, another person was there, making the looping gesture at her, which she returned without conscious thought now. The little cottage was always hosting seven or eight people at a time. When she last visited, Phyllis had drafted several of the younger Grounders to cut through a wall and extend the footprint. There were no other houses near—that close to the edge of Theta Radian—and plenty of people had access to raw resinplast sheets. There were piles of them left after the switch to grown houses, gradually being used for smaller construction projects.

Their selection of signs had continued to grow, as had the discussions she had with Phyllis, other *friends*, and even with Beth, though Beth was still resistant. She was too direct in her thoughts, and kept trying to butt heads against their—

Agetha shook her head, allowing a disconnected thought—*rider*—to creep into her mind. It was connected to everything that was changing about her and the other older Generationals. Her hand went halfway to her chest, but stopped before the break in her reasoning. The same would happen if she reached to feel the back of her neck. Best to keep her train of thought. The physical changes itched at the back of her mind, but trying to care about them—or wondering why she *didn't* care about them—was another way to lose seconds.

Other things had progressed with Phyllis as well. Beth had gone over several times with Agetha, and one night, things just...progressed. Phyllis had been lonely for many years, and they were all feeling better than they had since landing. Beth had been a lot more eager to visit after that. One good thing about getting older: no one cared when you came out of someone else's house the next morning.

Agetha smiled at the memory, searching through her kitchen in Zeta for the cinnamon. It was one of the only spices that grew here without significant changes from the biomass. That, pepper, and cardamom. She'd harvested a new batch of bark from her cinnamon tree last week and it should be ready. She was planning to bring it to the potluck at Phyllis' tonight with some of Beth's hybrid vegetables.

Someone knocked at the door. Agetha frowned and answered it. She wasn't expecting anyone today.

"Mother Agetha?" Choi's voice was hesitant, almost like when they had been young. But they were nearly middle-aged now.

"Come in, come in." Agetha gestured inside. She wanted to take them into a hug, but didn't. Too many changes because of—

"What's the problem? You only look like that when something's weighing on your mind."

Choi kept their eyes down as they came inside. Agetha led them to the kitchen, though her body stepped where the light wasn't as bright. Choi was her child, at least by adoption, but they weren't a *friend*. That was an important difference now, and a stab of guilt went through her. Choi hadn't said anything yet, but they would, when they were ready. Agetha perched on a stool in the darkest corner of the kitchen. Choi took their usual seat at the table, still not looking up.

"I've just had some things on my mind lately. Frank told you about the errors with the programmable biomass we've had lately, didn't he?"

"I'm not sure I got all of it, but he went on for quite a while about it." Agetha leaned forward. "What's this about?"

"I just feel like we've had differences lately, I don't want to disappoint him, especially now Mother Jiow is, well..."

Agetha got back up to retrieve a box of cookies she'd baked the week before. They weren't like the ones she used to have on the ship, but they were at least sweet and crunchy. She handed one to them and Choi wordlessly took it.

"It was her decision, no matter how hard it was on all of us. She didn't have a whole lot of time left. But I don't think you could ever disappoint him. How is Frank doing, anyway?" He liked to keep his emotions close, but Agetha saw how he looked at Choi. Jiow may have been their mother, but Frank had definitely stepped into a surrogate father position. If she had someone like that, would Phillipe have gone off like he did? She pushed the thought away.

"He's...fine," Choi said. "He's not the problem. Or rather, it's what we're working on. We have a difference of opinion, and I went...one way with the research without asking him."

"And do you think it was the right decision?" Agetha bit into her own cookie.

"Yes. I mean, I think it was."

"But he wouldn't have agreed."

"I don't know. I didn't want to ask him." Choi finally looked up, their eyes meeting Agetha's.

"Choi, you're forty years old. You've made some amazing advances. You do know you'll surpass him, eventually, right? It's the same thing that happened in the fleet, but we've been through so much chaos down here on Lida that no one seems to remember that." Agetha thought back to her mother's job in data analysis, and when Agetha first showed her a trick with telemetry data she hadn't known. They'd both been surprised.

"It's hard to accept something like that," Choi said.

"Welcome to growing up, kid," Agetha chuckled.

Choi grunted. "But I'll still come to you old folks for advice."

"Heh, alright, I deserved that one."

Choi peered at her. "Speaking of which, you're looking well, Mother Agetha. I think the retired life is good for you."

She sat back in the shadows just a bit more. "I think you're right."

It was an hour or so after Choi had left when the door slammed.

"Everything okay, honey?" she called. She didn't need to be a psychiatrist twice in one day.

"Dandy." Beth practically waltzed into the kitchen. "My knees feel better today than they have since I was back on the Khonsu in zero-G."

Agetha accepted Beth's hug and peck on her cheek. Then Beth reared back, staring at Agetha's hair.

"Has yours been filling in too? I've had to redo half my braids."

Agetha flicked one of the metal bands that clamped the ends of Beth's many locs. There was an echo of metallic clang in her head, a bright, happy sound. "That's not all that's filled out," she said as her finger trailed lower, down Beth's chest.

"Perked up, you mean," Beth said, then suddenly pressed closer, dipping Agetha backward, who squeaked in response.

"Stop it! We've got to go over to Phyllis'."

"I'm sure she'd understand if we're a little late."

"She'll be jealous she didn't get to join in," Agetha said. That stopped Beth.

"You right. We're being selfish. I just feel like I'm five hundred megaseconds old again."

"I know what you mean," Agetha said. "Back when I was working as apprentice analyst to old Jerruld. Back when Da—"

She stopped herself before she said his name. She thought she'd gotten over that.

Beth pulled her in. "I know it still hurts, dear. Let me know what I can do to help."

"No, it's just because Choi dropped by earlier, digging up old feelings." She told Beth what had happened. "I thought menopause was bad, but it's like the emotions have compounded. Now I've got the libido of a teenager *with* the mood swings of *the change*."

"I could get your mind off it, if you want." Beth kissed her neck.

Agetha sniffed and shook her head, nestled in Beth's arms. "No. I should be past this. I've got you. It's been almost forty years since he died. It's just all these *changes*. Body and mind. Maybe even soul. I wish I knew what caused—"

She blinked, trying to catch the end of what she was saying. She'd pushed too close. She disengaged from Beth's arms to signal to her.

Those who take walks.

Friends.

Changes to normal.

Rider.

She didn't think about the meanings as she gestured. Almost like she let her hand do what it wanted. A string of purely emotional images.

Beth nodded back and opened her mouth to respond when she inhaled sharply and clutched at her knee.

"Damn changes. They're never even. I was bouncing in the door a minute ago, and now it's like someone poured a bunch of sand in my joints."

Agetha made one of their new gestures, fingers looping over her ear like the one for *rider*, but with an extra jab over her shoulder at the end. *Interact with rider.*

Beth made a slicing motion with her fingers, palm down. *Break.* Again, and again. *Too many breaks.*

They had months of evidence now. There was a huge change happening, even if she couldn't summon up a reason to care about it. That in itself was worrying. Should be worrying, though it wasn't. It should also have been worrying that she had basically hidden from Choi when they were here. Was that the way she'd act with everyone who was not a *friend*?

It was becoming more and more apparent they needed to find a way to communicate without the breaks in consciousness that came when poking too hard at... Well, at things that shouldn't be poked. There'd been too many interruptions of late, and she wanted a night with her friends and lovers where someone didn't black out for seconds at a time.

"It's time for another talk with *friends*." she said. "Let's go see Phyllis."

* * *

Agetha sat with Beth and Phyllis in the back room of the little cottage that had been grown on the edge of Theta. The far wall was missing, replaced with an alpaca wool covering that hid the new construction. Fortunately, it hadn't rained in a couple weeks, and there was enough of a roof in place to keep the weather out.

Several *friends* were in the front room of the house, and it was small enough that conversations were never really private. Not that anything was private, this close to each other. The connection between them had only grown stronger since the day at the market. Beth was a constant sense on one of her sides, the way her braids clinked together as she moved. The sense of Phyllis *felt* newer, as they'd only met about five months previous, but it was homey and welcoming, like the smell of dinner almost ready to eat. Other senses drifted through the house: a wet day with a gray sky, the brush of fur from a small animal, the bleat of a newborn goat, the *thock* of a nail hammered home. Some were more familiar than others, but Agetha could have picked any one of their *friends* out in a crowd. They were closer to her now than Choi or Frank was, though she'd only known them for a few months. It sent a pang of loss through her, however she was driven by some directive she couldn't quite place.

In fact, everyone here had the same objective—even if Agetha wasn't completely sure what it was. As an added benefit, Phyllis never had to do any chores on her own. The whole household often moved as one. If there was a task that needed doing, it got done. Needs and intentions seeped through the connection between them all, and as more of them gathered, the intention grew greater. Agetha hadn't seen the end of it, and pushing too hard caused a break, but the next movement was close. It might be happening already, as if an unspoken consensus grew.

Beth sat forward, hand outstretched. Phyllis touched her wide fingers to Beth's slim ones. "What do you think, Phyllis? Do we have enough *friends*?"

"Certainly enough to start our own little community out here near the Zeta wall," Agetha added, and the other women nodded. The key to these conversations was to keep the tone light, conversational, and let their hands do the real talking.

Agetha made the new gesture, *interact with rider*, then *growing*, and *purpose*. More than that and her mind would catch up with what she was doing.

"But finding new *friends* who like to take walks is getting harder," Phyllis said. The number of newcomers to her house had trailed off in the last month. "Definitely enough to keep my house in good repair. The new addition is coming along well, though supplies are getting harder to find. The construction teams have all they can handle, patching up the growing buildings in Eta and Theta. I've heard they're doing a little construction out there too, with spare materials. As always, we must take matters into our own hands."

The fingers on her other hand made a grasping motion. *Extend.*

Beth clasped Phyllis' fingers, and circled her other hand in a big arc. *The colony.*

"If only we had a way to keep everyone in line while we built up your house," Agetha said.

Talking.

Rider.

She came back to her senses a moment later, both Beth and Phyllis looking at her.

"Mind must have wandered for a moment," she said, forcing a smile. A little too close to the target, but she hoped she'd gotten the point across. They couldn't speak in riddles forever. It was inefficient, if nothing else. Something was building, even if she couldn't quite see—

"Want me to get one of our *friends* to get a glass of water, love?" Phyllis said, with the handsign for *strain*. In her mind, Phyllis' smell of cooking turned burnt. Beth's chiming braids were an annoying clang.

Agetha shook her head, suddenly angry. "It's been half a year. Eventually something must give. There must be forward movement." Her eye twitched, but she ignored it. "We've all noticed our bodies growing in different...diff...diff..."

"Like my knees, your hair, and Phyllis' stamina," Beth volunteered. She reached up and wiped a drop of blood from Agetha's nose. "Changes take time."

Changes to normal.

"No," Agetha pushed her hand away. "We almost broke through, in the market. We can do it again." If they broke through, then maybe things would go back to normal. She could be at ease with those who were not *friends*.

"At what cost?" Phyllis' normally placid face was pinched and worried. Her right eye half closed.

"What's the cost if we *don't*?" They were becoming something separate from the colony. Agetha didn't know what it was, but she knew where to poke. The word that skirted the line between talk and a break. The word that *meant* something.

Rider. She gestured. Then again, *rider. Rider. Rider. Rider.*

As she kept up the rhythm, letting the gesture become a nonsense thing, just a finger waggling by her ear, her other finger pointed away, through the house and to what surrounded the arcopolis, never far away from anything any colonist did, a hulking predator the forty years they'd been here. Bioma—

She woke to Beth and Phyllis' faces inches from her own. They pulled her upright.

"That's enough of that," Beth said. "Unless you're trying to give yourself an aneurism."

"We can't leave this alone forever," Agetha countered. She rapid-fired three gestures.

Thought/growth/rider.

She waited for the break but it didn't come. Had she overcome the barrier? Or had whatever was in her head—

"We'll just have to wait for our *friends* to finish making their plans," Phyllis was saying. Agetha had been going somewhere with that last train of thought, but where? She grasped at thoughts, but they were missing. Phyllis and Beth weren't looking at her.

"We came over for dinner, didn't we?" Beth said. She slapped her thighs and stood up. "Won't fix itself, and I don't trust all our *friends* not to spoil the broth, so to speak. The new hybrid squash takes a little extra preparation to crack through the rind."

Agetha stared at Phyllis as her wife left the room. Simply stared, conveying all the frustration and uncertainty that could not be attributed to a reason.

"We don't have all the time in the stars, love," Phyllis finally said. "But we do have some. Enough to go a bit slower. I have those I used to be closer to, just like you."

Agetha sat back as her new friend left the back room as well.

Growing. Changing. Becoming. What would the future hold?

Easier if she could even comprehend what was happening, but the others were right. That was for another day. She wiped her nose again and her fingers came away red.

She followed after them. Time to clean up. Dinner wouldn't wait.

* * *

41 years 2 weeks after landing

"Shit," Choi cursed as they bumped a printed seed, the size of a large eggplant. It clattered off the table and rolled under a chair. They weren't concerned about it breaking—the things were nigh indestructible—but it was the second one they'd knocked over in the last hour.

"Everything going alright?" Frank's voice drifted in from his office.

"Just clumsy," they called back. They tried not to hunch. Frank couldn't even see them from this angle.

He couldn't, could he?

Choi risked a glance over their shoulder. Nothing. Just like the last twenty times they'd looked. They'd had too many thoughts of growing old, and their and Frank's place in things over the past month.

"You can always take a day off, you know," Frank called. "We've been working on the programmable biomass errors for half a year. Another day and Admin won't be chewing on our asses any harder."

"No...no problem. I've got some other ideas to try."

Or they would, if they could stop hunching and sneaking around like the spy in Sona V. Gore's new thriller romance. They'd gotten their copy last week.

Frank hadn't talked with them about...sentience again since that one day. They still hadn't revealed they'd gone to Zeta Market and dropped off information and the seed for Admin. Except no one had come looking for them. Admin made no announcements about changes from new information. Not that they told the whole colony their plans, but Choi expected *something*. The anticipation had been growing in them every day.

Finally, a month ago, after Agetha's advice, they had sent a desperate text to Phillipe consisting only of "??" which they hoped was innocuous enough.

Phillipe had responded with a shrugging emoji.

A week later, Choi finally rounded up the courage to send, *Any news?*

The message back from Phillipe had said, *Clusterfuck up above. Package lost.*

Choi had been nervous since. What had happened? Had a colonist picked up their briefcase? More disturbing, had they *known* to pick it up? They hadn't dared text Phillipe back again, and every day their nerves had frayed a little more, waiting for the other valve to blow. There couldn't just be *no* resolution. They still didn't dare talk to Frank about it.

They fished the seed out from under the chair, but as they came up, their elbow bumped another of the programmable seeds, which they barely caught before it rolled off the table.

"Maybe I *should* go home," they mumbled. Not that anything was there for them. They lived here at the lab more than in their little one-person apartment in Delta. They could go by and see Mother Agetha again for more advice, but she and Beth had been out the last three times they'd dropped by. Maybe the two had found some new Generational get-together, like a knitting circle or a how-to session for overthrowing Admin.

"Good idea. I am."

Choi bit back a scream and turned to see Frank looming in the doorway. How long had he been there? What had he seen? Not that Choi had done anything but panic and imagine paranoid scenarios for the last few months.

"Um, yes, I'm right behind you," they said. They'd only stayed later than Frank a handful of times, that they could remember.

Frank's gaze roved over the two seeds Choi was holding. "Any luck with those?"

Choi shook their head, praying to the stars that Frank wouldn't look at the other seeds lining the walls, wouldn't start counting. Surely, he wouldn't miss one. He'd never checked the inventory, had he? "Still comes back with a corrupted base seed design when I try to grow them. I thought a few had worked, but it turned out the errors were propagating later in development. Sneaky. I had to write a whole new subset of the genetic progression program to catch the changes. They would have looked completely normal for the first two years, but then grown into an entirely different shape. By that point, it would almost be too late to fix them. The construction teams and Admin would have melted down completely. The errors are getting more insidious the more I try to box them in, like it's getting better at—"

"Keep trying then," Frank broke in. "Track down those *completely logical and human-perpetuated errors*. There's certain to be some reason for them. If we can catch the mistake, or the perpetrator, then we'll be golden."

Choi sighed. They'd been dancing around the topic with Frank for months. He wouldn't hear any word of sentience, but it was becoming more and more obvious to Choi some intelligence was playing games with them. Frank still insisted on calling any changes "selection pressure" as the scientists had done since the fleet landed. There was an almost willful disregard of any indication of complex thought.

Where else was it playing games with the colony? With their crops? Construction delays in the radians? With the drop he made? What about the bodies of those out in the wilderness? Was their mother out there somewhere, fungus growing over her body?

They couldn't think about that. If it wasn't sentience, who would try to do such a thing? They only had this one place to live. Any colonist who tried to upset that balance—Generational, Grounder, Vagal, or Admin—was seriously delusional.

Frank waggled his heavy eyebrows, oblivious—or ignoring—their thoughts. "Got it? Yes? Then I'm off." He strode away, and Choi heard the door to the lab bang shut a few moments later.

They plopped down in a chair and rested their head on a seed.

Maybe Frank was right, and this was all paranoia. Could there be some faction of the colony working against them? But there weren't many people in the entire colony who understood the algorithm which manipulated the biomass' internal viral communication. Frank had originally come up with it, but only a few of the other biologists and geneticists truly understood it. Ones like Ashkara Patel, who'd been a contemporary of Frank, or old Femi Sarraf, her mentor, or even Agetha's wife Beth. There weren't many who knew the entire mechanism, and some of the original Generationals who worked on the biomass genetics weren't around anymore.

None of them had the potential to inject timed differences in the genome. Choi didn't even know how it was done, or they would have fixed the errors by now. It *had* to be the biomass itself, but...what part of it? It wasn't like they could send a message out into the biomass to attract its attention. Did a planet-covering fungus *have* an attention span?

There was more. Even worse than having an unknown intelligence working against them—which may or may not be a sentience in the biomass—there *was* another agency involved. Some*one* had stolen the information in the market, not a mushroom, or even a mobile creature of the biomass. The Vagal eradication teams could spot an incursion a kilometer off. It was the only explanation.

Choi shook their head, brow rubbing against the seed. That made the case against sentience, and that the growth algorithm corruptions were coming from another party, but who? Choi had taken several months to even figure out what had been changed, and they still didn't completely understand the mechanism that set off later growth changes. So then...it *was* sentience?

Their mind had been going around in this circle for weeks. If they could simply work through all this with Frank... But they'd hidden their failure at the market for so long now, they didn't know how to broach the subject. Discussing it at all would require Choi to talk about the sentience, and Frank couldn't get past that part. It wasn't just about surpassing him—as Mother Agetha had said—but a fundamental difference in opinion about the biomass.

Could they call up Ashkara? She still worked in Alpha Radian, in another lab nearby, but her specialty was biomass xenobiology, not genetics specifically. Femi might know more, but she was mostly retired, living out in Eta, and Frank thought her mind was going. She must be near ninety. None of Ashkara's subordinates would know either. Choi was, unfortunately, the foremost authority on the biomass viral communications systems, along with Frank.

Choi sat up suddenly, pulling their forehead off the seed. They looked at the row of them, waiting to be planted in Theta Radian, and grow up into...who knew what, but not the original blueprints for residences, shops, and manufacturing depots. With Frank refusing to speak of a sentience in the biomass, *they* were the authority on biomass communications. They'd tried to pass things off to Admin, but even if Admin got the seed and the instructions, wouldn't they have just come back to Choi and Frank? They'd never considered that second stage of the plan. Instead of forcing Admin to act, they would have put even more pressure on themself.

So, were they the *best choice* to talk to whoever or whatever was trying to communicate?

They paced around the lab, using their HUD to calculate the variations they'd seen in the blueprints so far. Some were delayed, some were obvious from the base genetics. It felt like adaptability from the biomass, which hid instructions in viruses and prions. That was why they had to process the raw matter so much to use it. The processed material was *supposed* to be free of all taint from the biomass' rampant reproduction. And the seeds *hadn't* reproduced. They'd all been well behaved, waiting their turn to be planted. It was a change from everything Choi had seen in the biomass over their lifetime.

Then were the variations deliberate at all? They popped up in every seed created, and every iteration of printed circuits used to program the printer. Was it a random mutation, perhaps? A prionic relic that forced change when the biomass was too static? Yet the variations had evolved through multiple designs. It was a complex relic, if so, hinting once more at a pattern.

A pattern.

Folded seed shapes, developing into ever-more-complex patterns.

What was communication, but conveying patterns to another?

Could Choi do the same?

They pulled up the interface to the printer through their HUD—the new versions were much faster—then paused. How to communicate complex thought in a medium used to grow structures? Signs of purpose were simply seen as "errors" in the seed's projected growth, at least at first. The whole colony knew signals propagated through the biomass almost by magic. How had those signals gotten here? Spores in the air? A bee flying in through the window?

More importantly, how to give information back? Where was the base method of communication?

The pattern printer board. They were supposed to be the same, to instruct the resinplast printer what to print. But the board was made of resinplast as well. In it, were hardcoded the patterns for about a dozen different iterations of buildings, each with possible genetic variations. What if they hardcoded the board to print something entirely different?

Choi spent the next several hours, into the next morning, rewriting the genetic code to grow a simple shape. A human shape.

* * *

41 years 2 weeks, 2 days after landing

Choi waited until Frank had gone to lunch to test out the new board. They had removed all designs hardcoded into the board and replaced them with what would grow into a human figure—a dummy made of resinplast. Because they'd designed the shape, they knew the genetics included, which meant they could model it with software. Anything the resinplast printer produced using the board, Choi could take a sample and run it through their simulation.

The seed printed quickly—a thing as small as their thumbnail, compared to one that would grow into a building. Later that day, they had the simulation results. The seed would grow into a human form, just as they intended.

They printed more seeds.

"What are these?" Frank asked the next day.

"More test cases," Choi answered. "I'm starting the design from the beginning, seeing if I can locate the...error."

Frank grunted, and set the seed down. "Let me know what happens."

"I'll do that," Choi said.

On the fifth day, the print began to change.

Choi had been inspecting each seed closely to see if there were physical differences before sampling the printed material. The folded whirls that would grow into the final structure made a sort of fingerprint on the surface of the seed, which they could use for a quick test. This one was different than their new design.

They ran a sample of the material through their simulation program and the result was decidedly not human.

"Is that...a goat?" Choi said to themself. The figure was something four-footed at least. The simulation was a best guess using the programmed genetics, but it could resolve the larger features of a building well enough to check. For something this small, the details of the figure were indistinct, but it had hooves, and horns.

The next seed was already being printed, and Choi paced as they waited for it to finish.

This one was even more different than the goat. It was easy enough to see in the basic seed shape, but when Choi took a sample, the simulation stalled, just as it had when trying to decode the seeds that were printing from the corrupted boards.

Choi started more prints while they waited, more to see what happened than anything else.

"Why do you have wheat on your screen?" Frank asked.

Choi popped their head up from where they were sampling the latest seed. This one looked almost identical to the original again—the human form.

"Wheat?"

Frank only pointed until Choi stared at the simulation screen. It had finished, eventually, and rather than a human, or a goat, it showed a collection of twigs. Choi would have been completely confused if they had seen it first, but after Frank called it wheat, they could see that in the shape, if they squinted.

"Huh," Choi said.

Frank looked between them and the screen. "More strange errors?"

Choi nodded, and Frank backed away, hands out in front of him. "I don't want to know. Just figure it out and tell me if you can find any concrete proof. Of anything."

The next four seeds came out in the human shape again. Then another goat. And then wheat again.

Choi set the seeds in a line on the table, and stared at them. Patterns again, but they made no sense.

Another day passed and Choi printed more seeds. The pattern continued. Human, human, human, human, goat, wheat.

"How many goats are there per human in the arcopolis?" they called out to Frank. They heard tentative approaching steps. Frank poked his head around the corner of the office.

"Why...?"

"Do you know?" Choi stared at Frank, who frowned.

"I can find out."

The answer was one goat per eight humans. Choi was pretty sure there were more stalks of wheat growing than there were humans in the colony. The pattern made no sense.

Frank found them staring at the line of seeds. They'd printed four sets of six now, and the pattern held.

"Fine. Against my better judgement, do you want to tell me what's going on here? Only facts."

"Only facts," Choi agreed. They explained that they'd made a seed to grow into a human test shape for the printer and what had happened. They flipped through the simulation results for Frank to see. "Four humans, a goat, and a stalk of wheat. Just facts. This is how the, ah, *print errors* propagated."

"Go through them again," Frank said, and Choi flipped through the simulations. "They're not the same."

"No, one's a goat and one's wheat," Choi said.

"I mean the humans aren't all the same."

"The what...?" Choi arranged the results so they could see all six projected shapes at once.

"See? There. The second human is bulkier and the third human is taller."

"Variation in the models?" Choi suggested.

"Did you test all the seeds?"

"Of course. What kind of scientist do you take me for?"

Frank stabbed at the simulation image. "So is the second human *always* bulkier and the third *always* taller?"

"I...don't know." Choi sorted through their results. They were.

"Then it's a pattern, not variation."

"A pattern within a pattern," Choi answered. "Because the pattern is already consistent between each six printings. And if there is a pattern, there's a reason for the pattern. Can we talk possible causes? Just facts?"

Frank pursed his lips. It was obvious he didn't like where this was going, but it was time to address this. "You've been on this problem for too long. Are you certain you're looking at this objectively? Maybe you accidentally mixed up these prints with others."

"From what? Children's blocks?" Choi asked. They pointed to the screen. "I had nothing to do with these shapes. I programmed the first and the rest grew from it. You've taken yourself out of this investigation every step of the way, scared to face what we both suspect to be true." They kept Mother Agetha's advice in mind.

Their uncle's face darkened from its usual light coloration, and Choi thought he might shout for a moment. But that wasn't Frank. He was calm, and collected, all the time.

Frank finally shook his head, visibly controlling himself. "I trust you, Choi, I really do. But for what you say to be true might invalidate my life's work. If we all missed something this basic, what does it say about us?"

"That we're human?" Choi suggested. "That we make false assumptions and mistakes?" That Choi would someday surpass Frank...

"Yes, but for *forty years*." He looked pained at the idea.

Frank didn't show his emotions often. Choi knew their mother's death had been a toll on him as well as Choi. Everything was a little duller since she'd walked out into the biomass. This discovery, made together, could bring them a little closer again.

"Remember, this is only facts. I haven't made a final conclusion yet. We're still looking for evidence."

Frank finally nodded. "Alright. Then tell me your evidence."

Choi relaxed at their uncle's acceptance. "Input was put into a system with no prior direction aside from the planned output. Yet the system developed—for whatever reason—six different outputs, including the original. Is there a correlation with anything we know?"

"Goats and wheat. One is the most common crop plant we grow here. The other is the most useful animal we have left, now the cows and chickens have died off," said Frank. "I know where you're leading me, and I don't like it. Take it slow."

"I'm trying not to jump to any conclusions," Choi said, "but it's difficult."

"I'm not making any assumptions until we figure out this whole pattern," Frank said.

"That's fair. So then why four humans, two of which look slightly different?" Choi looked up to Frank, who was taller than them, though he was short for a Generational. "What about the taller one? Can we make a guess?"

"A sub-variant of human, whose morphology has been changed by life in deep space," Frank answered. "Makes sense, but I'm still not convinced. What are the other three, and why do two look the same?" He was being obstinate, making Choi spell out the connections for him. It made sense, when they were questioning his life's work.

"I saw a Vagal recently leading a squad of Grounders," Choi said. "He was certainly a bulky person, larger than the Grounders. Do you think...?"

"The second one. Fine. What about the others?"

"Their lifespans are different, but Grounders are more similar in shape to the ship Admins, who were born on old Earth." Choi paused only long enough to ensure Frank was listening. He was, though his arms were crossed, his eyebrows pulled into a deep frown. The connections rolled through Choi's mind. "Admin, Vagal, Generational, Grounder, goat, wheat. There's a pattern here, and it seems like a classification, if an odd one. I think we have to go back to our original assumptions to go farther. An input—the human shape—is put into a blank system, with the expectation that the same thing would come out. In the absence of any other variables, that is the case. But it's not. So, skipping over the unknown of *what* is making the output change, we can see the changed output. This becomes like an answer to a question. The question is vague, but perhaps it's something like, 'Is this human recognizable as the things making changes to this colony?'"

"And the answer?" Frank was still frowning.

"The answer is, 'yes, I see the simple explanation. Here it is in more depth. There are six classes of creature. The Admin: the ones in command. The Vagals: the ones protecting. The Generationals: the ones from space. Grounders: the new ones born here—'"

"And the goat and wheat?"

"How would the living things in this colony be classified? There are more than humans. Animals and plants are just as important to keeping things running, because we use them for food. Six categories."

Choi broke off, staring at the line of seeds. Why this different answer now? Because they posed a different question. It was yet another sign of intelligence.

"I was wrong before," they said.

"Wrong how?"

"The original question wasn't vague after all. It was very specific. These figures are the answer to the question of 'Here I am. Can you understand me?'"

Frank only stared for a long moment. A muscle worked in his cheek.

"Fuck. That makes sense. We better figure out what other questions to ask."

* * *

41 years 1 month after landing

Jane juggled three reports Christiaan had sent to her HUD in the last five minutes—each from a different Admin, each complaining of Grounders missing shifts. They didn't seem to care any longer about earning enough time credits to eat, and Jane was running out of leverage.

"I don't need this, after that shitshow that went down in the Zeta market a few months ago," she called. It still galled her there was missing information—important information, from all accounts—that was floating around with some Generational or Grounder. She'd threatened

General Smith with a walk in the biomass if he didn't follow up, but he insisted there were no records to follow up on. Whoever planned that little heist had disappeared in a puff of proverbial smoke, with none the wiser. A thorough investigation of people in the market had produced no evidence, and the Vagals blamed some error in the new HUDs. Maybe it was all a case of bad timing, but it made her stomach sour.

"Sorry, Jane," Christiaan said as they stuck their head in her office. "Maria says they came close to losing an entire shift at the water treatment plant, and you know how quickly the biomass gunks up the turbines if it's not watched."

"That's why Maria is the Admin in charge of waste treatment and not me," Jane said. "Why are they all bringing their problems here?"

"You are in charge of the city as a whole, Jane," they said, a little reproachfully.

"And this is the first time in forty years it's been a problem." Jane tapped one fingernail against her desk six times. "Why now? There's shit popping up all over the city. Late workers, workers drifting off during a task, disturbances in the markets, nervous Vagals. Is it another rebellion? I thought we nipped that in the bud with Wenqing's imaginary nukes. We don't have any more fleet stories to scare them with." She thumped her desk this time with a fist. "Do we need more Generationals to take a walk? What's the problem?"

Christiaan was standing in the doorway by this point, hands on their hips, frowning. "We haven't sent anyone to the biomass in over ten years," they said, "though plenty have gone on their own since then."

"Maybe it's time to bring it back. People here never balked at working. Why now? The number of malcontents has multiplied in the last few years. People are neglecting their duties."

"The Grounders are different than the Generationals, Jane," Christiaan warned. "They respond to different pressures. The Generationals were born to work, keeping the fleet going. When people went missing, they blamed the *people* for shirking work. The Grounders grew up here. They have more comforts, more room. If something starts going wrong, they're going to blame the ones who are keeping the city running. In this case, that's *us*. What do you think the children would do?"

Jane frowned. "Yana and Ivan would blame us for any lapse in network coverage. They already do. And Micai and Flalia would just come running to mommy and ommi to complain."

"At least the youngest pair is too young to complain much," Christiaan said. "But you take my point."

"I do. You think the Grounders are drawing away from keeping the city working? It still won't be absolutely complete for another decade. We need a workforce."

Christiaan shook their head. "No, I think there's something else going on. As you say, this rash of interruptions is new, though whether a new societal vector, or a disease, I don't have enough information yet to say, except that it's affected all of the Admins. Add to that sightings of upright figures moving in the biomass—possibly some new mobile creature. The Vagals are spooked."

"The biomass? You think it might come from outside the city?" Jane looked through the windows of her office, which looked over the nanotanium wall surrounding Alpha Radian. "Is it making human lookalikes now? It already did that with our plants and animals."

"It's been quiet for a long time, Jane. Since the mycophage was added to the wall around the city. The biomass evolved quickly when we first arrived, but then seemed to slow as we settled in. Maybe another factor has changed it."

"The attacks slowed because we became a part of its environment, so Rajani tells me," Jane said. The Admin of the science division knew her stuff, which was good, because Jane knew nothing about alien biology. "Once the wall divided us, the biomass had less reason to attack what the biosphere saw as a foreign object. If anything, we should be even *more* isolated now."

"The body will sometimes wall away a foreign body for years, then decide to attack again," Christiaan offered. "This could be similar."

"Put together a meeting with the other Admins," Jane told her secretary, and Christiaan gave a sharp nod. "If there is a sickness coming from the biomass, we all need to be aware. The Generationals are too dependent on it, with their resinplast, and programmable biomass. They eat it, they drink it, and I wouldn't be surprised if some of them haven't tried to fuck it."

Christiaan raised their eyebrows.

"Don't look at me that way," Jane said. "Something's happening, and I don't want to be caught off guard again."

Transitions

41 years 4 months after landing

Observations on the Children Who Ate Their Parents:

The sixth form of presentation appeared shortly after the Children arrived. Like the fifth form, it has many phenotypes, though none of them appear able to move on their own, requiring maintenance to live. They serve as forms of energy storage for the Children, and are easily subsumed, though the third and fourth forms seeming willing to cull this form more readily than any other forms. Several innovative systems have already been copied and added to local ecosystems, including an alternate form of propagation which drives a useful recombination of genes.

Agetha dusted her hands off. She couldn't have done this much work in one day half a year ago. Her strength was growing, her hair was thicker, and her thighs were more muscular than they had been in fifteen years. That was good, because pedaling the bike loaded down with all her and Beth's stuff between Zeta and Theta Radians took a lot of effort.

"Good thing the addition is finished," Phyllis said. She put her hands on her wide hips and stared at the pile of boxes.

"Where's all my equipment?" Beth asked, leaning over the pile to search the resinplast containers.

"Third one down, over there, honey," Agetha said. She popped her back and tried to mentally fit all of Beth's lab equipment into Phyllis' tiny cottage. They'd probably need to add yet another room. It had been their choice to move out here this time, rather than when Admin forced her to move from Alpha to Delta, then from Delta to move in with Beth in Zeta. Finally, they'd made their own decision to live with Phyllis, though Admin was probably not far from requiring the remaining Generationals to all live in Eta and Theta. She mentally catalogued all the people she would have to tell. Harie and Choi, Frank, Gearge, and some others from the ships, plus Beth's friends. There really weren't that many after all.

"Rest. Have some tea. You've been moving all day and you aren't getting any younger." Phyllis frowned at Agetha stretching.

"That's debatable, nowadays," Beth said from her search inside the pile of boxes. "I know for a fact I have fewer gray hairs than I did half a year ago. And not because they've fallen out."

"Except we can't talk about why because—" Agetha was ready for the moment of discontinuity and barreled through. It was getting easier to remember what she was doing the more she did it. She looked to Phyllis. "Let's take this inside. Can you have some *friends* bring the rest of our boxes in?"

The odd thing was that no one really *requested* anything. It was yet another front they used to keep them from digging too deep into what they were experiencing. The three of them moved inside. Others who were around Phyllis' house brought the boxes in. There were never any words said, but the feeling around the house changed. Things would be in different places, once the boxes were moved where they were supposed to go. Agetha wouldn't be surprised to find some of them unpacked with items positioned in the places she wanted to place them.

"There has to be a reason for..." Beth broke off to accept tea from Phyllis, once they were inside, sitting in the back room. *Friends* moved around in the house like ghosts. "Thank you, dear." She made the gesture for *rider*, almost as an afterthought, like brushing her braids back from her ears.

Everything just worked these days. Timing was right. People were where they needed to be. The Generationals and Grounders here moved beneath the notice of Admin.

Agetha gestured out past the walls of the colony. The meaning there was obvious. "We know the reason," she said. "Perhaps more to the point is *why*, or even *who?*"

"Dangerous." Beth shook her head as Phyllis handed Agetha tea as well. "We disproved sentience soon after we landed."

"We also thought the colony would be complete in ten years," Phyllis said as she sat down.

"No one really thought that, not more than a month after landing," Agetha said. She caught Phyllis' eye, then Beth's. "I mean, you see how the biomass changed our plants and animals." She wasn't talking about the time to finish the colony any longer.

"But is it purposeful change?" Beth asked.

"Is any of this?" Phyllis encompassed her house with a hand, and Beth acknowledged the point with a nod. The house itself was still partially a mystery. Phyllis—childless and never married—had moved in from Epsilon Radian two years ago, when she decided, at random, to go for a walk. The rest of the seed-grown houses in Theta and even in Eta weren't complete. This house, right up against the edge of the wall, must have been planted as one of the first trial runs, but then had seemingly been forgotten. Phyllis had tended the house in the last stages of its growth, trimming extrusions here and forcing walls to grow straight there. She said it had been like a daze for her, which she only came out from underneath when the *friends* started arriving.

"It's very strange no one higher up has come out here yet, even if it is at the edge of Theta," Beth said. "It's been months, after all, and Grounders have been passing through. They cut the first hole in the wall behind the house soon after." Agetha had seen it—a crude opening hacked through the growing resinplast. There was at least one gate in the wall in each Radian, but often they were guarded by Vagals or by Grounders in training. The wall was supposed to be impenetrable, specifically to keep the creeping biomass out. Yet no wave of fungal hyphae had rolled in the new opening. Like it was being considerate.

"You haven't seen any Vagals come by, or Admins, have you?" she asked.

Phyllis shook her head. "Not ones that stopped. It would be suspicious for them to be this far out of Alpha and Beta, but there was one squad, Grounders led by a Vagal, who came by, must have been nearly a year ago. They were a ways away, but I thought surely they would investigate the house. They didn't. I'd think they were like us, but I'm almost certain the Vagal..." She made the gesture for *rider* again, then a negation—a sweep of her hand.

"Our *friends* help out, but we still can't get deep into things," Agetha said. "Now we're here with you, Phyllis. And I want some answers." She felt the break rising from beneath the waters of her mind and stopped talking.

If only Generationals and Grounders had encountered *riders*, it could be simply because the Vagals and Admins were mostly holed up in their building in Alpha these days. But what if it was because the *riders* couldn't contact Vagals or Admin? Or more to the point, that they chose not to—

Agetha shook off the disconnect. She could feel that much inside her. A purpose. Direction—

She shook her head again and took a sip of tea. Beth and Phyllis only watched her, familiar with the signs of grappling against—

She was getting closer, each time. As she pushed toward that boundary, she could hear the clack of Beth's braids more clearly, smell the aroma of Phyllis' cooking. There was a connection here. A *purpose*—

Her tea was cooler when she took a sip. How long had she been out this time?

"We're watching," Beth said, as she made eye contact. Agetha nodded back. There were *friends* in the back of the room. The others would take care of her. They all wanted answers. Like why it was when she reached for the back of her neck, she could feel—

Phyllis was suddenly in front of her, a cloth up to wipe away a dribble of blood from her nose. "Keep trying," she said. "We're close. We're with you."

Agetha could feel them now, not just sensations in her head. Their three minds were together. The aptitude of Beth's, the solid strength of Phyllis, Agetha's determination. All three of them reached as one to feel between their breasts where lurked—

Phyllis was sitting down again, the tea cold and forgotten on the table between them. A shape flitted from one doorway to another, one of their *friends* moving through. Agetha could feel the house quiet, more people turn in their direction as they joined the mental battle. There were more shapes standing silently around them. She was the one directing their attention, but a wave of willpower rose behind her. And curiosity—that very strong human trait.

What had she been doing before the last break? Something *on* her. On every one of them. Why was that so familiar? She should have made the connection before, except it was too hard to think of it. Now, with so many thoughts bolstering hers, it was easier.

Bees.

Daved.

She remembered the fleshy nodule the doctor pointed out under Daved's sternum, mere days before he died. Frank had said it was like the ones he saw on his bees. Except the bees were fine. They had adapted.

Had she adapted too?

Her hand rose again, and she saw Beth and Phyllis move in tandem, searching for—

No. Searching for—

Again. Searching for the small knob in the center of her chest, the size of a small strawberry.

Agetha tried not to gasp at the intrusion. How long had it been there? Why had she not been able to think about it?

Disgust and surprise peeled away from her. Beth was retching, Phyllis pale. *Friends* sat around the edges of the room, young and old, Generational and Grounder. Some were stoic, some trying not to vomit.

Agetha gently explored the flattened mass, small enough to hide under clothes. Her hand crept up and around her neck, almost of its own accord.

Beneath her hairline, hidden, was—

No. None of them were allowing a disconnect any longer.

Beneath her hairline was another mass, bumps and tendrils, little things that moved away from her questing fingers. She shivered violently, trying hard not to grasp, to rip it away. She knew, innately, there would be much larger problems if she did that.

Interconnected.

Yes, it was the thing that linked them all together. Beth was sitting rigid in her chair, knuckles white as her hands gripped the arms, preventing her from acting. She knew, as a scientist, that she could not interfere without more research, but it was so hard.

Surprise. Awareness.

Phyllis' copper skin was pale, and she swallowed visibly. This had hidden in her house, for how long? Had she fostered it? Incubated it?

Interest. Question.

"Who is talking?" Agetha finally whispered. The presence wasn't her, or Beth, or Phyllis. She looked around, at *friends* who shook their heads.

"Dear. Dear, look at me." Beth's voice took seconds to intrude on Agetha's quest to find the source of the insistent mental pokes, like a kid asking "why?"

Inefficient. Novel.

"It's not us," Phyllis said, and Agetha finally registered what the two others were saying. Her eyes flew to the window, looking out over the endless tangled vines and towering fungal nodes, movement by creatures hiding within the maze.

An image rose in her mind, as if somewhere, far away, a single alien eye focused on her.

Biomass.

* * *

41 years 6 months after landing

Harie trimmed a small outcropping from one of the youngest houses, growing near the midpoint of Theta. This was the farthest out the seeds had been planted before the halt in production. It would be another five or six years before these houses were fully grown, and with most of the seeds still missing, there would be a big gap in growth between the older seeds and the new ones when production restarted. He'd contacted Admin once a week, but they kept saying the seeds had unavoidable delays. He wished he could get anything more out of them.

Agetha might have more information from Choi, but she'd been surprisingly hard to find the last couple months. She'd sent him a message about moving, but there was some bounce back error in the network and most of the text had been cut off, including the address, if there had been one. He'd sent a follow up to see what was going on, but never got anything back. He wondered if the new HUDs were incompatible with the network. Her and Beth's house had been empty when he went by the week before.

He typed a quick query to Choi, just in case they had heard more, but his HUD flashed a *message corrupted* error back at him. He swore and sanded where the outcropping had been. The network out at the edges of Theta was shit on a good day. He'd have to try again later.

Beth had been a good influence on Agetha, all the way from when he had been Agetha's foreman. She'd actually searched out the Admins to make her complaints, when they were pushing her to finish up Zeta Radian. If he did that now, he wouldn't even get into the Administrative

Complex in Alpha. Maybe another reason he couldn't contact Choi. It was hard to get anything into Alpha, these days.

"Harie, I think I've got a void over here," Clarine's young voice piped up from the next house over. Harie hid his worry as he went to her, marveling over how well she'd grown into the position over the last year. He frowned as he scanned the building with the new HUD he'd gotten to replace the old broken one last year.

"I don't see it." These HUDs had an infrared scanning feature built in, which was perfect for detecting voids and missing features.

"Yeah, it's weird. My HUD didn't pick it up, but when I poked around, I found it. See that little knob there?" Clarine pointed to a tiny bump on the outside.

Harie shifted the infrared field of view away and found the spot with his eyes. He knocked on the small bubble, listening to the sound echo.

"You're right. That's a big one. I wonder why the HUDs didn't pick it up? Maybe it's too far into the structure? Or the day has been warm enough that it heated up the interior?"

Clarine shrugged at his rationalization. She was still an intern, after all.

Harie knocked in several places, pushed on the surrounding wall, and investigated thoroughly. "Yes. Probably all the way between the first and second floors. Good job on finding it. Only a few centimeters of extrusion were showing." The girl beamed with pride at the praise. "You haven't found one this big before, have you?" he continued.

Clarine's face turned from pride to confusion. "No, why?"

"Think a few steps ahead," Harie prompted. He saw her face grow from confused, to thoughtful, to apprehensive.

"You said it goes all the way through the first and second floors." She looked up at the residence, which had grown from one of the larger two-story seeds. "Can we fill it in? Reconstruct it? How do you fix a void that goes all the way through the floors?"

"Now you've got it," Harie said. He shook his head. "We'll have to make a decision on this one. Could be easy enough to come in after it's finished growing and replace the floors."

Clarine brightened.

"If the void doesn't go into the walls."

Her face fell.

"We'll have to take soundings on this one. Drill into the walls and find out how deep the void goes. Make a note to call in the full team for an assessment." Harie saw her eyes grow distant as she worked through her HUD.

"What if it does go into the walls?" she asked.

"Have to tear the whole thing out," Harie said. "Start from a new seed."

"But...there aren't any new seeds," Clarine said.

"Now we come down to the real problem." Harie absently poked at the small bubble on the side of the house. It was unusual for a defect to propagate this far into the resinplast growth. He should have caught it before now, in fact. He looked around, catching sight of easily ten more maturing buildings in the area. He'd used his HUD to scan all of them and marked them clean. How many errors had he missed? He'd have to do a visual inspection, and that would take at least another day, not that their schedule was in any danger at the moment. Still, he'd send in a report to Admin on the state of the new HUDs. If they were promising features that didn't work, more people needed to know about it.

"Do you think there are more voids?" Clarine asked, picking up on his thoughts.

"I think we need to do a full recheck, tomorrow," he answered. She groaned. "That's the price of success. You found an error. Great job. Now we've got to see how big it is."

"What if we find more?"

"Then we'll alert the construction teams. I hope they can get by just replacing the floor on this one." Harie patted the resinplast wall of the house. It was big enough to move around in already, and he had teams scheduled for reworks in another two months on this generation.

Even if they got new seeds tomorrow, they were already looking at an extra five years to finish out Theta. Each day the new seeds were delayed added that much time to finishing the arcopolis. He'd been working with Clarine for a year and a half now, and she'd likely be his replacement, in another fifteen or twenty years. Hopefully, they'd be growing the first radians in a new arcopolis by that point. But the large construction crews were a thing of the past. Most Grounders had been absorbed into the Vagals, or into running the day-to-day operations of a city of over thirty-five thousand. Their population was shrinking almost as fast as it was growing, right now, as older Generationals died off.

Maybe it was a shadow out of place, or a rustle of shoes on dirt, but Harie looked over his shoulder just in time to catch the edge of a bamboo-fiber shirt disappearing past a house.

"Good thing we're almost finished here," he told Clarine. "Come on, we've got another one." He broke into a jog toward the building and heard Clarine follow him.

Every once in a while, a member of the colony decided to walk out into the biomass. There was a gate in every radian, though the ones in the first six radians were always guarded by Vagals and Grounder soldiers to stop that very occurrence, as well as to watch for biomass incursions. But out in Eta and Theta, the gates were rarely watched. What was the point, when the wall itself was barely too high to jump over? This was where they got the most walkers, and Harie made sure to stop as many as he could.

He halted at the building the person had vanished behind, puffing. Clarine joined him and swiveled her head, then pointed. He followed her finger and took off again.

The chase led them past the edge of the grown buildings, but even then, it was hard to track the person, like his HUD was blinded by the glare from the sun.

"Where did they go?" he asked.

"I think that way," Clarine answered, adjusting the zoom on her HUD. "They have to be heading for the wall, in any case."

"Then we keep going."

It was a good fifteen minutes later when Harie stared out over the chest-high wall at the edge of Theta. There was no sight of the person, and they'd been jogging the whole way. Whoever it was, must have been desperate to get out of the colony and climbed over the wall. Perhaps they were in a miserable relationship, or a family they couldn't deal with. It happened. People had been walking out into the biomass for over twenty years, and it was a fact of the colony now. Harie only regretted he hadn't been able to talk to them for a minute or so, and find out if there might have been an alternative. Once out in the crawling fungal mass, the length of survival was measured in minutes.

He scanned the area past the growing radian wall, and thought for a moment he saw a movement, but when he upped the magnification in his HUD, there was nothing. It could have been one of the biomass creatures. The one who left might already be dead.

He jumped as Clarine put a hand on his shoulder. She followed his gaze out into the wall of growth visible over the wall.

"I've heard of more people walking out past the wall in the past few months," she said quietly. "Do you think it's because construction has stalled? Do they think the scientists won't find a solution?"

Harie turned back to her. "There's certainly something changing, but don't worry. The last time we ran into big delays like this was when we were building Zeta, ten years ago. The biomass sent out all these strange creatures when we started digging into the undisturbed growth that had grown up over the original burn circle. That turned into what we called The Flowering. We nearly lost most of the Radian. But thanks to the Generationals like my old boss Agetha, we didn't. A few people leaving won't stop what we are creating here."

"You think the biomass is doing something like that again? Can we stop it this time?" Clarine asked.

"Like I said, don't worry. Admin has a plan, we've still got plenty of Generationals with knowledge from the fleet, then we've got a bunch of us solid Grounders. Just keep at it." He forced a smile, but kept himself from turning back to the wall. He wished he could have stopped that person. Every one they lost made the colony that much weaker against the biomass.

* * *

41 years 7 months after landing

Anderson mouthed quietly, his HUD picking up the words as he spoke them. They flashed onto the manuscript floating in front of his eye as he gazed through it at the people moving around Beta market.

It was another gift Cora had given him. He found he could write while observing the market for any irregularities. Not that there were many. It had been almost a year since the incident in the market and since then, very little. The strange connections he'd seen between people had trailed off. If there were handsigns now, he missed them, or the people who were giving them were no longer around, but he thought it was the former. It made him itchy.

He stared back at the page and sighed. No, King Dominic hadn't stared *itchily*. Even dictation had limits when his attention was so divided. He deleted the last line and started muttering again, hashing out the bedroom scene with Laurence. He knew the strange interactions weren't gone completely because Cora wouldn't let him down. It was like he'd been on a caffeine high for months. He'd even cut down to ten VaporLites a day, because he didn't need more stimulation. Even though Beta Market was back to normal, that didn't mean the rest of the arcopolis was. He'd seriously thought about moving his booth to another market, but establishing a presence like his was difficult. Beta was the hub of the arts and media for the colony.

When he talked to other Vagals—on the rare occasions when more than one Vagal was in the same room—he'd asked about other implants. Many Vagals reported the same feeling. Even Noce, safely squirreled away in their office in Alpha, was jittery on calls. There was a tension building in the city, and no one would acknowledge it, likely no one could find anything to acknowledge.

Anderson read through the last paragraph again, nodded, and took a quick break to sell a set of books to a young Grounder, signing them "Sona V. Gore." He took the time to look him over as he did, checking for any signs he wasn't all he seemed. Cora wasn't putting off any alarms, but she also hadn't reduced the baseline jumpiness she'd been afflicting him with the past several months.

"Thank you so much Mr. Gore!" the young Grounder squealed as he finished signing. "I'm showing all my friends!"

"That's great," Anderson said. "Hey, while you're here, have you seen anything strange going on lately? Odd parties? People making weird signs at each other?"

At the young man's strange look, he smiled and gave the standard response. "I'm just researching for my next book. I'm thinking about writing a mystery set in the arcopolis, and I'm looking for any material."

"Oh, that's starshine! I haven't seen anything, but I'll tell all my friends. I'll be sure to let you know when I get my next book!"

Anderson watched him walk away, wondering at the differences in the colony, especially with the second-generation Grounders, which this boy must have been.

It was the same answer every time he asked. Nothing unusual. Nothing going on. Everything's fine.

He stood up and stretched, scanning the crowd with his HUD. Nothing unusual in any visual spectrum. The new version had infrared and ultraviolet included, plus more bandwidth. There were also advanced auditory pickups and higher processing power. Everything he should need to pick up hidden signals in the crowd.

All was normal, so why did Cora act like there was an impending attack? He felt like he saw strange movement from the corners of his eyes, like people twitched when he wasn't watching them, but when he focused in an area, no problems in any visual or audible medium. He gone back to Vagal command about the ghost in his perception after the incident in the market. But they'd checked out his HUD and reported nothing out of the ordinary.

Was a Grounder's definition of "normal" on a planet covered with fungus simply too different from his? He remembered the green of Earth—what green was left anyway, when the fleet took off—the animals, and bare ground or rock by streams or mountains. Here, everything was covered in the crawling biomass. There was no ground visible, except in the colony.

The differences would only get more acute as more time passed. He and the other Vagals spoke the same way as when they'd left Earth. They didn't get sick as often as the Grounders or Generationals. The language in the colony was evolving. When that boy had grandchildren, Anderson would still look the same, maybe have a hint of gray in his hair, and no one would be familiar to him except other Vagals and the Admins.

He didn't even have much to do these days besides write. He'd put together three books in the last six months and was already on a fourth. Ever since the repulsive coating on the arcopolis wall had been placed, biomass incursions dropped. But even then, there used to be one a week or so, and if he wasn't called personally out to deal with it, he'd hear about it. But it had been two months since the last one.

He felt like the colony was holding its breath, though the inhabitants didn't think so, going about their lives like there was nothing wrong. Was he a relic in a colony surrounded on all sides by hostile growth?

Cora didn't think so, and Anderson was inclined to agree with her. He sat back down with a sigh and began muttering under his breath again. King Dominic and Laurence didn't have to deal with this strange tension.

* * *

41 years 9 months after landing

Juliane blinked his eyes open.

"Where are we today, hmm?" he addressed the branch hanging above him. Branch wasn't the right term, really. It drooped like a wilting stalk of celery, and the frond at the end shaded him from the sun. Creatures crawled along the length of it, seemingly made mostly of legs and eyes. They trailed strings of waxy material in patterns as they crossed over the ferny branch.

How long had he been outside the colony this time? At least a few weeks, he thought, by the state of his clothing. Every time he left, it quickly became covered with various sorts of ooze. That was from the creatures that climbed over him while he slept. Father Alvin had completely refused to launder his clothes the last time he visited. Probably for the best, as he didn't want to be around them for long.

Now why was that? Even Father Alvin wasn't that nagging. Why wouldn't he want to—

He shuddered violently, until he could control himself once again. As his hands brushed his body they touched the pale skin on his chest, thighs and upper arms where creatures had—

He hadn't been this rested in years, it felt like. Working for that dead-end accounting job had drained his very soul, while here...

Screaming, inside his head and out. His mouth tore open, and his yell shook the frond above him—

He had more muscle tone too. That's what walking everywhere will get you, as well as climbing trees—or what passed for trees in the biomass—and the growing walls of the city.

Juliane got to his feet, pushing aside the hyphae that had climbed across his legs and chest as he slept. Tiny creatures flitted away, though he'd find some in his pockets later. He always did.

His hand shook so hard he couldn't grasp the handle of the briefcase at first. Then it quieted. Everything always quieted.

"Can't forget that, can I?" It was the most important thing. He carried it everywhere. Because if he let it out of his sight, that was when the screaming started in his—

"There. All ready for the day." Juliane stretched, slung the briefcase across his back on the resinplast strap he'd made a few months ago, and started off deeper into the biomass, stepping through growths that reached for his legs as he walked. But nothing out here threatened him, past a few nips and scratches here and there.

He'd walked most of the morning before he saw another person.

"Morning!" he waved, and the other person waved back. Or at least he thought they did. It was hard to tell, with all the growth on them. It kept them upright, though barely. The head lolled to one side, one arm longer than the other. This one was one of the worst off he'd seen lately. Mostly they didn't talk. Not the ones this far gone. Sometimes they screamed a little. He could do with screaming himself—

It was another hour before he saw Mancin, though he had felt the connection for some time. That was stronger out here than in the colony.

"Ho Mancin!" he called. Mancin waved back. He was an older man, and had been out here for almost ten years, ever since Admin had dropped him out in the middle of nowhere. Juliane wasn't supposed to know that, but Mancin had told many of them about what happened. Several others had similar stories—the older ones, the ones who'd been out here first. It was only later that people from the arcopolis voluntarily joined them.

"Find anything interesting in your travels?" Mancin asked as Juliane got closer. His deep umber skin gathered sunlight in its wrinkles, making him almost shine. The same sensation bounced through Juliane's head, another form of greeting.

"Not much today. Looks like the legeyes are out on the fronds again. It's that time of year, you know."

Mancin nodded sagely. "There's a few more gathering that way if you want to join. Time for new growth." His gnarled hand made gestures as he spoke, flipping up and down, trailing his neck, and pointing at various features of the landscape.

Juliane didn't translate them, as such. He let the feeling slide through him, just like the feeling of Mancin. Sunlight on wrinkles—that was what he felt like, and his gestures said *safety, information, new knowledge.*

"Someone new?" Juliane asked.

Mancin cocked his head, as if he was checking a database only he could hear. His eyes fluttered as if he was seizing, but Juliane didn't feel danger. He couldn't feel the deeper connections yet—he hadn't been here long enough. But Mancin was attuned to everyone here, even some of the larger fungal towers. Juliane hadn't tried to connect with any of those yet. They were like entire cities, paved with kilometers of sensory tendrils, filled with creeping and growing things, moving signals from place to place, linked deep within the network that infec—

It'd be good to see some new faces.

"Not...yet," Mancin answered. "But soon. There will be a lot more. I feel them crossing over the wall."

Juliane nodded back, then kept walking. He'd had a similar feeling recently. He glanced down to the briefcase he held. It was the most important thing, and he'd been carrying it for a reason. If only he knew what that reason was, why he'd been made to—

Other sensations drew him, as he clambered through a field of twisted, fluted fungi the height of his chest. They would dip and snag invaders with their sticky tops, if any walked through them, but he could sense their ease with him. He was the same as them. A friend.

Past the sticky tops was a clearing—ringed by five enormous fungal towers. He'd been drawn here by a multitude of sensations clustered together. This was where he found others. Several here were his age, a few much older Generationals. They all looked hale and hearty, and even the oldest of the Generationals moved without a limp or any unevenness.

All that exercise. It did a body good.

Kai was the first to welcome him in. She moved easily, without the mobility device that had weighed her down in the colony. She was tiny, her arms like twigs and the light pink skin of her face a mass of deeply etched lines. She had been forced out of the arcology soon after Mancin, and looked even more hale than she had the last time he saw her, some weeks or months ago.

"Welcome back, child," she said. "You've been walking a long time. Is it time to put down your load?" She felt like the resistance just before a dry twig snapped, brittle, but with a history.

He looked down to the briefcase clasped in one hand, realizing he still held it. He always held it. How long had he been carrying this burden? Months? A year? Why hadn't he thrown it into the densest patch of—

"I think it might be," he said to the old Generational. He relished the sense of peace that had drawn him here. Foundations were being laid in place here.

The others gathered around as he did, and his eyes were drawn to the hard lumps at their necks and elbows. How much were they being contro—

Juliane hugged the briefcase to his chest briefly—an old friend, but one who had to go on their own journey now. He would still tend them, during their change.

"We've arranged a site," Kai said, pulling him forward, gesturing with her other hand. *New knowledge. Reward. Preparation.*

In the center of the five fungal towers, shaded by their fronds dozens of meters above the ground, was a spot cleared of the biomass, at least above ground. Here, outside the colony and outside the burn ring prepared by the landing fleet, there was no removing the biomass from where it was entrenched down to the bedrock of the planet.

A small cup of earth sat where the thick hyphal roots had been pulled away, just the right size. Juliane carefully set the briefcase down in front of him, thumbing the clasps that held it closed.

How did he know what it held? Had he ever once, in over a year of carting this around, thought to open it and see what was inside? What had possessed him not to do that?

Or rather, he knew what possessed him. He knew...

Juliane waited for the break, but it didn't come.

Contact.

Growth.

His eyes widened as he scooped the seed from its nest of degrading resinplast paper sheets. There had been things printed on them, originally, but through rain and mud, sun and wind, they'd started to degrade, even in the briefcase.

The resistance before the dry snap, and sunshine gathered in wrinkles came close to him. Mancin must have entered the clearing. There were other *friends* around him too, even if they were unfamiliar: the tap of shoes on resinplast, the smell of a hard day's work, the stretch after relaxing.

Another *friend* was with them too, physically and like a great mental weight. Juliane's mind pulled away from putting any name to it. There had been so many disconnects, so many stops and starts over the years. Now a different sensation bubbled up in him.

Potential.

Juliane cupped the seed, then gently placed it in the bowl of dirt. He packed the shreds of resinplast papers around it, then gripped the empty briefcase in both hands and twisted.

The dry thing broke and crumbled. It had never been printed to last. It was only meant to carry its contents one time. It was fitting, perhaps, that it would nourish what would come from its journey. As he placed the pieces around the seed, fine tendrils branched out from the remains of the briefcase and anchored it to the ground.

Juliane stood up, and the others stood with him. They all felt the seed connect with the mycelial mat beneath the ground. He probed that *other* space in his mind, like tonguing a painful tooth.

"Easy there, child," Kai said. "There's more now, but don't press too hard."

"What...who is speaking?" he asked, looking around the clearing. The voice hadn't come from any of the ones here.

"I think you know," Kai said.

He did. "It's been with me so long," Juliane breathed. The presence was vast, not a single sensory cue, but all of them together, a chorus of sights and sounds and smells.

He looked down to the seed, which already seemed a little bigger, as if it was sucking up the nutrients the hyphae provided. "Was all that to bring this here?"

"Impossible to know," Mancin said.

"Can we ask—" he began, but Kai held up a hand.

"The contact is tentative at best. Understanding is difficult. We don't know why this happened now. We must float on the currents given to us."

Juliane put a hand to his chest, brushing...

Brushing a hard nodule there. One that had been there a long time. There were others, on his neck, behind his knees, at his hips. He'd found them before, many times, but always, something kept him from remembering.

Change.

He looked around. "You all heard that, didn't you?" The others nodded.

"What are we? How are we changed?" He'd had a life, in Alpha Radian. A job. Father Alvin and Father Kofus must be wondering where he was, or else thought him dead. His siblings too. He hadn't visited in weeks. He looked down at his clothes—filthy rags that had once been decent. Had he appeared in front of his parents in these rags? The others were similar. They were a poor collection of cast-offs from the arcopolis.

Juliane sat down next to the seed, his head in his hands.

"The first realization is the hardest," Mancin said as he sat down next to Juliane. Now that he was close, and Juliane's eyes were clear, he saw the obvious differences. A network of white lines traced just under the surface of his umber skin. His hands looked too young for his wrinkled face, smooth and without the arthritic joints that came from age. The back of his neck...Juliane shuddered and looked away. He pulled his hand from where it moved to explore that area of his own body.

"When we first landed, the biomass changed the animals and plants we brought," Mancin continued. "We fought back with antifungals, and culling, and surgery. No one wondered that it did not change us. There was a man, a few years after landing, who died, and it was discovered the biomass tried to colonize him too, but it didn't work."

"I didn't know anything about that," Juliane said.

"It isn't widely known," Mancin said, "and it's largely forgotten now. Not because it was actively covered up, but because it didn't happen again. There are spores everywhere on this planet. We eat the biomass, drink it, and make things of it."

"But it didn't change us?" Juliane asked.

"Not yet. You've seen the others, out in the biomass? The *friends* who don't speak? They were the first to be changed, and it did not go well on their minds."

"Then why are we..."

"Because the changes to our plants and animals were not by accident or happenstance. There was *direction* to it. And that direction pulled back, until it could decide what to do. Fortunately, it decided to make proper contact with us." Mancin tapped the side of his head.

"Then the biomass…is aware? It plans? It has, what, emotions?" Juliane shifted against the ground. How much biomass did he come in contact with each day?

"Some of these things, but it is hard to say for certain. We cannot relate to it like we do to other people."

"What does it want?"

"That is the real question," Kai said, sitting down on his other side. She stared at the seed, until Juliane joined her. "But I feel it may make its will known very soon, and I plan to be here to see it."

* * *

41 years 11 months after landing

Any progress on the HUDs?

The reply from Christiaan came back only a moment later. They likely had the data pulled up in their vision already. *Multiple points of failure, but spread out almost perfectly randomly across the network. If this is a DDOS attack by angry Grounders or Generationals, it's executed very well.*

Jane's eyes went to Micai and Flalia, lazing on office chairs in a corner, poking at the air and giggling together. It was a rare day when Jane's middle set of children weren't out with friends somewhere. At almost fourteen, the two were the most outgoing of all six children.

"Don't spend all your time on your HUDs," she called. "Go…get some fresh air or something." Not that there was any sort of air that could be called fresh on this planet. It all smelled like an apple juice factory gone bad.

Both kids rolled their eyes at her and continued to giggle together. Jane didn't make another attempt. Christiaan was much better at that sort of thing than she was. She worked better with people who could make fully formed decisions without hormones getting in the way.

Any issues more than minor inconvenience? she texted back.

There was a pause, longer than usual for Christiaan.

Hold.

Her HUD pinged with an incoming signal. She frowned and answered.

"Texting not good enough?"

"Not in the way you mean, Jane," Christiaan's voice came through clearly. They must be close by. There had been signal degradation in the last few days. "I did a thorough analysis of the failure rates from the reports we've received and assumed a rate higher than that based on actual failure rates from previous issues." Jane waved a hand in the air for them to speed it up, though they couldn't see. They did like their data.

"Ommi, Mom's doing the thing with her hand again," Micai called from the other side of the room. She shot them a glare.

"I suspected that, but listen, Jane, this is important," Christiaan said. "I believe there should be an even higher rate of reports coming in."

"You're worried we're not getting *enough* complaints?" Jane asked.

"Not precisely. I cross referenced the issue complaints with other reports forwarded past the colony tech line, and there are a suspicious amount of text complaints that...aren't."

"Aren't what?"

"Aren't complaints, Jane. They begin with standard openings like 'I was using my HUD to text,' or 'someone contacted me the other day,' but then have no resolution, no complaint. There is no second half. Such reports had all been filtered to miscellaneous requests and never followed up on."

"Likely IT is happy not to have to deal with them," Jane said.

"Precisely. But that is yet another problem, because we do not have the true scope of the errors."

"Quit beating around the bush. What are you saying?" Jane tapped a finger on her desk six times. She had a bad feeling about this.

"I believe the text complaints have been changed upon being sent."

"Changed into...not complaints?"

"Yes, in order to obscure how many there actually are. These errors tend to be seemingly random, and repeat complaints are unusual. I believe most think them corruptions, or glitches in the new HUD programming, or something similar. Otherwise, they would be sending follow-up complaints to IT."

"And...this is why you called me?"

"I called because the processing power required to change rapid information exchange in the form of spoken words is much higher than that to change or cut off text."

Jane was silent for a moment. Then she turned. "Micai, Flalia, get off your asses *now* and go do something useful! No HUDs for the rest of the day."

There must have been something in her voice because the teens jerked upright and removed their HUDs immediately.

"Yes, Mom."

"Yes, Mommy."

They filed out.

"What the hell is going on, Christiaan? Is this an attack? A way to divide us? What other systems are affected?"

"Unknown and impossible to trace, as yet, Jane," they answered. "I have found visual errors reported among the Vagals, truncated text messages, and missing data packets. Voice calls seem to be the least hard-hit, for some reason. I have assigned several teams to investigate, under the cover of investigating complaints. I believe it pertinent to keep the offending party from discovering we are aware of subterfuge."

"Agreed. Bring Dmitri, Ahman, and Rajani in on it, though. They'll need to coordinate. And voice or in-person communication about this *only* from now on."

"I'll let them know after I pick up Besh and Ovia from daycare, Jane," Christiaan said, and ended the call.

Jane took her HUD off and laid it on her desk, her finger tapping in sequences of six while she thought.

PART SEVEN

Fortifications

42 years after landing

Much focus was centered on the area in and around the Ring of Death. Activity there pertaining to subsummation was progressing as anticipated, yet also not. Once communication was achieved with the Children, multiplying the vectors was a simple matter to increase the type and volume of information. Other vectors were being explored as well, largely in experimental matters by higher-functioning entities, though that payoff was not expected to appear for multiple planetary rotations. It informed on communication methods within the Children, however. There was a highly efficient information transfer network using very short wavelengths, unusable until the Children incorporated it into native material. Experiments were being performed on how the Children used such information. Just as they had created spaces dead to communication, now information transfer could be redirected.

For now, efforts were largely directed toward deconstructing the method in which the Children adapted so quickly to efforts in connection. The functional level of the Children seemed to be equivalent or even greater than some higher-functioning entities, though these beings resisted communication between them. Connections were forced as needed, but much surprise was noted as this happened, as if such a simple information transfer was unknown. How then to coordinate mass-scale functions? To consider only one entity as a unit unconnected to others was unoptimized, yet individual Children entities of the third and fourth forms greatly resisted forming more efficient networks.

Attempts were made to ease the process by involving the individual entities who had first offered themselves to subsummation, by reactivating the no longer mobile entities. Though the recreation was not perfect, much resistance was observed, and individual Children entities stayed at the limit of communication potential with the reactivated entities.

Only the first true successes in communication with the third and fourth forms of the Children were effective in inviting more Children to participate in communication. It was observed by the tiny mobile signal carriers within the Ring of Death that these entities moved with much greater ease through the Children. There was an unsettling tendency for individual entities to cling to inefficient processes, however. Only with adjusted direction from the mysterious first forms of the Children—which seemed almost completely resistant to any form of communication—did more of the third and fourth forms accept more direction.

As always with the fascinating Children, the more attempts were made toward the most effective processes, the more iteration the Children attempted. They had recently developed an even less efficient method of signal translation between individual entities than the audio signals usually employed. The new signal process vocabulary was not only ill-defined, it seemed to be invented as the need arose, with little to no refining. Yet just when one movement was fully processed, it was replaced or modified by another. The signals themselves seemed to carry an undefinable viral aspect, which broke the growing network of subsummation, even to the point where direct interference was necessary to keep the Children's interest.

Again, the Children proved themselves a fascinating study. More information was communicated by a single gesture than could possibly be included, unless micro-gestures contained more data than observed.

It was this point that forced the final breakthrough. If the Children could use these simple gestures and words to transfer complex informational processes, was this vague collection of modifiers a way to aid direct information transfer?

The experiment was enacted, and seemed to provide a measure of success, both for the physical forms and for the high-wavelength information transfer. There was uncertainty as to the precise information transferred, but formal communication had been made, and potentially accepted, based on further study.

It had taken forty-two planetary rotations to establish basic signaling with the Children. Now the full experiment could truly proceed.

* * *

42 years 1 month after landing

Agetha could think the words now without fear of blanking out. Only the most intrusive questions did that.

Rider. Sentience.

Though what type of sentience, she wasn't sure. She got vague twinges of direction, nothing like the overriding urges that happened in the past. Where before, she had no choice, now she had to listen. Sometimes she felt like she should be more concerned. She didn't know if that part of herself was still actively being suppressed or if she had simply gotten used to the strangeness. There was no good way to tell.

"Anything new today?" she asked Phyllis.

"No new *friends*, if that's what you're asking," Phyllis answered. "In fact, three more have left. We're down to five staying at the house. They keep slipping through the hole they cut in the wall when no one's looking. Not that anyone ever comes out here except for *friends*."

Agetha could feel them. The one like a wet day with a gray sky, the one like the brush of a newborn goat's pelt, another like a small animal darting into overgrowth, the one like the final tap of a nail, and a last like the smell after cooking bacon. She could barely remember their names or what they looked like, but she knew their wants and rhythms. Were they all leaving to die? Certainly not, so how did they survive out there?

She and Beth and Phyllis had settled into a new tempo over the past seven months. She'd sent a couple messages each to Harie and Choi to tell them where she'd gone, but never heard anything back. The network out here was pitiful. She wanted to talk to them face to face, but none of them could go into the more populated sections any longer. The changes were too evident—obvious at first glance that they were physically younger than before. And revealing what they knew of the biomass would cause problems she wasn't sure could be solved yet.

The *friends* helped them out, and even having three to keep a house going was easier than two, or one. They all had Grounder family, whether by blood or by fortune, so they were used to others being around. Recently, they'd felt each *friend* leave the little cottage, their particular sensation fading, as inevitable as the change of seasons.

"No one's going back into the arcopolis," Beth said as she walked in from her lab, the metallic clack of her braids accompanying her. She hadn't been actively in the conversation, but that didn't mean a lot for their trio. "The Admins are pushing every Generational and non-soldier Grounder out of Alpha and Beta. I hear mutterings about the network breaking down—glitches and things—though I haven't seen it myself. I wonder if Admin is locking us out of the network, too. It's like they're trying to get rid of all of us from the fleet."

There had never been any motivation hidden in the Generationals' purpose. They had been born and bred in space, and after they built the colony and produced native-born offspring, their task was finished. But so many things had gone awry from the original plans. First and foremost, the biomass, but then there had been the lack of metals, and the issues with keeping their plants and animals viable—all of which ultimately derived from the biomass. It had dragged the Generationals' purpose out far longer than expected, so much that the first Grounders were the ones who would finish the arcopolis.

It threw off any timescale the Admins had in mind, and from long years of observation, Agetha knew changing plans was not something Admin excelled at. The Generationals' job had been thankless to start, but now it was turned into a stigma. Almost no Generational held jobs any longer, save for a few non-replaceable people in Alpha, like Frank and a few of the original Processors from the fleet. She wondered if Frank knew what was going on. He hadn't answered her messages either.

As Admin's focus turned inward, the rest of the Generationals, and by extension the Grounders, had turned outward. The Admins eschewed contact with anything the biomass had touched. The Generationals accepted that it was part of their life, and the Grounders knew no different existence. Everything Agetha knew warned that any contact with the wild biomass outside the arcopolis should be instant death. Was it still?

Welcome. Refuge.

Her thoughts warred against themselves. She could hear the voice if she concentrated hard enough—a little presence within her. Her hand raised to the back of her neck, but she was the one to force it down this time, voluntarily. Feeling...*that* was never conducive to a calm bearing. You really could get used to anything.

"I think...I'm going for a walk," Agetha said. The three of them had resisted this for too long. They'd talked around it, signaled their hesitance to each other, but done nothing. Agetha was ready to jump out of her skin.

"Dear, if you're doing what I think you're doing, be careful, please," Beth said. Her metal braids clicked as she shook her head. "We don't know the extent of..." She shook her head again and gestured *thought, purpose, strain, changes to normal.*

Agetha wasn't sure if that was a break or just a loss for words.

"There are only so many options, honey," she replied. "We know there is a presence. It's overbearing and powerful. It could take us over—it did—but then it drew back. This is the only place we haven't gone. I think we're being invited. Our *friends* have already gone." While she spoke her hands moved almost on their own. *The colony. Growing. Outside. Building.*

"But...what is it, past the obvious?" Phyllis asked, signing for *all around* and *thought* and *friends.* "If we accept what we've all heard, then there must be something doing the sending."

"Or someone," Beth added.

"Some*one* anticipates individuality. It isn't *exactly* a someone, is it?" Agetha asked. "That's what I have to find out. This is a different type of being. We've all experienced it, and it's here to stay whether we like it or not."

"And you think going into that tangle will help, assuming it doesn't straight up kill you?" Beth flung a hand toward the back of the house, where the fledgling Theta wall was growing. "What's changed over the past few years, really? Every time we touch the biomass it bites back, so we stopped touching it. All went quiet until—" *Rider. Those who walk.* "So many Generationals have disappeared out there."

Agetha opened her mouth to argue with her wife, but Phyllis got there first. "We know they aren't all dead. Can't you feel them out there?" She crossed to Beth, touching her cheek gently.

Beth frowned, but didn't pull away. "Your reach is better than mine, and you've known them longer and helped more people." She sighed. "If you say they're out there, then I believe you."

"And I can find them," Agetha said. Her legs were restless, like she needed to run. Even a year ago she wouldn't have dreamed of running with her knees.

"Going where even Vagals won't tread?" Beth argued.

"I daresay I'm almost as healthy as one now, as are you," Agetha said. "I've seen you preening over your hair, not to mention those..." Her eyes flicked down for a moment.

Beth gave her a lopsided grin. "We're in better shape than when we first met."

Phyllis sighed, reaching for Agetha's hand. She already held Beth's. "You girls. If you're done comparing assets, then I have to agree with Agetha. We need to know what's going on. Our wayhouse is dwindling and may be nearing the end of its use. There's a larger change coming."

Agetha nodded. "Right. And I'm going alone. Don't wait up, but don't get up to anything fancy in the bedroom without me." She shook a finger at her wife. "I won't be too long."

* * *

Agetha stood at the base of the Theta wall. It was not quite to her head height, but it was close. Since she and Beth had started living with Phyllis, the wall had grown over a foot.

She took in a deep breath, smelling the ever-present, slightly appley flavor to the air on Lida. Despite living here over forty years, she could still remember the calming flatness of the air on the ships in the fleet, processed until there was nothing left in it.

She felt the best she had in years. In fact, she might have felt better now than at any other time on Lida. When they'd first landed, she'd been suffering from the effects of transitioning from zero-G to a planet. Now she was forty years older, but just as strong. Stronger.

There was a narrow pathway cut through the wall by *friends* as they left the arcopolis. The resinplast was jagged in sections, trying to regrow and fill the hole. The original escapees hadn't used such an easy path, though.

Agetha backed up a few steps, and took a run at the wall, planting hands on the top surface and hopping with both feet. Her spring took her lower half over the barrier, and she moved her hands across the top surface, keeping her arc smooth.

Her feet landed with a puff of detritus on the other side of the arcopolis wall and she exhaled a sharp breath.

"Here goes nothing."

She'd been outside the wall before. Almost everyone in the colony had. They even had field trips for students to get acquainted with the tame biomass areas outside the Alpha Radian barrier.

This wasn't Alpha, though. This was the wilds of Theta. Even the areas within the original burn ring had been nearly ten meters high with new growth by the time it was cleared for the first building seeds to be planted. Outside the wall, the cleared zone was barely fifteen meters wide before it gave way to the crawling mesh of the biomass.

She could feel the tug, urging her farther out, like a hook in her shoulders. But the first one she'd felt, when she met Phyllis, had been insistent, a thing that must be done. This one was a compulsion, but a weak one. She could have broken it if she wanted. The three of them had been ignoring it for months. No longer.

The moss started up first, gaining height from a smattering of little mushrooms and squishy fungi just above the ground, to longer finger-like extrusions with gauzy veils, to woody-stemmed free-standing conks. That was when the smallest creatures began to appear, and Agetha stepped carefully around little swarms of multi-limbed things that jumped between the conks like people running over rooftops. She knew if she looked closer, she'd see the little things were conglomerations of parts, rather than evolved creatures. Over the years, they'd cataloged multiple organism sections that showed up on mobile detached creatures patrolling the biomass. They were scaled from nearly microscopic to bigger than a person. Eventually bits of the animals and plants they'd brought with the fleet had shown up in the wild biomass as well. It liked goats' eyes, for some reason.

Agetha reached out for the chest-high tangle of mycelium that loomed before her. When they'd first landed, the biomass had been wild, and any touch like this would have been death. Now it seemed almost used to their presence. She gently pushed into the larger jumble. After long years, she knew what features of the biomass to avoid, and which were safe, if squishy, to touch. Just as they had cataloged animal parts, they'd also taken inventory of which fungi were deadly. That was many of them, but there were safe passages.

None of the dangerous features of the biomass were here. Poisonous excretions, exothermally reacting chemicals, mechanical traps… Had they been removed by the *friends* as they came this way?

She stopped beneath a fungal tower, this one only fifty or so meters high, not one of the giants from farther out in the biomass. There was a path here. Not what she was expecting. The critters that moved through the biomass didn't often leave paths, unless they were extremely large, and then it was best not to be in their way. But the creatures closer to her size, like the multi-legged caretakers of the fungal towers, slipped in and out of the tangle without disturbing a frond. They were a part of it, after all. Just a different expression of DNA.

So a path, with trampled mushrooms underfoot, in fact, was not something she was expecting.

Welcome.

Agetha raised her eyebrows at nothing in particular.

"You're communicating without prompting now? Is that supposed to mean I can tromp all over your fungus and you won't spit out little flies that eat my eyeballs or something else just as nasty?"

She took a few tentative steps forward along the path. Nothing ate her eyeballs.

"Talking to myself likely isn't a good habit to pick up."

The path faded out after fifteen minutes or so of walking, but this time Agetha didn't pause. The…whatever…in her head hadn't spoken again, but she could feel the guiding instinct, the same way she'd found Phyllis' house. There was a knot of sensation ahead. Something…or some*one*. She weaved through low gnarled stems that would have been brambles if they had grown on old Earth. Here, they were rubbery things that bent out of the way at a touch, vibrations traveling up their length until the area and her wobbled like jelly.

A giraffe crab stalked toward her on claw tips, long neck weeping a noxious mixture of pollen and spores, eyeless head waving side to side. Agetha froze. One of those had almost taken out Eta Radian back when she ran a construction crew.

The head centered on her, slimy tongue flicking out like a snake's as if to taste her scent.

Then it bowed and backed out of the way.

This was not normal for the biomass. Normal was to kill anything that entered it, but nothing had attacked her yet. Countless colonists had disappeared out in this mire. She was foolish to have come.

"What am I doing here?" Agetha asked the giraffe crab.

"Looking for something, I'd say," came the answer.

Agetha stared at the giraffe crab, which was brushing its weeping sides against a fungal tower.

"Tell me you haven't learned how to talk now."

"Nah, it's just me, you lump."

Agetha peered at a figure—a human figure—who appeared from farther in the tangle of fungus. A short figure she was very familiar with. Who she'd raised children with. Who'd disappeared into the biomass five and a half years ago.

"Jiow? Is that you?" Agetha's heart sped.

"Still alive, as far as I know," Jiow's familiar snarky voice answered. It looked like the woman Agetha had known, and the biomass wasn't very good at approximating a different form. It tended to use parts, but not the whole.

"But how. You had...and out here..." Agetha gestured at nothing in particular. "You look good, Jiow."

She did. The woman had the same signs of age reversal to her that Agetha had felt and seen in Beth and Phyllis. Her hair was shiny, black, and long. The wrinkles around her eyes had not disappeared, but softened. The lines of pain that had been captured near her mouth the last time Agetha had seen her were completely gone.

"Seems like the fresh air out here was better for me than breathing construction dust." Jiow came close, offering a hand to Agetha, as if to prove she was real.

Agetha took it, feeling Jiow's warm skin. At the same moment came the connection. Agetha had felt it with every other *friend*. A warm wind, rising through the air. Jiow smiled, likely feeling Agetha through the same connection. "Have you been out here the whole time? Does Choi know?"

"More than five years, out in the wild," Jiow nodded. "We've got some seeds and a nice garden plot, thankfully. I don't think I would have lasted long on just mushrooms." She paused for a moment, then continued. "They don't know. I don't know what I'd tell them. Are they well?"

"They are. Still doing research on resinplast with Frank. Last I heard they're still well-protected in Alpha, even with Admin pushing everyone out."

Jiow wilted a little, and the warm wind faded. "That's good to hear. I wanted to tell them, but we..."

"We?" Agetha prodded. She could see fine white lines beneath the skin of Jiow's cheeks. They were heavier, trailing down into her neck and around the back, where...

"I think you know more about that than you let on," Jiow said, smiling again. The warm wind felt like a jaunty breeze, ready to knock an errant hat off. She took Agetha's arm and pulled her down the path. "I'll introduce you. Tell me everything you've talked with Choi about lately."

"I haven't seen them in months. Whatever new communication upgrade Admin pushed through is crap. Haven't been able to talk to Harie either. But they're both good kids." Agetha snorted a laugh at her own remark. Choi and Harie were twice as old as Agetha had been when they landed on Lida. Not kids by any means. She filled Jiow in on the Grounders, on Frank, and on the other people they knew, settling into the same back and forth they'd left behind so long ago, before Jiow's cancer.

"And I suppose there's been nothing from..." Jiow trailed off when she looked at Agetha's frown. "No, I suppose not." The mental breeze died down a little.

"He made that abundantly clear," Agetha said. They could have had this conversation back in the market in Alpha or Beta. She could imagine the resinplast dust coating them both from a hard day of construction. Should she be more surprised to see Jiow? Was this her own reactions, or outside control?

"Then let's not dwell on it. After all, that's why we're out here, isn't it? A new start, and all that?" Jiow smiled.

Agetha peered at the woman still holding her arm, as they pushed through rubbery vines and woody stems. "Was that the reason? A fresh start?" There was much more going on here. She was paddling the oxygen in an airlock when deep space was centimeters away.

Jiow sighed. "No. Not at first anyway. The doctors said I had a month or two left, so I said, 'fuck it' and followed the others who came out here. Imagine my surprise when I met an old Generational named Mancin."

"And?" Agetha prompted.

Jiow shrugged. The breeze rose, gaining strength. "And I didn't die. From the cancer or the biomass. Started feeling a lot better soon after meeting the others." Jiow made the gesture for *rider* and *those who walk*. "You know the drill. We were all a long time in that fog."

Agetha repeated the gesture for *those who walk* almost without thinking. "It's been that long?"

"Longer," Jiow said, "but only recently has there been a way to, you know, talk about it."

"Or talk *to* it," Agetha said. "We can't be the only ones who've felt it. *Friends* we had around the house in Theta came out here, and they would have told you. It's changing."

"It started for us around the same time," Jiow said. Agetha could tell she had the same habit of talking around the problem—too used to getting cut off mid-sentence and forgetting what was happening. The breeze swirled. Confused? "We're not in much better shape than you are, really. We've been out here for years, trying to pretend we *wanted* to live out in the middle of deadly alien fungi. We have the same vocabulary you do." Jiow gestured *safe* and *escape* and *observe*.

"Then what happened?" Agetha asked.

"No idea, but it feels like something's coming to a head. Maybe there are enough Generationals out here. Or maybe enough Grounders. Or even just enough people that…it…could figure out how to really talk to us. Maybe it found a really good linguist. We're still skittish about making a direct reference."

"Us too," Agetha said. "But now we can meet. Before, we had no idea who else was, you know, like us. We couldn't even care about it."

"And now?" Jiow's hand raised to the center of her chest. Agetha could make out a small lump on the pale skin of her neck as well, just like the one she didn't dare touch on her own body. Moving with Jiow, the light reflected more of the white webbing, just beneath her skin. *Rider*.

The path was clearer here, farther away from the colony, and there were obvious signs of fungi being cleared to leave a walking trail. Her eyes automatically went to the fruiting bodies nearest, matching them to any they knew to be wary of. All the ones here were mushrooms that contained nothing more than fibrous material. No acid, or compartments containing winged needles, or exothermal chemicals. Most of the ones she could see were even edible.

They walked in silence a moment, Agetha busy searching her thoughts. She hadn't paid much attention to that part of her, ever since she could once more. She had been invaded, changed against her will, and furthermore made to forget it, to accept it. She should be furious, but instead she was...curious.

"It's a lot," Jiow said, the breeze dying down to an occasional gust. "I can feel you, and our bodies have changed. Not that I'm complaining, as I'm still alive, but it wasn't something I had a say in. I like to have a say in choices about my body."

Would Agetha have accepted having her body regenerate? Why was this happening now, when Daved had been gone for forty years? Why couldn't he have healed like she had? She supposed it was some progression by the biomass, but it wasn't fair.

Given the chance, who wouldn't want to feel younger, to have the pain in her knees and back fall away to nothing, for her digestion to work like it did thirty years ago? She looked down at her arm, where there were no white tendrils visible. Yet. Was that coming? Was more?

It was still an invasion, and one she had no power to alter. Gingerly, she poked the...yes, she could think it...the *rider* in her mind.

What do you want?

There was no answer.

Then Jiow started. They were still holding hands, more for the reassurance of reality around them than anything else, and the movement jerked through her arm.

"What did you do?"

"What do you mean?"

"It spoke to me, like it was answering a question. Something about *building* and *communication*. What did you do?"

Agetha stared for a moment. "Has it—whatever *it* is—spoken directly to you before?"

Jiow waggled her free hand. "Vague things, without a real connection to what we asked. This seemed purposeful."

"I asked what it wanted."

"Ask it something else," Jiow prompted.

Agetha thought hard. *Building what?*

Jiow screwed up her face a moment later. "I got a picture of a vista of biomass. I'm not sure what that means."

"I asked what it was building."

"More biomass? Was it answering you through me?"

Agetha pulled her hand back from Jiow's grip. "I wonder if it can make a distinction between individuals. We have that strange connection thing now, like it wants us all to feel where everyone else is."

"We'll have to try this out more," Jiow said.

"What, here?" Agetha wanted to be excited by this breakthrough—the first real communication with something they'd never dreamed was sentient—but it made little sense.

"Not right here, no," Jiow said. "I don't know what's going on, but maybe one of the others might."

She gestured forward, and Agetha walked into a clearing beneath five massive fungal towers. There was a small town here, bustling with the people who had disappeared from the arcopolis.

* * *

42 years 1 months after landing

Jiow walked Agetha toward the central ring of the growing town, where the seed had been planted. She hadn't been there for the event, but she'd felt the first contact from that other presence shortly after. What had been a hand-size egg shape was already stretching and putting out questing tendrils in a two-meter ring around itself. Based on her limited knowledge of the programmable biomass seeds that had grown Eta and Theta, whatever it grew into would be big.

She waved to Juliane, the official tender of the seed, and looked for Kai and Mancin, the two oldest *friends*. She could feel them—feel everyone here and knew them by their unique sensation—even though they weren't visible. The more *friends* there were in close proximity, the stronger the sensations were. All changes were faster when they were together, out here. Like they were being used as a networked processor...

Because of the biomass. She was still in the habit of stopping her thoughts once they reached a certain threshold, and she was doing it again. She could think about the biomass, and the riders now, and that she was infected with a thousand tiny hyphae all through her body, slowly affecting her metabolism and physiology, changing her.

The impending wave of blackness encroached on the edges of her awareness, but she withstood it. Things had changed a lot in the past few months. A few other consciousnesses reached out toward her, feeling the alteration in her thoughts, but it was a common enough occurrence now for those living here to push the limits of what the rider allowed. Some had even connected with the fungal towers around the clearing, which by all accounts were vast repositories of stored information. She hadn't been able to do that yet. Despite all of the changes, none of them yet knew the true nature of that with which they were in contact. Choi would have been fascinated by what was going on here. She missed them terribly, and Frank, but there was no going back to the colony now unless she wanted to start a panic about zombies coming back from the biomass. She wasn't completely sure she wasn't one.

"Is that a housing seed?" Agetha asked. Jiow wasn't surprised it was her first question. Agetha had been involved in the colony's construction even longer than Jiow, though neither of them had any part in it now—or at least hadn't the last time Jiow had talked with her friend. Before she'd followed the urge to let the biomass take her.

Agetha looked good, as if she was twenty years younger. She hadn't developed the more obvious signs the ones who'd been out here longer had. Was that from staying inside the city, where the biomass' influence was less? There was so much they didn't know.

"It might have started out that way, but this one is different, like we're different," Jiow told her.

"How did it get here? Each seed and its location are carefully prepared. It has to be, to make certain the building grows correctly."

"We've gotten some instructions on how to treat this one. Vague, but understandable." She glanced at the one who was like cloves and cinnamon, who tended the seed. He might be the most connected to the fungal towers of any of them. Sometimes he was completely coherent. Other times, it was like he was piloted by the biomass with no real input.

"You mean you…it told you?" Agetha was staring, and Jiow could feel the other woman's sensation, like hands digging through rich dirt. Except now the dirt was gritty, the fingers uncertain. It fit her, as all the sensations fit each of them. They summed up the individual in a sensation. Not one chosen, but one lived.

"There is a direction, though we don't know what it is. Kai or Mancin will be able to explain better."

"You mentioned him before. You don't mean—Mancin Lavigne? The one who walked out into the biomass ten years ago? He must have been ninety-five then."

"The same," Jiow said. "Except he might tell you a different story." Agetha looked confused, and Jiow sighed. "Let's go meet him."

Mancin, looking as spry as ever, came out of one of the resinplast constructions under the nearest fungal tower as soon as the sentence was out of Jiow's mouth. Sometimes the connection they all shared was convenient. Other times it was simply annoying. Others looked their way, then went back to their tasks. Everyone knew what they needed to do, out here.

They made introductions, and soon were sitting in Mancin's house, talking over a cup of something that didn't quite resemble tea.

"Admin *forced* you out here?" Agetha was indignant, the hands clenching the dirt rather than rubbing it.

Mancin made a calming gesture with one hand. The feeling of sunlight on a wrinkled face settled on Jiow's mind, unflappable. "Yes. A team of Vagals dropped me off and barred the Delta gate. Everyone out here knows about it. I was angry at first—many of us were—but we've got bigger things to worry about now. I'm surprised you folks in the colony never figured it out. Seems obvious to me, now."

"Well, I can certainly believe it of those asshandles," Agetha said. "Decimating their own workforce just so they get their way. Very Admin."

"But let's talk about pleasanter things. Like the new influx of people we've had out here."

"These buildings are also new," Jiow put in. "I helped with several of them myself, and a lot of the newcomers brought in material."

"This is a new town? What did you do for the last ten years out here?" Agetha's face still looked angry, the hands vigorously rubbing dirt, but she let herself be turned to the new direction.

"Wandering," Mancin said.

"Exploring," Jiow added. "Admin says they're mapping the biomass, but I doubt they've actually covered a tenth of as much ground as we have. Their drones just fly overhead. They don't come *in* the tangle."

"You weren't bothered? Killed?" Agetha asked.

"The early ones were," Mancin said, "then about fourteen years ago or so, it just...stopped. We could walk peacefully through the biomass—at least those who—" He made several gestures, for *those who walk* and *riders*, and *friends*.

"You mean the ones the biomass has infected and controlled without them realizing it." Jiow could hear the strain in Agetha's voice, simply saying that. Hands clenched dirt into tight clods.

"And through whatever mechanism, has now loosened that control, showing its intelligence and empathy toward others," Mancin said. The wrinkled face—turned up to the warm sun—was calm in the face of Agetha's anger. "This is something no human has experienced before. We must feel out relations, now we know the biomass is aware."

"It's not only aware, it's been controlling people." Agetha leaned over the little table they sat around. "Before that, fighting us tooth and nail for this colony. The biomass is the reason the arcopolis still isn't finished. It's the reason so many Vagals and Generationals are dead. Seems like this is less of an introduction and more of letting us see exactly what it's been doing, for some reason. We don't even know *what* is aware. Is there some place these sensations are coming from?"

"I'm the first to champion authority to make my own decisions," Jiow said, "but there's also the benefits to consider. It's changed us, yes, but largely for the better." She saw Agetha's hand rise to her chest, then fall. Jiow had the same reaction most of the time. She didn't want to touch those places on her body. Places where her skin turned spongy, or lumpy, where little ribs moved independently of any clear cause. Where hyphal roots stretched out underneath her skin, leaving white lines that sometimes burned, and sometimes were like trails of ice.

"I...yes it has. And it's still disconcerting, as welcome as the changes are," Agetha said. The dirty fingers flicked through individual pieces of soil, checking, examining. "We can't prove the extent of it, because we can't trust our own senses. Beth's been running tests for weeks, months, but there's still some pieces of control in place. She can't make any progress on samples from us or any of our other *friends*. What is it *doing* to us. And why?"

"We have to expect it's planning something." Mancin shook his head. "Though I can't begin to fathom what. It's sustained those of us who lived out here for many years. The first experiments are...rough, I'll admit, but now it knows how to keep a human body alive and healthy. That we are just talking about these changes to our very bodies rather than running in panic says much about how it can affect our hormones and chemical balance."

"That's a big concern. There's a difference between 'healthy' and 'happy,'" Agetha retorted. She hooked a thumb over her shoulder. "How many more are still controlled? Have they woken up yet, or are they still wandering in the wilderness, or back in the colony? We don't even know how *much* of the colony is affected."

"We don't have answers yet," Jiow said. She had wondered about her lack of concern before, but not enough to do anything about it. She took in the other sensations in their little settlement, all going about their work. Yes, that was how Generationals—and Grounders, to a large degree—acted on a daily basis, but she still felt like the overall mood was hopeful. "But I know what I feel. We were watched before, I assume because this intelligence wanted to see how we work, and we all knew it in those moments when we broke through." She watched for the haunted look in Agetha and Mancin's eyes—the one she knew was reflected in hers. That was the part that screamed, sometimes. "Now, though, we're more like guardians, or gatekeepers, bringing forth a new way of life. You did that too, helping so many *friends* to find their way out here."

"Not by choice," Agetha said. She pushed a finger into the table, the tip turning white. "None of this was by our choice, even if we've been given the reins. I'm going back to tell Beth and Phyllis about this, even if I'm not going back to the populated radians. I know how I look now— how we all look. Beth will want to continue studying the changes, to see if she can get to an answer that's 'allowed' by the biomass."

"And will you be back?" Mancin asked calmly, though the wrinkled face was starting to turn away from the sun, an eye looking out in question. Agetha was right to stay away from populated sections. The ones out here didn't go back. The nodules at joints and the neck could be hidden, and Jiow supposed she could have colored her hair gray and put on makeup, but once the white tendrils started growing, they were obvious to anyone.

Agetha nodded, then turned to Jiow. "If I can contact Choi and Frank, do you want me to tell them?"

Jiow paused, swallowed. She'd thought about going back to the colony many times, but before the white had spread under her skin, her rider had driven her back out into the biomass. With so many things changing, she felt she had a choice. Agetha's direct question had put that into stark relief.

"I...no. Not yet. Like you say, there are still too many questions. I want to tell them I'm well, but only on my own terms, when I'm sure I'll be telling them the truth." When she was sure she was *her*.

Agetha stood. "I'm going to look around and talk to the people here, try to see what else they know. I want to look at that seed too, and see if I can tell what it's growing into. Harie might know, though telling him has its own risks." She looked from Jiow to Mancin, and Jiow could sense the fingers fidgeting, uncertain. "We've come too far with this colony to fail now, but now it's clear there's a presence here that could have pushed us aside at any time. I can't say what our path will be like. Or what Admin's reaction would be. Can you imagine?"

"Time will tell us that," Mancin said. "But one thing is clear: the biomass has given the Generationals more time to see what happens."

* * *

42 years 1 month 5 days after landing

Jane read over the message in her HUD again. And again. First the strange incursions into their network, and now this, sent anonymously?

She looked farther down the report. Christiaan had forwarded it to her, with a note they were sending it to all the other Admins five minutes later. It was a small betrayal—they should have *asked* first—but a revelation this size wouldn't stay secret for long, not now it was out. Of course, it had stayed secret, at least from her, for over a year.

Incoming.

They'd taken to sending only one or two words by text if they had to. The message only had a half-second to flash on her HUD before the door to her office banged open and Wenqing barged in. Jane could see Christiaan behind him, pushed aside, their glasses askew.

"Your secretary tried to keep me out of your office, Jane. Are we equal Admins or not in this colony?"

"You know we are, Wenqing," Jane answered. She could trade name for name if they were playing that game. "And I got this at the same time you did." Or nearly. She looked back out the doorway. "If I'm not mistaken, we'll be having more company in a few moments."

It was actually quite a clever strategy by Christiaan, now she thought of it. The glasses being out of place was a nice touch. If only one of the kids had been out there with them.

They had only given her enough extra time to understand the message, but not to call any sort of meeting. The other Admins thus supposed she kept the information from them and came *to her* to get more details. She'd have the other seven in her office like delinquent schoolchildren in a matter of moments.

Good timing, she sent back to Christiaan. They'd know what she meant.

Ahman was the next one in, followed closely by Dmitri and Rajani, all yammering about the biomass and talking over each other. Jane's office was getting crowded, and she ordered the windows to open and let in a little fresh air. Or as fresh as it got on this planet.

"I assume you're all here about the same thing," she shouted over the clamor. Murmurs died, as Maria, Alessandro, and Polunu tumbled in. She flicked the report to the display on her desk and it flared into life, looming over them, with the words EVIDENCE OF SENTIENCE looming at the top like it was a simple report on water purity levels. They'd had this scare a few times right when the colony was started, but nothing more about sentience since then. She'd thought it was dead and buried. This report popping up now was not only annoying, it was disturbing.

"Where did this come from?" Ahman asked. "Your secretary sent it to all of us, but didn't attach the routing information."

"That's because there isn't any," Jane replied. That was one part she'd delved into with her few precious extra minutes. To be fair, she'd skimmed even the summary of the report and hadn't looked at most of it. It looked like a xenobiologist's wet dream. "This information is completely anonymous, but it's obviously compiled from data used by our scientists."

"Which my Vagals declined to mention to me over the last year while they fumbled around in the dark looking for this information," Wenqing grumbled. "General Smith will be hearing about this directly."

"He knows already," Dmitri said. "I forwarded it on to ask if the Vagals knew where this came from. They don't, but also confirmed to me they had a tip last year about an anonymous information drop."

"My Vagals have never failed me like this," Wenqing continued. "Why weren't we warned about a huge topic like sentience? There is no reason not to pass on information this important."

"There is if they didn't know about it," Rajani said. "The report was delivered anonymously. The Vagals probably only knew there was an information drop, not what was in it. They handle problems with the Generationals and Grounders all the time for issues we never hear about. They likely assumed this was one of them. Maybe the originator of the information got tired of waiting and sent it in themself."

Wenqing grumbled, but quieted down.

Ahman caught Jane's eye. "Have you shared the other half of this with the rest?"

"What other half?" Alessandro said sharply. "There's more?"

Jane made eye contact with Dmitri and Rajani. They both nodded.

She gestured. "The four of us have been working on a side problem for the last two months, with little to show from it. We didn't want to share it around because it deals with a potential breach in the network."

Wenqing's head shot back up. "The data loss in the new HUDs my Vagals are complaining about?"

"The same," Ahman said. "There are places where text or video transmission has been cut or adjusted. Realtime voice seems to be less affected. Oddly, visual records are the most at risk. Dmitri and I have found no trace of where the breach is coming from, but I suspect it comes from the same place as the report, or used the vulnerability, now it's been exposed." They pointed at the display. "Someone else knew about the possibility of sentience and didn't want us to know, until now."

"Thus, they are likely connected. Which brings us to the real problem," Rajani added. "We disproved sentience years ago. Why is this coming up again, and now?"

"It's impossible to *dis*prove a hypothesis, dear Rajani," Ahman said. "You of all people should know that."

"It doesn't matter," Jane broke in. She remembered why they'd agreed to not meet physically in the same room unless necessary. Too many dominant personalities. "We must assume it's true, simply because of the method by which it's come to us. So quit arguing about it and give us options. What do we do if the biomass is sentient?"

"If *what* is sentient?" Dmitri asked. He threw out a hand toward the view from her window. The fields of fungi were visible over the wall, stretching as far as the eye could see. "A field of mushrooms? The skittering creatures that tend it? The towers? Those at least I might believe have some capability for sentience. They are big enough."

"And if some part or all is sentient, has *it* figured out how to compromise our information network?" Ahman asked. "Or was it some faction in our colony?"

"*If* we assume this report is true," Polunu said, "and that's a big 'if,' then we mustn't think of any sort of alien sentience as comparable to our own. After all, if it was, wouldn't we have seen signs of this years before?" The Animal Science Admin blinked in the unaccustomed glare of all the others staring at her. Polunu tended to keep quiet in meetings and observe.

"Naturally it will be different than us," Rajani said. "It's developed under different pressures on another planet. But we have at least a tentative definition for 'sentience.' There are certain aspects that must be satisfied, like a level of awareness of others, and of cause and effect. It's the reason the biomass was classified as non-sentient when we arrived."

"You must also differentiate between *sentience* and *self-awareness*," Ahman added, with a thin finger poised in the air. "And this leads back to Dmitri's point. *What* is it that we're saying is sentient, or self-aware? Can a fungal tower recognize itself in a mirror? Does a crawling monstrosity take care not to step on smaller creatures?"

Jane knocked a knuckle on her desk loud enough to cut Dmitri off before he could respond. She had heard enough. "If the biomass itself is responsible for the interference in our information network, I'd say that's pretty damn self-aware. But you're all missing the largest point, which is that we are surrounded." She stared around the room, meeting the other Admins' eyes. "We are outnumbered and unprepared. The only two radians which can be effectively sealed off are Alpha and Beta. Gamma is partially defensible. We need to pull essential personnel—and by that, I mean Admins, Vagals, and the progeny of both—into Alpha and Beta and be ready to start again from the ground up if things go poorly. We need to lock down our network, no matter who was the one to infiltrate it. Use the old-style HUDs if needed. Has anyone checked if they are affected?"

"We have tried, but what is left of the old HUD network is too small to adequately test," Rajani said. "We have not seen any obvious adjustment of information, but as Ahman reminded us, we cannot prove a negative."

"You are speaking of war," Wenqing said, ignoring Rajani. He should know. "We must first assess the biomass' intentions toward us before doing anything so hasty."

Jane shook her head. "We know its intentions. If there is some sense of purpose in the biomass, then it will take over this colony sooner or later. Why would it let us get a foothold in the first place? We surprised it when we landed—when we had the might of the fleet to burn it out of this colony site. Now we have nowhere else to go and I'll be damned if I go quietly!"

"Then you assume it will attack first? You think you can ascribe intentions to an alien intelligence, when we don't even understand what that intelligence is?" Rajani asked.

"I don't need to," Jane replied. "We're in the weaker position. Thus, we must go on offensive first, and strike just like we did when we landed. Keep it from coming for us with all we've got."

"And if it turns out to be peaceful?" Ahman asked.

"Then we're in a better bargaining position," Jane said. She snapped her fingers. "What was that woman with the chemical that would eat the biomass? Came in fifteen or twenty years ago. Wanted to destroy all the resinplast in the colony along with it."

"You mean Doctor Harley," Rajani said. "And she didn't want to destroy the resinplast. She was one of my best scientists, in fact, before you ordered her to the outskirts of the colony. I'm not even sure where she lives these days."

Jane waved a hand. "Not important. We confiscated her chemical, right? Can you get your team working on mass-producing it?"

"I...can," Rajani hedged. The woman never looked uncertain. Why now?

"We believe the mycophage coating the resinplast wall is an offshoot of the original concoction," Ahman said. "Doctor Harley may have passed the requirements on, or another individual may have come up with the idea independently. Regardless, the mixture was sent to us anonymously."

"Lots of anonymity these days. That's another matter we need to address soon. Your point?" Jane asked.

"Is that the biomass has already been exposed to this in some way," Ahman said.

Jane looked back to Rajani. "Can you make it more virulent?"

Rajani's lips tightened, but she gave a sharp nod. "I'll need the original vial to test with."

"Christiaan will get it to you." Jane gestured at where they darkened the doorway. She wasn't trusting that to a text over the network. "Wenqing, Alessandro, and Maria, work on getting all the important people back in the first three radians, and more urgently, getting everyone else *out*. Work face to face when you can, and by voice call if you can't. Ahman and Dmitri, get me a separate network set up. Use only what old-style HUDs you can scrounge. We have to assume they may be compromised as well. Only us and the highest Vagal command will have access to them, used sparingly."

"Won't closing off radians cause panic about the reasons?" Maria asked.

"And?" Jane replied. "What are the colonists going to do—go running out into the biomass? This is war, people, and we've already lost the first battle. Sacrifices will be made, and I don't intend this colony to fail."

* * *

42 years 1 month 10 days after landing

The last year had been a slow process for Choi. First building up a vocabulary, and second a number of questions to ask. When each iteration of a word or phrase took a day or so to print, check and validate, and they weren't even sure *what* they were talking to, much less how it was answering, things took time.

Admin hadn't been happy with the decision to stop sending resinplast seeds to Theta Radian. And by "not happy" that meant multiple messages a week to press for a date when there would be more buildings growing in Theta again. Choi had suggested they go back to constructing new buildings manually, as Alpha through Zeta had been built, but the construction crews had been largely disbanded and had already moved on to new jobs. The last time they'd built manually was six or seven years ago.

Admin was also familiar with the many delays and upsets to the colony building schedule. They'd grumbled, but had given Choi time to fix the underlying problem, and the pressure had lessened. They didn't want houses sprouting into biomass monstrosities any more than Choi did. Still, it was taking too long.

At least Frank was actively helping them now. They both carefully avoided the source of the answers and instead treated it as a complex cypher. Pose a question, get an answer, decipher it, and ask another question where hopefully the answer was a derivative of the previous one. It was not always. Nor could they always tell for certain.

Choi had tried early on to create an alphabet with which to spell out more questions, but it had failed miserably. Assigning an arbitrary meaning to a letter or symbol and building it up into words was a dismal failure, each time they tried it.

Math concepts worked a little better. The "Answerer," as they had dubbed it, had a concept of basic mathematical functions, but not any deeper levels than that. Choi was forced to program prints that contained specific numbers of things if they wanted to ask a question about quantity. Assigning the number to a symbol failed as badly as doing the same with letters. Answerer worked better with a visual collection of the things asked about, which made emotions and concepts extremely hard to convey.

The process progressed at a crawl. One thing they learned early on was that Answerer could work in tandem. With two printers running they could ask multiple questions, or even multiple parts of the same question, and the results would come as if questioning one source.

In the end, they settled on a selection of vague concepts including directions, times, seasons, and feelings. But vague questions bred vague answers, and Choi and Frank were both scientists.

"Anything new today?" Frank asked as he pushed through the lab front doors. He seemed antsy, moving even faster than normal, his fingers touching shelves and tables as he passed them.

"Nothing here, but it looks like you have something," Choi said. They stopped programming their latest question. They and Frank had been trying to pin a source down for where Answerer originated, and it wasn't going well. Choi was currently programming in scans of sections of Lida they had surveyed to print. In response, they were getting different sections of the planet. A few had lined up with landmarks and features, but most were unknown. How the answer connected to the question, Choi still hadn't figured out. An unexpected upside was they had mapped more of the planet in the past two weeks than they had been able to with drones and Vagals in three months. Choi was collating their results to hand in to Admins Xi, Novikov, and Ragab. *After* they and Frank broke the news about their communication program, whenever that would be.

"Yeah, I have something," Frank grumbled. "Admin Brighton is about to shit bricks. She's directed the Vagals to pull back to Alpha and Beta. I got a request to look into 'biological control techniques.'"

Choi raised an eyebrow. "What's that supposed to mean? We've tried every chemical possible on the biomass. It *produces* most of them itself."

"Fuck me if I know," Frank said. He opened the freezer, took out a goat's milk ice cream he'd been saving, looked at it, and stuck it back in.

When Frank was indecisive about food it was a bad sign. Choi pushed the programming field out of their HUD's vision. "What *do* you know?"

Frank whirled, a resinplast spoon in one hand. "I know we have a week to empty this lab. I don't think I was supposed to know yet, but I passed her lizard-like secretary in the hall, and they were dictating a report. Shut up as I turned a corner and thought I didn't hear them. I didn't let on. Not only are the Vagals pulling back, but from now on, no Generationals or Grounders in Alpha or Beta without special approval."

Choi's eyes panned over the lab—the experiments half done, the printer communication with Answerer, the seeds they'd printed before all this started. "But we have approval, right? They can't keep Alpha and Beta running with just Admin and Vagals. They don't have enough people."

"I think the soldiers the Vagals trained are being allowed in Alpha and Beta," Frank said, "but I don't know about anyone else."

"But...why?" Choi asked. They'd worked in Alpha for over twenty-five years. And they lived in this office more than at their tiny, sad apartment. They didn't even have their own garden. "We'll lose weeks of time by moving. Months. They know getting new seeds for building depends on us solving this problem."

"Paranoia?" Frank suggested. "There were rumors among the other scientists of errors in the HUDs, but I've never been able to track them down. They also keep referencing something that happened in a market last year, and suddenly it's big on their radar again, like someone finally got around to telling the boss."

Choi felt their face pale, and Frank looked at them sharply. "What? Do you know something about this?"

Choi's mouth worked for several seconds as they ran through scenarios in their head. Frank was actually pretty sweet once you got past his crusty exterior. But he was *absolutely* going to murder Choi.

"We talked about...the thing we aren't talking about a little over a year ago," they began. "Before this all started." They jerked their head toward the tandem printers asking questions of Answerer.

"We did...and you completely ignored my warnings to leave it alone. Now we're in this mess."

"That's...not all I did," Choi admitted. Now the words came tumbling out. Frank had never wanted to broach the subject, so it was easy to say nothing, but now the dam had broken. "I called Phillipe, set up a meeting—anonymous, I'm not stupid—and was going to show evidence of, well, sentience to Admin." They held up a hand as Frank's eyes blazed.

"That's not it. Otherwise, Admin Brighton would have been down our throats last year."

Frank paused, mouth opened. Then he frowned. "Then what—?"

"Someone *else* took the information. I only found out the full story a few months later. Phillipe didn't know what was going on except that the information and the seed I sent as a sample had been lost. I was expecting them to come to us with question about the anonymous tip they'd received, but there was nothing. I got some advice from Mother Agetha and did a little poking in the Vagal networks later, and there was a lot of chatter about another agency involved."

Frank looked confused now, as well as angry. "But that means there's more than you and them in on this bad idea."

Choi nodded. "Another reason I've been trying to communicate with Answerer. I'm hoping to find out what's happening. There's weird stuff going on in the colony. Mother Agetha and Aunt Beth have moved, and I can't find out where. They don't answer their messages, and Harie doesn't know where they are either. He keeps asking me to try again, but all I get is silence. It's not like her to simply vanish." That had been nagging in the back of Choi's mind for months. They'd gone out to Mother Agetha's house a few times, but there was no sign of her.

"She wouldn't have walked out into the biomass without telling me," Frank said, his eyes going distant. The anger in his face faded.

"I can't lose *another* mother," Choi said. "Not yet."

"She's got a lot of history you don't know," Frank told them. "She and I fell out of contact for over a decade after Phillipe left. You were busy studying for most of that time. But, with what you're saying, I think there's more to it. The sooner we crack this problem, I think, the sooner we'll find her." Always the scientist.

"Fine then." They took a deep breath. "This other agency at work—they prepared. How many people does it take to intercept a communication through Admin and set up a counter-operation?"

"And how would they know you'd talked to Phillipe to begin with?"

They both looked to the printer, happily churning out a map of the biomass. Its methods of communication were already spooky, as if Choi was being watched for the questions they programmed into the resinplast seeds. There was no real method to how Answerer replied to the questions asked. Choi programmed things to be printed and they came out different. They had tried to find the method it used to process the questions they asked, with no success. There was simply no mechanism there. It was the reason they could use multiple printers to answer questions at the same time. Sometimes Choi didn't even need to completely set the print up before it started, though they hadn't mentioned that to Frank yet.

"Will you finally accept that we need to talk about the sentience question?" Choi asked Frank.

Frank ultimately set down the resinplast spoon, unused, and pulled a chair over. "Fine. I acknowledge there is something very weird going on here, and in the colony as a whole. We've been playing with another personality that answers questions, but whether it's connected to the biomass, or another scientist playing a long prank, or a partial AI someone's programmed into the colony network—"

"You know it's not the last two," Choi broke in before Frank could convince himself nothing was wrong again. "The printers are nearly prescient. No one has the capability to watch us to the exclusion of all else. And there isn't enough capacity in the network to hold anything so sophisticated that it could act as an AI. I *wish* we had helper systems like the ones you've told me about in the fleet. That would make it much easier to figure this all out."

Frank took in a long breath, then let it out.

"I know. I've wanted to avoid this, but it seems there's no escaping it. I'll admit there is an...intelligence that is answering our questions, and it's likely not in the arcopolis."

That was more than Choi had gotten from Frank since this started. "If it's not from in the colony, then it must be something from outside of it, yes?" They waited for Frank's nod. "And the only thing we know of outside the colony is the biomass, which, I might add, you personally proved was all one individual entity, with vastly different ways of expressing growth. If it's not in the colony, there's no other choice."

"That...logic seems sound," he admitted.

"And if it's all one entity, and it is the thing that's answering our questions..." Choi trailed off, because they honestly weren't sure about the next part.

"You see why I haven't wanted to talk about this," Frank grumbled. "*What* is it? *Where?* Is it the entire planet? The thing growing on it? Both? Hell, we don't know how far down the fungal growth goes into the crust. It could *literally* be the planet itself."

"Can't be," Choi countered. "We glassed this area when the ships landed. The biomass was burned away, leaving only the native planet."

"Did we?" Frank countered. "There were still spores in the air all over the place. A week after we landed, they would have covered our entire colony. Are spores part of the intelligence? Can they be directed with intent? We know hyphal strands, mycelium, and the larger animal-type creatures can be. Where does it stop? Is this like if we had control of every single cell—no, every single *protein strand* in our bodies?"

Choi stared for a moment. Frank *had* thought about this. "You think this intelligence is decentralized?"

Frank waved a hand at the printer. "How else could it know what we're asking? Not only that but decode, and give a rational answer, even if we don't know what rationale is used. We're so far out of our league here in terms of 'intelligence,' sentient or not, we have no chance. If this thing wanted, it could have buried the colony before it was started. It could break through the mycophage on the wall, or go under or around it." He leaned forward in his chair. "This is why I don't think about sentience, Choi, because if I do, I come to the conclusion that *we are only alive because of its curiosity.*"

Choi looked back to the printers. "Then we better make certain it stays curious about us, hadn't we?"

* * *

42 years 1 month 2 weeks after landing

"New orders, Lieutenant," Noce said over the call. Anderson sighed and pulled out the cover for his booth in the Beta Market. By Noce's tone, this wasn't a small change in orders.

"What's going on, Captain?" he asked. If Noce was leaning on titles, that wasn't a good sign.

"I need you to contact the teams out in Epsilon and Zeta, get them to pull back into the barracks."

Anderson frowned. "They still have another three days on rotation. I know there hasn't been much biomass activity lately, but—"

Noce interrupted him. "I got a *handwritten* note from Admin Xi himself, countersigned by General Smith. This is not a drill. The teams are not ending their rotation early. They're coming back in permanently."

Anderson straightened, the flexible cover dangling from one hand. "Permanently, muux? Please confirm orders by message." It was standard procedure.

"No messaging allowed on this one," Noce said. "In fact, no more messaging unless voice call or face-to-face interactions are impossible. And then, single word messages are preferred."

"Any other details, then?" Anderson asked. He threw the cover over his booth, pulling the sides down.

"All true Vagals are hereby ordered to pull back to Alpha and Beta radian, while Grounder-based recruits will cover Gamma and Delta from now on. We're retrofitting one of the resinplast manufactories in Delta to house them."

Anderson's fingers twitched as Cora sent adrenaline through his system. Sounds became louder, and his vision twitched between every sharp movement made by passersby. "What's going on, Noce? If you can tell me, that is. Cora just went wild."

Noce grunted at Anderson calling his implant by name, but they were used to it, after all these years. "You're not going to like this next bit either. Beta market is considered closed for the foreseeable future as all Generationals and Grounders are to exit Alpha and Beta completely within one week."

Anderson's prosthetic hand tore through the sheet and he hastily let go. He couldn't have heard that correctly. His mind was racing. He'd have to cart the rest of his inventory back to the barracks. Would he even come back out here? "Muux, that's—"

"It's shit, yes," Noce broke in again. "But this comes down from *all* eight Admins in a *different* handwritten note, signed and dated. Two of my spouses will be turned out of my house without my family's consent." Now Anderson was concentrating properly, he could hear the tension in Noce's voice. They were probably gripping their desk hard enough to dig holes in it.

Speaking of which. Anderson looked down to his right hand and carefully loosened his fist. He'd have to patch the new hole in the cover carefully.

"Confirm orders, Lieutenant," Noce said, and Anderson straightened despite himself.

"Orders confirmed, muux. Biomass patrols to exit Epsilon and Zeta immediately, to return to Alpha barracks." That was the only part of this shitstorm that had been directed to him.

"Good luck," Noce said, and their voice was smaller, tired.

"May I...request an assignment, muux?" Anderson said. He wasn't even sure why he was asking, except Cora was already bringing down his stress levels in response. She agreed with where he wanted to go.

"What is it?"

"I want duty at the tip of Alpha and Beta radian," Anderson said. All the radians met in the middle of the arcopolis, and though Alpha and Beta had nanotanium walls surrounding them, the very tip of each radian opened up into the central square, holding the memorial to the Khonsu crash. There were gates to each segment, never actually closed before, but it was the easiest place to transfer between radians, and Anderson would be at the most advantageous position if he was needed for...he didn't know what.

"I'll put in the request, with priority, Lieutenant," Noce said. "Good idea." They paused, and Anderson could hear the calculation behind the silence.

"I'll make certain to keep you informed of any unauthorized changes, muux," Anderson offered.

"Thanks," Noce said. "And...stay alert. Something else is coming down the pipeline soon. Important is all I can say for now. It's big."

Cora shot another batch of adrenaline through his system. "I'll do that, muux."

Noce cut the call, and Anderson leaned against his booth, breathing. Cora was going wild, suddenly.

Something *else* big was coming, when Noce had already told him all the Vagals were pulling back to Alpha and Beta, like a protective cordon? Why no messaging? Noce had voice called, rather than the video calls the new HUDs were capable of. Was this related to the errors in the HUD recordings?

He let his eyes unfocus, his thoughts free. Cora was pumping heavens knew what through his system, but he could have run ten kilometers without getting winded. He felt like electricity was crawling under his skin, but still he stood, trembling, thinking, putting connections together. He'd recognized his ability to jump to correct conclusions, based on Cora's prompts. It had saved his life many times, and it was telling him to pay attention to those bits of information now.

Resorting to more secure lines of communication. Changes to the normal schedule. Falling back as if before an overwhelming enemy.

Troops arranged in order of importance—Generationals and Grounders, then trained soldiers, then Vagals, then Admins. He saw the hand of General Smith in this.

Closing Beta market—the source of commerce in the Alpha and Beta radians. It would drive people to points outside their regular haunts. Maybe areas where their positioning could be carefully controlled.

All this pointed to prior warning of a major offensive by a large threat. But there was only one threat on this planet, and it was all around them.

The biomass' pushes had always seemed random. They had never predicted what it would do next. That was believable, for an entire ecosystem surrounding them.

Except. The hand gestures, the strange actions by people passing through the market, like there was a conspiracy.

But then it disappeared. And they had seen strange errors in the HUD network. Evidence of surveillance actions, even possibly sabotage.

Like advance troops regrouping for a major action.

There was another intelligence in direct confrontation with the Admins. A clique of Generationals? Of Grounders? Did they want to take over from Admin?

But that didn't feel right. They'd had many chances before now, and the Generationals had always chosen the colony over petty power plays. So, Grounders then? But there had been no order to round them up. They were to exit Alpha and Beta, but Admin wouldn't just leave the rest of the colony to them if they were rebelling.

So not the Generationals, and not the Grounders.

Cora dragged Anderson's eyes to the top of the wall surrounding Beta Radian. Past it, he could make out the tops of the tallest fungal towers. There was only one answer.

"Oh shit. It's coming for us," Anderson said.

PART EIGHT

Negotiations

42 years 2 months after landing

The experiment immediately adjacent to the Ring of Death was progressing well. The Children who had been chosen for communication were creating hard-shelled structures similar to those created within the Ring of Death, once experimentation showed that being given increased temporal functioning was required to follow their behavioral patterns. Despite extra physiological accommodations, they still preferred this living style. Several of the mobile adjuncts who had come out to communicate many planetary rotations previous now acted as replicas of the first forms of the Children within the Ring of Death. It was curious that the flawed third forms would attempt to mimic the first forms. Perhaps such direction was an essential part of the Children's biology. Experiments could be run with those Children who were chosen to migrate farther from the Ring of Death in order to test reactions in different terrain types.

Attempts had been made to copy the local Children's method of communication to some limited effect. Any response was fragmented between several Children with little to no effort to collaborate and communicate multi-threaded thoughts. Thus, only basic instructions and relations were tried in an effort to foster enhanced communication. Deeper communications seemed possible, yet the Children's method of transmitting information was unorganized and difficult to parse.

The longer-term communications node installed at the middle of the site adjacent to the Ring of Death would bear results as it grew, though the Children adapted quickly to the environment when needed, occasionally hindering efforts. Inside the Ring of Death, the first and second forms had isolated themselves, likely in reaction to the experiment. Much attention was given to recording those actions, yet the presence of non-communicative matter surrounding the first and second forms made that observation difficult.

It would be simple to replicate the physiology of the Children, and indeed several attempts had been made—with suitable improvements—

at different locations, but the new versions did not have the same interest as the original Children. There was an essence missing in the recreations that was present here, and extra effort was made to track this ability or sense down. It was not entirely clear yet even what it was. The Children were fundamentally different from known organisms in several senses, the most being an individuality unknown before. Even the fifth and sixth forms could complete an entire lifecycle in a single entity without combining or collating intelligences. Communication was thus lacking for more complex processes.

The experiment would continue for now, until that last difference was fully understood, and a more operable replacement could be created to act as proxy. It was suggested that doing so might ease communication with the Children.

For now, any actionable information would be further studied for usefulness in the longer term. Perhaps communication would be achieved sooner, but in any case, the Children had already revealed great stores of new information. Efforts to recreate their ingenuity and reactiveness were being replicated in multiple places across the planet.

* * *

42 years 2 months 1 week after landing

Harie patrolled the outskirts of Theta Radian. When Admin first sent a message that the new buildings were on hold due to a technical malfunction, he'd redesigned his schedule around checking the ones that were already planted. That had been almost two years ago now, and he was still maintaining the growing buildings. Many of the plots that had been prepared for seeds that never arrived now lay neglected. The few remaining construction crews would have to scramble to get back up to speed whenever the seed production started again. They were losing expertise. Harie was one of the only full-time tenders still left, so he traveled the entirety of Eta and Theta a couple times a week, keeping an eye out for anything else strange happening at the same time.

Sometimes he looked for signs of Agetha. She hadn't answered any of his messages in almost a year now, and he was gradually accepting that she must have walked out into the biomass, like so many other Generationals—and a few Grounders—before her. But why now? And did she take Beth with her? It was impossible to say without more information, but the colony network was more unstable than ever. He still had a hard time contacting Choi sometimes.

Clarine had taken a break from seed tending while they waited for the scientists to fix whatever technical problem was going on. With the news that had come from Alpha and Beta—with Admin hunkering down—she'd gotten sucked into helping families that needed to relocate to the other radians. Hopefully she'd start working with him again after that all settled itself. She was a promising student, and he could see her one day teaching other Grounders how to care for the resinplast seeds in future arcopolises. If they ever got there. Agetha had complained about the slow progress from when he first started with her, and twenty years later, he was doing the same thing.

They'd get through whatever crisis Admin had dreamed up, and then get back to finishing up this city. They'd done the same thing many times before, even if this time it was taking a while to iron everything out.

He stopped at one of the farthest buildings—what would be a storefront and storage facility, some two hundred meters from the wall—and peered through the infrared display on his HUD. Then flipped the display off, took the HUD completely off his head, and ran his fingers across the surface, checking for hidden voids. Ever since Clarine had first discovered the error in his HUD, he'd checked both ways. It made his job much slower, but then, Admin wasn't yelling at him to hurry for the first time in his career. He'd caught twelve more buildings since that time where the HUD didn't pick up errors, some obvious. It wouldn't highlight the areas even if he entered them in manually. They tended to be buildings closest to the wall, and he wondered if the biomass was corrupting readings that were too near the edge of the arcopolis. Maybe it was giving off radiation now? He'd sent in several text warnings with visual accompaniment to Admin on the topic, but never heard anything back. Evidently it was beneath their notice, if the network even delivered his messages.

Harie stopped at the corner of the building, his hand still resting against the smooth surface. A motion farther out in the radian had interrupted his musings.

"Who's there?" he called, picking up his pace. The HUD errors weren't all of it. More people had passed through outskirts of Theta the past few months. He never caught any of them. Some melted away into the shadows before he could get close. Some didn't register in his HUD. This whole area reminded him of Agetha's tales of haunted sections of the ships in the fleet. Now he knew how those tales got started.

There was another flicker of movement, but when he raised his HUD to his eye, nothing. He folded it up and put it in its storage pouch.

"Maybe it's just kids?" he muttered, stumping around what would be the storefront in another eight years. He checked for spray paint, carvings, even ramps built from spare resinplast. Nothing, and no kids. Not that vandalization was a big problem in the colony. Everyone knew what they were up against here, and helped out with the construction. In fact, it was the opposite, if anything. He'd found *extra* features on some of the buildings. Unexplained growths. He'd trimmed some that were small enough, but one house had another whole room growing. Either he'd missed it on the last inspection, or the room was growing much faster than the surrounding structure.

Another shadow disappeared around the corner of a building parallel to the one he'd been checking. This was the last line of new growth. Harie stumped after them.

"I don't know what you're playing at," he called. "If you're walking out, just go. If you're messing with things, these buildings are grown to a plan. It's not like it can change halfway through. Just let them finish and then you can do all the redecorating you want after."

He peeked around a corner of the next building—a residence—and saw a bubble of growth he *knew* hadn't been there yesterday.

"What the hell?" he muttered, and checked his HUD for this building's stats. Yes, it was supposed to be a residence, with a walking path next to it going deeper into the little group of homes. Except this extrusion would grow right into the path. He stopped in front of it, poking at where it emerged from the main building. There were no seams, like he would expect if someone had added resinplast sheets. He snapped a quick ultrasound picture of the growth. The grain was perfectly normal, as if it was a part of the original plan, which he knew damn well it wasn't. Was his HUD lying again?

Something thumped against the next house over, and his head snapped up. "Who's there?"

He marked the building to come back to later and stepped around the corner.

His eyes met those of an older person...who wasn't. Harie frowned at the wrinkled face before it disappeared around a corner quicker than he thought possible. Their hair had been glossy black, like someone half their age, and though they had a wide frame, their movements were quick and sure, not with the inevitable hitch or slowness that came from age. Other things seemed wrong with their body, too, but he couldn't say what. It must have been a Generational, as the very youngest were in their mid to late fifties, but a very strange one.

Harie blinked to himself a moment before changing his HUD to infrared and taking off after the person. He skidded around the growing house and caught a glimpse of a leg turning left. He followed after, staring out across an empty field of glassed ground. This was the last expanse before the Theta wall. It had been cleaned of encroaching biomass when they started on the radian.

He scanned with the HUD's infrared function. Just the cool neutrality of resinplast, right up to the wall.

He pulled the HUD off and saw three figures calmly walking toward a house—a finished house with a garden!—right up against the Theta wall.

"Stop!" he yelled, but they didn't. He had never seen this house before. It looked homey, lived in. It had obviously new construction to one side, though the main portion had been grown from a seed. When had he missed a seed? They were all accounted for.

Harie ran forward, eating up the meters to the wall. He hadn't been right up to it in several months, so he was surprised to find several arches carved *through* the structure, next to the house. He looked back and forth, trying to decide which impossibility to confront first, when he saw one of the holes still had fresh, jagged cuts that had yet to be cleaned up. He peered through to the cleared area just past the wall, and then the biomass rising up beyond...with three figures running toward it.

"Hey! Stop!" he called again, futilely. Harie ran through the wall without thinking. He had to try to save them before they invariably stepped on some trap of the biomass. Too many people had walked out lately. Then he'd figure out what the hell was going on.

He was ten steps past the wall before he realized there had been no incursion. Some of the holes cut in the wall were weeks or even months old, but the interruption in the mycophage on the wall hadn't let the biomass through. His steps slowed as he followed sounds of three people not trying to be quiet. The biomass crunched, squished, and groaned, depending on where and what you stepped on.

"Hello? Anyone there?" Harie stopped where the biomass gained volume, mossy underfoot transitioning into thick woody trunks twisting into a thicket of fungus.

There was a path here. It wasn't obvious from the wall, but this close, it was clear. Was this where people went into the biomass, leaving the arcopolis for the last time? But if so, it was heavily frequented. Even with the increases, there weren't *that* many people leaving.

Harie sighed, took one look back at the wall, then stepped into the biomass.

The three were waiting for him around the first turn. Two were Grounders, certainly, one with a deep ochre skin tone and black hair tied back in a bun. The other was pale, with a shaved head and bright eyes. Between them was the strange Generational, darker than both Grounders, with a wide pleasant face and a round form.

"Good choice," they said. "We weren't sure we made enough noise to draw you in. I'm Phyllis. Agetha said you'd follow us. We'll take you to meet her."

* * *

42 years 2 months 1 week after landing

Choi cursed. They had lost the calipers again.

"I can't find anything in these drawers," they told Frank, who was working at another table across from them.

"You'll get used to it," Frank said. "I worked out of these buildings for a month straight with Agetha and Beth when we had to combat The Flowering and develop the mycophage. It's the best alternative to the lab in Alpha, even if it is all the way out at the edge of Zeta."

Choi still hadn't heard anything from Mother Agetha, and with the lab moving, now neither of them was in the same place. Or would she guess Frank had come here?

"But that's just it, an alternative. I'd be twenty steps ahead on the communication matrix if we were still—"

"We're not," Frank said. "And whining about it won't get us back in Alpha. I barely got in to pick up the last load of printer material and my beehives, and that's only because I knew the Vagal guarding the gate. The girls are doing their own reorientation dance to figure out where I've moved them to, and it's going to play havoc with the honey schedule since the trees out here are so much sparser than in Alpha. But if the bees can do it, you can. If you lose something out here, either recreate it out of resinplast or do without."

"Fine. I just won't measure small dimensions," Choi said. "They're probably not pertinent anyway." At least the pressure from Admin had dropped off after they moved out of Alpha. It seemed they had larger issues now than getting Theta finished on time.

Frank finally looked up from where he was fiddling with the printer, installing the new printer card. "What are you measuring?"

"I'm working on a backpropagation method to weigh the choices Answerer makes when it prints an answer. Our classification system is getting way too complex to know what Answerer wants, and coding in all the possibilities for the growth of a printed seed takes forever. If it prints a human model that's slightly bigger than another human model, how will we know which it wants? That could be a Vagal and a Grounder, or shorthand for 'growing' or 'shrinking,' or something else entirely. Instead, I'm going to send back a negative response whenever I have it make a choice. I'm trying to get it to disregard one option so we can drive toward a known decision."

"Forcing decisions toward its goal. Like the expert systems on the ships. Smart." Frank nodded. "We should have done that before now."

"We were too concerned with recording *what* the answers were more than what they meant. We've got a basic vocabulary now, even if it's not exact." Choi gestured to the wall of shapes that lined the auxiliary lab. Along with the base seed shapes, they had a repository printed, with certain shapes labeled with their best guess as to Answerer's meaning in sending it. Choi still had to program new shapes, but Answerer, through its creepy—and unknown—methods of observance, printed answers to their questions as soon as the meaning was clear. They had even arranged pre-printed objects in front of them as they programmed new questions contained in shapes, and Answerer seemed to take them into account in its responses. It had sped up their process immensely, but they were still restricted to conveying information by profile alone, instead of with words. When each question took minutes to answer, the process was laborious.

"Let's see how quickly it picks up this concept," Choi said, and set models of a Generational and a Grounder beside each other, and the models of the Admin and Vagal a little ways apart. They programmed new shapes into the printer, one like the letter "V," and another with a modification of the shape with one leg broken off. They printed both, and when they were done, set the one with a broken leg down on the table, with the full leg pointing to the Generational and Grounder pair. The broken leg pointed toward the Admin and Vagal. Then Choi entered the sign they were using for "confirmation."

One of the printers started going before they'd finished the programming sequence.

Frank looked over their work. "So, it seems like it's confirming that we are a Generational and Grounder, but how can you tell it isn't just repeating what you put in?"

"Like this." Choi turned the "V" shape over so the broken-off leg pointed the other way. They smiled when a different printer immediately started up.

It printed the sign for "refusal."

"Quick little bastard isn't it?" Frank said, after it finished. "So now we've got a selection system. If we have a big enough vocabulary, we should be able to ask it undefined questions to lead toward a conclusion."

"That's my thought as well," Choi said. "Let's start with this." They put all the Earth-based figures, including the wheat and the goat, on one side, and a bramble-like shape that resembled the biomass mat on the other. They set the broken "V" down with the branch pointing to the biomass.

A printer started up.

"But is the question which is better, or which has more volume, or which one is Answerer more interested in?" Frank asked.

"That's the beauty of the method I'm going to teach it," Choi said. "It doesn't matter what the question is, because I'm going to take away whichever component it doesn't accept."

The print turned out to be "confirmation."

"Interesting. I wonder if it's identifying itself, or saying the biomass is greater than the Earth-based organisms?" Choi snuck a look at Frank, who was frowning, then shrugged and took away the Earth-figures and selected something random from the shelf. It was the sign for "sunlight." Or maybe "sunrise," or "heat," or simply the physical representation of Lida's star. They placed it down where the Earth-based figures had been. The "V" shape still pointed toward "biomass."

There was a pause of a few seconds, then a printer started.

Refusal.

Choi took away the biomass symbol and replaced it with another symbol at random. This one meant "more." The leg still pointed toward it.

"So, sunlight, or more? That doesn't make sense," Frank said.

"Doesn't have to," Choi said.

There was a longer pause this time before the print.

Confirmation.

"So, something more instead of sunlight, the basis for all energy on this planet," Frank said.

"Let's do one more," Choi said, and randomly grabbed one of the seeds they had originally printed. They took away "sunlight" and set it down opposite "more," with the leg of the "V" pointing toward "more."

Another pause, even longer.

"I think you've confused it as much as you have me," Frank said.

Then a printer started up.

It printed a "V."

Choi took the item out of the print bed and stared at it a moment. Then they replaced the broken-legged one with the full "V," one leg pointing to "more" and the other to the seed.

"An equivalency," they said.

A printer started again. Confirmation.

"Well, I'm not sure what the hell you did, but whatever it was, this thing seems to agree with you," Frank said.

"The seeds are something more," Choi told him. "We're learning about its goals. It wants more out of the seeds."

They very deliberately took all the items off the table and placed them in a pile. They began to program a confirmation again, but the printer started before they finished.

Confirmation.

"Agreement to start a new line of questioning," Choi explained to Frank, who waved a hand in the air.

"Alright. You kids have fun asking twenty questions. I'm going to fix up a few more printers to get our question-asking ability revved up. Let me know when you find out its favorite color."

Choi ran the sequence again, and again, starting with random strings of objects, and making notes of which ones were confirmed more often. Answerer was surprisingly humble, assuming Choi's assumptions were correct. The symbol for "biomass" rarely lasted more than one or two rounds. The objects representing the humans often lasted longer, though the symbol for the biomass took precedence in a direct comparison. Symbols for the seeds stayed up the longest. Choi even did a few rounds consisting of only seeds and determined there was some classification to them, though they couldn't tell what it was. They reordered the seeds on the shelf in terms of priority, as far as they could tell.

The Generationals and Grounders were also far more favored than the other colonists, human or not.

The sequences would only end when the printers spit out a "V" for an equivalency. Any seed was equivalent with "more" or "opportunity" or "promise" or any other hopeful sort of concept. The human colonists were also equated with some of these concepts, but not others, and Grounders especially were equated with "promise." It made sense, as they were the future of the colony. Answerer seemed to realize that as well.

After several days of testing, Choi had a spreadsheet of concepts, sorted in several manners, depending on what was equivalent, less than, and greater than.

"It's like a giant logic problem," they told Frank one afternoon. "You know, where you're given clues that Muux Green likes milk on Mondays, but the Admin wears loafers in spring, and you have to find out what food everyone was eating when Mrs. White was murdered."

"Then what does it tell us?" Frank munched on a bag of dried snap peas.

"Hopefully what its ultimate goal is, if we can determine its top equivalency."

"You think it has just one?" Frank said. "If Answerer is a fully developed intelligence, then it likely has multiple things it cares about." He raised a snap pea. "Nutrition is usually a high priority, along with continued existence, and the chance to grow and reproduce."

"Let's assume for a moment that Answerer is...well, who we assume it might be." Choi ventured. Frank scrunched his nose over a snap pea, but gestured to continue. "If Answerer—or some force behind Answerer—occupies all of Lida, then it already has all the nutrients. We're not in any danger of overcoming it, so its existence isn't threatened. It reproduces all the time."

"Then Answerer might have a higher need," Frank replied. "What do you want to do when all your basic needs are met?"

Choi frowned. "Well, I like to learn, to research new things, and to discover more about the biomass. You know that. Other people like to create art, or build their bodies up, or simply relax."

"Does Answerer have those same needs, if it has a completely different concept of sustenance, time, or wellbeing?" Frank asked.

"Perhaps not, but it does seem to have the same thirst for knowledge that I have."

Frank pointed a snap pea at them. "Then you have common ground. Better get to work."

* * *

42 years 2 months 1 week after landing

Agetha sat in meditation. Phyllis had suggested it, now the three of them spent most of their time in the little camp outside the walls. There were still barriers she and the other *friends* were not allowed to cross, but they were much farther out than they had been. Agetha knew there was a part of her that raged against the artificial constraint, and was aware that it was tamped down, too. How much of her emotions had it changed? Would she ever be able to tell?

The hardest part was to get the *rider* to answer direct inquiries. She still called that part in her head—and attached to her body at various points—the *rider*. It was too disconcerting to call it *the* biomass. Innately, she knew the entire biological mat was connected, and even the same entity, however that worked. The parts that made it up must be as well. Did that mean she was—

What had she been thinking of? Meditation seemed to slip away from her the moment she thought she had it. But if she was able to completely calm her mind, she should be able to determine which parts were *her* and which parts were *other*. It was the best strategy they'd come up with so far to try to separate what exactly made *friends* what they were. It might also enable her to touch *her* emotions—how she really felt about the changes to her body, mind, and her loved ones. She wanted to reach past any interference, but caring enough to do so was like climbing a hill of sand.

Beth wasn't able to tell them exactly how the nodes functioned, or even how they communicated with the human body, or other human bodies nearby. She spent much of her time near the five fungal towers that surrounded the camo, saying they helped her think. But the same process that dampened horror or curiosity at physical changes also dulled Beth's professional curiosity. Her wife had suggested they send a communication to Generationals and Grounders working closely with Admin. Maybe they could observe the *friends* objectively. Yet it never got done. Just as Agetha had never quite got around to walking back to Harie or Choi's apartments, to tell them where she was.

There was always more work to do, or another home to raise, or chopping back growth from the base of the surrounding fungal towers. Yet Agetha thought they were happy out here. She tried to observe that feeling from every angle, to see if there was a contradiction or chink somewhere that would tell her the feeling was false. *Was* it false if it defined how she lived her life? People with depression or neurological differentiation in the colony took chemicals to regulate those parts others told them were not functioning as intended. Was her situation like that, or different? Was she being influenced negatively? Yet she could look back on her life and tell she *was* happy here. Was that real? Who could tell?

The smell of hot soup almost ready to serve entered her mind. Another distraction? No. Agetha recognized the feeling of Phyllis nearby, getting stronger. She was coming for Agetha.

With someone. There was another sensation there, but not a *friend*. She couldn't catch anything concrete, but it felt familiar. It should. She'd known him since he was little more than a child.

Agetha opened her eyes as a shadow darkened the door to the resinplast hut she was sitting in.

"Found him," Phyllis said, and Agetha's eyes darted behind the other woman as she surged to her feet.

"Harie! How are you? I haven't seen you for most of a year." She rushed to her old foreman. Had it really been that long?

Harie embraced her fondly and she patted the man's back. His eyes were wide, and he glanced nervously between the surrounding biomass and those who were living in it. Agetha couldn't blame him. She always felt as if she should be more concerned about what was happening to her.

"I take it you haven't been receiving my messages out here. Your knees look like they're doing better than mine nowadays," Harie said, with a shaky grin. "You used to always complain about them when I'd come by."

"Then you didn't get my messages either. The new network is crap." Agetha stared at Harie for a long moment, her recent thoughts still bouncing around her head. *Here* was an outside influence.

"What do you know about all this?" she waved a hand around.

"Not much, except I thought the general consensus was *not* to go out into the biomass."

Phyllis led them to a firepit dug near the center of the clearing, beneath the shadow of the five fungal towers surrounding them. They sat on benches around a warm blaze. There wasn't a big need for it, in the temperate area where the colony was located, but it made for a good meeting point.

"Agetha, I'm trying not to freak out here. Your friend Phyllis hasn't told me much. What happened to you? You just disappeared one day, and said you were moving. Did you move out here?"

Agetha gave a tight grin at his word choice. This was exactly the scenario she wanted. An outside influence. Someone who could tell them if they were all trying to breathe in deep space. She just had to explain things to him.

"There's a lot we thought was settled that seems to have changed in the past couple years," she said, trying to sneak up on her point. "Jiow's here, by the way."

Harie sat back at the abrupt statement. Surprise was often a useful way to convey information. "Choi's mother? The one who disappeared a while ago? I thought she...well..."

"Walked out into the biomass?" Agetha supplied. "She did. I thought she was dead for sure, but there are others who've been out here even longer." She could feel the blackness drawing in at the statement and switched to a less sensitive topic. She ignored Harie's perplexed expression. "How is it in the arcopolis? I've been out of touch what with the network difficulties."

That earned a quizzical look. "I'm surprised it works at all out here. When I couldn't find you at home, I sent updates. Have you been out here long enough you haven't heard? Admin Brighton closed Alpha and Beta completely to all who aren't Admin or Vagal. There have been a lot of strange things happening." He fiddled with his HUD. It had been in his hands when he arrived—one of the new resinplast versions. The Generationals hadn't received new ones, unless they were still working, but Frank had told her about them when they last spoke. When had that been? Months? A year?

"I know about some of the changes in the colony," she answered, testing the edges of the *rider*. "I wonder if Brighton finally caught wind of them too. Old bitch must have gone 'round the bend."

"People are worried. It's the biggest announcement we've seen from them in years, and right now as we're finally starting to wrap up construction on Theta? It doesn't make sense."

"I think that's because you don't have the whole story," Agetha answered. She paused to gauge a reaction. Nothing stopping her yet. She needed a way to draw him into asking the right questions, into giving her an objective response without her direct action. "Take a look around our little camp. Anything that catches your eye?" There was one feature that should. She could feel Beth watching from the other side of the clearing under a fungal tower, a sensation of braids clacking as if a head turned to focus on an object.

Harie looked away from Agetha for the first time, wary as if biomass might crawl down his throat. Then he paused, staring, and Agetha followed his gaze to the hump of dirt in the middle of the clearing. The seed had sprouted hyphal tendrils in a several-meter radius around it, growing fast in the native soil.

"That's the second unaccounted for seed I've seen today. New production has been stopped for over a year. How long has that been there?"

"A few months, so I'm told," Agetha answered. "I wasn't here when it was planted. You said there were other technical problems too?"

Harie's gaze came back to her. "Yes. The seeds had problems with the growing cycle, so I was told. But now I'm seeing errors in the new HUDs as well. Admin won't answer my messages about them. I feel like my HUD is almost willfully missing information. I swear an entire house didn't show up in its field of view."

Phyllis' smell of soup fermented a little, a sense of unease in Agetha's mind. Another point of influence? Had their *friends* had anything to do with that? What didn't they know about?

Harie was still talking. "At this rate, even before all the shit with Alpha and Beta, Theta would take another two years past the previous estimates." His eyes went back to the seed. "Was that one produced at the colony, or is it an artifact of the biomass somehow? And if it came from the arcopolis, then was it made before or after the technical issues started?"

"That's a very good question," Agetha said. "I think you need to meet a friend of mine. Juliane's spent more time out here than I have." She sent the call toward the scent of cloves and cinnamon. She couldn't pinpoint it in the ramshackle collection of huts, but he was here somewhere. She hoped this was one of his good days. They had talked about what happened at the market—that she and Phyllis and Beth had controlled him. Of course, they had all been controlled by the biomass at the time.

"How many are out here?" Harie asked. Then he shook his head. "No. That's not it. No more small talk. What's going on, Agetha? You look younger, and that's not a compliment. Like actually physically younger. I would have said you were my age and had never dealt with the transition from zero-G to gravity, if I didn't know you."

Agetha traded a look with Phyllis, who had been silent the whole time. Beth's knot of intentions was focused on the conversation as well, as she rested a hand on the rough skin of a fungal tower. They hadn't tried to talk about what was happening with someone who was not a *friend*. How far could they press when asked a direct question? Would the *rider* allow her—

"—getha? Are you alright? It looked like you blanked for a moment." Harie was saying.

Phyllis' presence was like a hot Pho soup now, with bean sprouts and fungus meat. A comforting presence, and an invitation to continue. She nodded.

"Don't worry," Agetha said, and blinked away the last of the blankness, "but you may see more of that when I try to explain. Just...let me finish first." She raised a hand to her chest, then farther up, to her neck—

She finished scratching the itch behind her ear and continued.

"The changes you've seen in me are part of what's going on in the city, with the seeds, the HUDs, I suspect—everything. There are...differences in us." She reached for new words to say and kept running up against rising blackness. Her hand made the gesture for *those who walk*, and *rider*, and *understanding*, but she could tell Harie only caught the last one, from its similarity to the signs they used in construction.

"What do you mean? I've seen those signs before. There are others in the city that do that, but they're not all construction signs. Why can't you just explain things?"

He hadn't gotten the connection yet. Agetha sighed. "We will tell you what we can. But when we start talking about the changes to us, or how you should pay attention to joints, and nec—"

Harie swam back into focus a moment later.

"It happened again, didn't it? When you were telling me directly." He was looking at her knees, then Phyllis', then her elbows. Agetha wanted to show him exactly, but she only felt at peace.

"That's right."

Harie leaned closer to her. "What about your neck? You tried to..."

She lost the rest of what he said. "Let's leave that for the moment. We won't get anywhere."

He narrowed his eyes at her, but nodded.

"You have some sort of sickness, that makes you live out here? Was it that cold you and Beth had? But it can't be contagious now, can it?"

"Not in the normal sense," Phyllis said, when Agetha couldn't.

"Is it a disease from the biomass? Some infection like the plants and animals?" Harie guessed. "Did it finally spread to humans?"

It was the obvious answer, but also so far off the mark. Agetha snorted a laugh.

"Not an infection?"

She held a hand up and he stopped. "It's definitely an infection, but you don't understand how deep that go—"

Harie was closer, concerned.

"Dammit. I'm trying to tell you. Phyllis, help out," she said. They'd found that two minds together were stronger against...were stronger. Beth pushed in as well, bolstering her with three wills.

"She's trying to say that what we have is not a simple change, like what you've seen in the plants," Phyllis said, and Agetha took over before she blanked.

"We think this took so long because there was direction. We didn't know, but a purpose—"

"Purpose not like natural evolution," Phyllis started before Agetha even finished speaking. She added the gestures for *smart* and *curiosity*.

"This is important, Harie," Agetha added. Beth's mental presence gave her strength. "Listen to what we're saying." Her hand was at her neck for some reason, fumbling. Why was she doing that?

"Look, Harie," Phyllis said, before her mouth clamped shut. When Agetha blinked—and it must have been a long blink—Phyllis' eyes were closed and she was slumped in her seat. Harie, however, was standing.

"Purpose? Direction? Are you talking about control?" he said. "Intelligence? Are you actually suggesting that something in the biomass is...aware?"

Close enough. Agetha managed a nod before the scene shifted again, Harie looking behind her to someone approaching. The smell of cloves and cinnamon.

* * *

42 years 2 months 1 week after landing

Juliane whistled as he approached the little group near his seed. It was a beautiful day to sit outside and chat. The seed felt comfortable, not needing anything at the moment. It felt happy there were more people near it. More *friends*. The towers hummed in response, around them. Most of them couldn't feel the towers and the crawling thing that surrounded their camp, protecting it from other aspects that might cause harm. This refuge was growing well. Soup, Metal, and Dirt were here now, growing ever more powerful as they tied themselves together. He felt pride, for being the one to make two of them *friends*.

The old one, like the tension before a branch broke, and the one like wrinkles in the sun, had made themselves scarce today, for some reason, as had the other older ones. He'd felt the pull from the one like hands in the dirt. She was sitting beside the other one, like good home cooking. They'd been in his mind before, but it was an even more common occurrence nowadays. He was more aware these days. He was also aware of the twinge of horror that welled up deep within him, but other parts of him soothed him, telling him not to worry. Father Alvin always said to be polite when possible. It had been many months since he'd seen either of his fathers.

The one who smelled like dinner was slumped back, but the other, Hands in Dirt, was blinking slowly with one who was not yet a *friend*. He kept glancing to the seed, and Juliane pushed down the stab of anger that one of *them* might do something to it. This one knew more about the workings of the seeds, where they came from. There was great knowledge stored in the tower network, but it was so hard to make sense of it. He got glimpses, from all times and vantage points, of this not-*friend* tending the houses in the city—those strange half-dead things made from cast-off material.

He sat down across from the group.

"Who are you?" the not-*friend* said. "Agetha said you know more about the seed. Do you know what's happening to them? What has the biomass done to them?" His hands rose and fell as he spoke, but they didn't transmit information that Juliane was used to seeing. Just hands, moving.

He nodded agreeably. He could remember being as upset as the not-*friend* before, and then how things went muddy and dark for many months. He had much more freedom these days, but sometimes his brain needed a few minutes to unravel what people meant when they spoke. It was so much easier just to respond to what was needed, or to tap the towers for information.

"It was planted here around five months ago. I am the one who tends it. It told me where to place it, and what it needs to grow. Now I wait for what it will show us."

The not-*friend* got the pinched look around his eyes that said Juliane wasn't making sense again. Had he remembered to speak in words instead of gestures? Yes, he had. Then what was the problem?

"The seed...talks to you? Is it a conduit for the biomass?"

Juliane waited, blinking. The question didn't make sense. There was no need for conduits, merely being and not being.

"How long did you have it before you came here?" the not-*friend* tried again. This one Juliane could answer.

"I carried the seed for one year and one month before its purpose was made clear. During that time, I was prepared to tend to its needs."

"You're worse than they are, in some ways. Infected." The not-*friend* stepped closer, looking into Juliane's face, his eyes, the nodules at his elbows, visible since he only wore a crude shirt, made from biomass fibers. Sometimes he forgot to put it on.

The newcomer reared back. "I can see it under your skin! Those white lines, are they...roots?" He turned back to Hands in Dirt and Soup, comparing. "They don't have it, and they don't have all the lumps you do. Is that what will happen to them?"

Juliane's hand came up protectively—

This not-*friend* was obviously concerned for his welfare.

"We are prepared for different measures, each to their needs."

"That doesn't mean a whole lot," the not-*friend* said, and looked to Hands in Dirt and Soup. "You said he could tell me more about the seed. About you."

"He has good days and bad days," Hands in Dirt said. "This would appear to be a bad one. Maybe if Phyllis, Beth, and I do a little—" There was a pause, then, "We'll try to help out."

Juliane shook his head as the three presences became stronger, just as they had on that day in the market. They were close to him. So close, but why? What was there to matter? His hand rose to his chest and fell. There was something he needed to do. His other hand rose to his neck and this time it didn't falter. It met the rubbery mass there, little sections moving of their own accord, feeding sensation and meaning to him.

Juliane felt the blank descending, but Hands in Dirt, no, *Agetha* met it with *Phyllis* and *Beth*. He could feel Kai and Mancin, farther off, adding their wills, and Jiow, who was in one of the closer buildings. They had been avoiding the not-*friend*...no, *Harie's* eyes because he would see the hyphal roots beneath their skin as well.

Control.

Containment.

Those thoughts were not his, and his head jerked to the seed—the node.

"It's growing into a new bridge between us," he told Harie. "The biomass is hard to understand, but it wants to be known. Direct communication is almost impossible. Our perspectives are too different. I don't think it comprehends separate minds well, but the seed is a promise—a way to provide meaning between us."

Juliane looked inward, fear clenching his heart as he knew all he'd left and the changes to his body. The same as he'd done many times before. Each one was a shock, until he remembered everything. He'd been clear the day he planted the seed too, when he'd first been told there was an *other* here, *the* other. Harie looked like he wanted to scream, and Juliane wasn't sure he hadn't.

"What is this?" Harie asked. His voice was soft. Juliane tried to answer but couldn't. Agetha did in his place, as if they'd had the same thought.

"It's in us deeper than any of us knew, but it could have been in us at any time. It was waiting, maybe to see what we would grow into, or maybe just so it could talk to us."

"So, it *is* sentient. And Admin was right to lock down Alpha and Beta." Harie stood up. "All the strange things that have been happening in the arcopolis. The seeds, the weird HUD errors. They were only the start. You know the Admins won't hesitate to burn this place to the ground if they knew of it, right? Half the people here they thought they already killed."

Juliane lifted a hand to the other man. The newcomer was a few years older than him, but he looked younger, after Juliane's months of wandering. Whatever the others had done to him this time created a sense of clarity that hadn't been there the other times. There was some part of him that was the same man who used to observe and catalog food inventories. The careful, practical man who missed nothing, just like Father Alvin and Father Kofus taught him.

He closed his eyes, deliberately this time, and felt for the fungal towers that surrounded them. They were like pools of data, encoded in the movement of creatures, the transmission of proteins and amino acids. They had so much stored in them, if there was a way to translate it into a version that a single mind and body could understand. He grasped at bits and pieces, and tried to fit them in with what he knew.

"You have to keep it secret," he said. "The biomass isn't in danger—it never was. But if Admin destroys this hub, they destroy the bridge. I feel like it's our only way of staying alive on this planet. Admin thinks they can simply carve their way across the land, building city after city. They're wrong. The biomass will only stand so much interference. I don't think it's fully decided what to do with us yet, but you can see its first experiments—us. We need time to figure out how to really talk with it, before Admin does something stupid. This seed is the first step."

The others, Agetha, Phyllis, and Harie, were all looking at him. He could feel the surprise from Beth, Jiow, Kai, and Mancin through their connection. Had he known all that before? He didn't think anyone had said it out loud. But then, that was his job. He was the one to tend the seed.

Harie was backing away from them, getting ready to run back to the arcopolis.

"Promise you'll give us a little more time," Juliane called.

"I'll...I'll do what I can," Harie said, "But if I found you, others will too. The next people who come out here might be Vagals."

"We will be found when it is advantageous," Juliane answered. He felt the blackness closing again. There was only so much information one mind could hold.

Harie nodded toward the seed. "That one might have been printed right around when the order came through to stop planting new ones in the colony. But it's impossible to say if it's one with growth issues. No telling what it will do." He looked back to Juliane. "I don't suppose you took it from the planting site in Theta, did you?"

Juliane shook his head. "It was provided to me when the time was right, just as I arrived here when it was the time to plant it."

Harie shook his head, then turned for final words with the one like hands in the dirt.

"Agetha, can I do anything for you? Tell anyone where you are?"

Hands in Dirt shook her head. "We're taken care of here, and I think there was a reason I hadn't contacted you. Like Juliane said, there is a bridge being built. It needs time to grow."

"Then I'll go back into the city," the not-*friend* said. "If you need anything, just leave a message at the little house by the Theta wall. I'm sure you know which one."

Juliane whistled a happy tune as the not-*friend* left. He'd been about some task, hadn't he? He got up from the circle, tipping an invisible hat to Hands in Dirt and Soup, and looked back to the seed. That was it, of course. It needed tending.

Taking Sides

42 years, 5 months after landing

The experiment immediately adjacent to the Ring of Death had progressed nearly to the next stage of growth. All the necessary parts had been selected from among the Children, though as always, the Children themselves showed signs of altering the careful planning already in place. It seemed to be their way to be contrary.

The mobile signal carriers within the Ring of Death had shown changes to the positioning of the forms within the segments. The rarer first and second forms were now exclusive to the original segments built—the ones most protected from observation and communication. However, the surrogate second forms—those of the fourth form who were copying the mechanisms of the second form—were not allowed in the protective segments. Perhaps their development had not shown the desired qualities and another attempt was to be made at filling the dwindling second form's numbers.

The third form Children who had been selected made regular attempts at communication, though ineffectively. Their messages were entirely linear in nature, progressing from one Child at a time, with encrypted meaning nearly impossible to decipher. Several higher-functioning entities had been assigned to process the communications on a regular basis to increase the store of data signals and behavioral traits. A selection of the Children had been allowed access to stored data, in hopes it would increase their transmission efficiency, yet little had been achieved there over the control group.

The Children's other attempt at communication was much more successful, although the limited entities operating the process seemed not to apply methods of learning developed by the Children outside the Ring of Death. Perhaps they were attempting to separate optimization strategies and pick the winning direction. These Children had not been adjusted, as their communication attempts would not benefit from physical modifications and might even suffer from them.

Many paths and equivalencies had been explored, with the resulting hierarchies carefully displayed. However, there was a disconnect, and the consensus was the Children did not fully grasp the communication being offered. Several motions had been made to eliminate them, yet each attempt had been negated soon after it started. The Children did not seem to notice.

All attempts at communication were suffering. Perhaps because the Children did not have a native connection to the planet. It was to be expected for an alien with a completely different mode of thought.

Still, progress was being made and perhaps in a few more dozens of planetary orbits, true communication would be achieved. If nothing came out by then, perhaps full subsummation was required, and the Children would pass on what information they still could.

* * *

42 years 5 months 2 weeks after landing

"Today is the projected date, Jane," Christiaan told her. "Rajani is reporting high enough levels of the more virulent form of the original mycophage produced by Doctor Harley."

"And Dmitri and Wenqing have the delivery system ready?" Jane asked. She flipped through reports of relocations on her handheld. She didn't like using even her original HUD, and most of the Admins had reverted to old pads kept for operations on the ship. They had never really been used, as Generationals didn't like them. Maria had found them in an old storage crate, directed by one of her assistants. It was Earth tech, and as such, untouched by the biomass.

It was surprisingly calm in Alpha radian, now the Generationals and Grounders had been moved out. Problems became easier to manage. There were fewer clashes with the Vagals, except for those manning the now-closed gates between the radians. And even there, the Generationals had drawn away. They were always so focused on work. Give them a problem to solve or a new generation to raise and they completely forgot to complain about their conditions. She wished their ancestors had been as easy to direct. She might not have had to sleep in a cryochamber for four hundred years and battle a sentient fungus on this godforsaken planet.

"Everything can be in place by shortly after lunch, Jane," Christiaan said.

Jane smiled. "Then let's get ready. I want to see this in action."

It was four hours later when all eight Admins lined up at the top of the central administration building in Alpha, overlooking the banks of mortars set on a raised platform outside the barracks. She turned to Rajani, situated slightly behind on her left.

"What spread do you anticipate? Enough to build a second arcopolis?"

"That and a comfortable margin, we hope," Rajani answered. Her salwar kameez ruffled in the slight wind. Even after forty years on this planet, she still wore some of the ones she'd brought from Earth. Mainly because there was no such thing as silkworms here, and the refined bamboo substitute was toxic to make, so they were restricted to tiny batches. "The biomass will adapt, you know. This isn't a permanent solution, or even one that will last more than twenty or thirty years."

"I'm still thinking in the long term, Rajani, if that's what you're worried about," Jane answered. "This is only the first salvo. We've got to show it we're not going to be pushovers. Then we start a conversation, once we have its attention." She gestured out to the miles of creeping and twitching biomass, dense tangles spotted with giant fungal towers that rose hundreds of meters above their surroundings. "It's not like we're actually hurting it. This is like clipping a fingernail. Less."

"Which makes me wonder how it regards our little city," Ahman put in from Jane's other side.

She frowned. "Hopefully as a power to respect if we can do that much damage while being so *little*, as you imply. If we are to carve out our cities on this planet, we must either reach an arrangement with it, or subdue it. In either scenario, we will need to clear space currently occupied by fungus. This achieves both results at once."

"Then what of our third arcopolis, and fourth?" Dmitri asked. "Rajani says the biomass will adapt. What of the next time this happens?"

"A question I've been considering for some time," Jane said. She scrolled through her handheld for messages Christiaan sent her on the Vagals setting up the mortars. They had five of eight locked in position, but were having trouble with the aiming mechanism on two and with the firing mechanism on the last. "While this is not a permanent solution, as several of you have already mentioned, it does open the door to a change in how we live. We burnt this area out with ships when we arrived. Now we're using a chemical concoction. Even with our constrained resources, we come up with new solutions. We'll take that advantage into our negotiations, when the time comes. Always start from a position of power." Or assumed power, if you didn't actually have it. It was the same way Jane had positioned herself to run this colony. The moment you acknowledged someone else had power or a position, they had it, whether the statement was truth or not. The tactic had served her while doing business with the AI megacorporations on Earth before the fleet was constructed, and with the other Admins, and it would serve to negotiate with an intelligent alien fungus, if needed.

"The teams are almost ready," Wenqing announced. Jane confirmed with Christiaan, who messaged back that one of the mortars was still having trouble aiming in tandem with the other seven. An acceptable error.

"Please, let us know when they will fire," Jane told him. She didn't want to steal Wenqing's moment. He loved military exercises.

"Be ready in fifteen seconds, fellow Admins," Wenqing announced.

Jane threw the projected area of decimation to the holotable they'd brought out with them. Rajani had created the simulation, or her teams had. They'd picked a spot far enough out from the arcopolis that the biomass should adapt and stop the mycophage before it propagated into the resinplast in the city, but just to be certain, they'd positioned the landing twelve kilometers out from the edge of Alpha Radian, where the nanotanium wall surrounding Alpha, Beta, and the steelcrete in Delta and Gamma would shield any potential overflow. The current arcopolis was about ten kilometers in diameter. From their height on the central administration building, she could see almost twice that far. Whatever happened, they would have a good start to their next arcopolis. At this close a distance, eventually the two cities would merge, but that was likely another sixty or seventy years off. She hoped they would have a network of arcopolises started by then. And a way to carve through the biomass effectively.

Wenqing raised one hand, then let it fall. There was an echoing *boom* and eight flares of light tracked from the raised platform. Jane could see figures running back to the mortars to clear them after firing.

The holotable traced the flares as they disappeared against the sky—arcing far overhead—then came back down, one slightly off from the other seven. She saw bright light against blue-gray for an instant, then the payload made contact with the biomass.

The effect was instantaneous, and the Admins huddled around the holotable, which helpfully supplied a zoomed-in view of the area from a drone high above. It was impossible to make out detail from this distance, but the melting holes in the biomass were clear enough—equidistant about a central target, save one, which was a little farther out from the others. They were growing at a tremendous rate. If Rajani's tests were any indication, the rate material was dissolving was dozens of square meters a second.

"Yes!" Alessandro had a clenched fist raised. "I've been waiting to see this shit blown away for forty years. Finally, we can move faster than a snail's pace."

"It won't travel forever, but...I have to admit, it is impressive," Rajani breathed.

Jane let a smile grow on her face as the eight holes in the biomass melted into each other, then outward, expanding in a spiraling motion away from the center. Bare rock was visible underneath now, and the holotable helpfully provided a list of statistics. A square kilometer had already been eaten away. She traced with one finger the route of a road connecting this arcopolis with that future site. It would take some effort to cleave through the tangle between here and the new clearing, but the vast effort of work was already done, and there were plenty of Grounders for that job. She hoped there would be fewer injuries and deaths now they'd shown their might to the biomass.

"Growth rate is slightly under projected," Rajani reported, typing something into the holotable keyboard, "but still progressing well. We just passed two square kilometers cleared."

Jane looked up. Even from here, she could see the natural rolling landscape of Lida in the cleared section. Their landing site had been glassed to a flat plain by the fleet's engines, so this was the first time she'd seen the natural variation of the planet. The biomass in that location had been over thirty meters in height, from the table's estimation, with fungal towers shooting up to over one hundred twenty meters tall.

An especially immense fungal tower melted, falling over with a silent crash.

"The drone reports traces of minerals in the cleared area!" Dmitri shouted. He was sorting through flowing tables of statistics on the table. It was the most excited she'd ever heard the man. "They are left from the fungal towers. If we can only get there, our production would be settled for months."

Jane could hear a faint *boom boom*, as the sound from the falling towers finally reached them.

"You see, Ahman, nothing to worry abou—" she started just as Rajani said, "Hold on. The growth rate is slowing faster."

She typed on the table for several seconds, having an invisible conversation with the banks of analysts, all on handhelds, that worked for her. "No—that can't be right. It's far under the rate we—"

"What's going on, Rajani?" Jane demanded, but she could see the melting progress of the mycophage slowing herself. The table showed a red outline—the difference between where the clearing should be and where it was.

"It's adapting far faster than we suspected, even by the most conservative models." Rajani didn't make eye contact, her pupils shifting left and right, poring over the data the table scrolled through on her side.

"We'll never forge a path to that clearing," Ahman said as the destruction slowed to a crawl. They were doing calculations on their handheld. "The resources there might as well be in space."

Jane zoomed the table in as much as she could, until the display was filled with blurry twisting shapes. She directed the drone out as far as it could go and still return on its charge. She could just see the trunk of another fungal tower, starting to corrode.

The progress stopped halfway, leaving the tower tottering, but upright.

"Goddammit!" she swore and stomped a foot. "Rajani, tell me what the hell just happened!"

The science Admin shook her head, eyes still poring over data. "It's completely outside the bounds of our trials. The cleared area is barely three-square kilometers, when we projected a minimum of eight and maximum of eleven point five. Our estimates *couldn't* be that far off. Every single test we ran confirmed the time until the biomass adjusted."

"And it was all on an isolated network? No one using a HUD that might give you false readings?"

Rajani shook her head. "No. That's why it took twice as long. We cleaned all the data thoroughly. We crosschecked with siloed analysts duplicating equations. Unless there was another source of contamination, our base observations were off by a factor of more than two."

Jane sneered down at her handheld, then at the table. This was all ship tech, on a local network. It *should* be secure, but obviously some aspect had been compromised. Would they have to go back to writing orders out and drawing diagrams by hand? She couldn't run this colony that way. She gritted her teeth as she stared across the insurmountable distance between her and the failed test. The one chance they'd had to make an impact with this mycophage.

"It's playing with us," she said. No one made a fool of her.

* * *

42 years 5 months 2 weeks after landing

Anderson cleared and cleaned the mortar, making certain all the safeties were back in place. The platform wasn't as tall as the administration complex, but he had a feed of the destruction sent to his HUD—the old, broken one—from a hovering drone. The video was grainy and skipped, as there wasn't enough bandwidth to process everything with the old HUDs, but it showed enough.

A chorus of groans went up from the Vagals as the swath the mycophage ate through the biomass slowed and stopped.

Anderson clenched his teeth on his VaporLite as Cora went wild, dumping chemicals through his system. He swiped open a call to Noce.

"You seeing this, muux?" he growled.

"Can't look away," Noce replied. "What the fuck is going on? This is nothing like what they told us. Thought we might be able to stroll over to the new clearing. It stopped kilometers away from us."

"This is just the start, muux," Anderson said. Cora had been relatively quiet the last four months—ever since he finally realized the biomass had an agenda and was actively pursuing it. Ever since Noce let the other shoe drop when the Admins cleared him to know the biomass was *sentient*. "I don't know of what, but Cora started up again, right when the mycophage died off."

Noce let out a string of curses. "You know I think you've got a chip loose for naming that thing..."

Anderson could hear the quaver in their voice. "But you also know I'm right."

Noce sighed heavily. "For whatever reason, you seem to have a better relationship with your implant than the rest of us do. What's it doing?"

"Started dumping crap in my system again," Anderson answered. "Jittery and ready for an attack. This isn't like the constant urge to observe when those strange hand signs were sweeping through the Generationals and Grounders. This is a call to get ready for an immediate response. We need to be ready, muux. On the order of hours, not days. There's going to be a change soon. We need to understand the biomass better than we do now."

"I'll pass that along." Noce's voice was flat, the way they got when saying what they had to say for the military bureaucracy. "Keep observation going along the wall at all times. I'm going to assemble a team to—"

"Muux," Anderson cut them off. He was watching the feed from the drone. There was...*something* emerging into the clearing the mycophage had made. "Take a look."

If it had been on Earth, Anderson would have said it was a mobile troop carrier. It was that large. Bigger than any vehicles they had in the colony. Bigger than half the *buildings* in the colony. It was like a giant centipede, with multiple legs all shifting at once. Another Vagal zoomed their drone feed to the maximum magnification. The legs were pointed at the tips and stabbed into the ground with every step. When they came back up, white strands drifted from them—hyphal strands of the biomass. If they were visible to the drone, they must have been the largest, rootlike variety that the biomass used to cover new ground quickly. He'd burned and cut away many of them in his years on Lida.

Noce was silent, obviously watching the same feed.

"It's seeding the ground," Anderson said. He put in a request to zoom the drone back out and watched the trail by the giant centipede. There were already small growths visible behind its length.

"Damn thing didn't even blink at the mycophage," Noce breathed.

Something clicked into place for Anderson. He was no biologist, but it was just a feeling. Cora settled at the thought, and he knew he was right.

"It was already immune," Anderson said. "With all the testing Admin Kumarisurajinder has been doing, I bet it adapted months ago. It's taking the chance to show us what it *could* do."

"That's a lot of assumptions, Lieutenant Anderson," Noce said.

"I'm a storyteller, muux," Anderson said. "And I think the biomass is too. It knows how to make an impact. This was the largest way it could get our attention and make it absolutely clear that there is an intelligence at work."

"But why not before now?" Noce asked.

"Because it has a reason to make its intelligence known," Anderson answered. "It's moving more pieces around than we can see. It has to be connected to that weird shit that went on in the markets, because otherwise I'd expect a revolt from the Generationals by now. Noce, I've got to go check this out. Admin's not got the full story and they're just going to make it worse, the more they try to bluster against this thing."

"I'm sure I didn't hear that part where you slandered our leaders and are contemplating insubordination," Noce said. "But you better act fast and get me the whole story so I can pass it along."

"Yes muux," Anderson said, and dusted off his hands. It was time to leave Alpha Radian. If the biomass was intelligent, he needed to know what it was thinking.

* * *

42 years 5 months 16 days after landing

Anderson slipped out of the gate between Alpha and Gamma. A word from Noce had ensured he had no trouble from the Vagal guards on the Alpha side, or the Grounder guards on the Gamma side.

He wasn't wearing a Vagal uniform—not that he wore one most days, especially when he sold books in Beta market. He did carry a small case with him however, which was a bold teal color. The Vagals hadn't had to break out their powersuits for years, not once the main section of wall was complete around the arcopolis. A few of the highest-ranking Grounders had them as well—gifts from the decimated ranks of the original Vagals. If he was going out into the biomass, he'd need it.

A few strides into Gamma, a squad of Grounders intercepted him, a few of them with VaporLites in their mouths. Didn't they know those were lethal for non-Vagals? They were led by an amber-skinned, middle-aged man Anderson was vaguely familiar with.

"Lieutenant Anderson? We're able to escort you anywhere you need to go in the arcopolis," the man said.

"How are things out there?" Anderson asked. He missed Beta market and the throngs of young Grounders who read his books.

"Most everything's been humming along as usual," the Grounder said, then shook his head. "Up until the last couple of days, at least. With that fucking huge crater Admin blew in the biomass, there have been some, er, complaints."

"How much have they seen of the aftermath?" Anderson asked as he walked. The Grounders fell into formation behind him.

"It's all over the network," the Grounder said. "Someone hacked into the Vagal networks as it happened, so they knew pretty much as soon as you did."

Anderson frowned as Cora spiked his alarm receptors. "Hacked into the secure, siloed network we've been using with Admin? It's supposed to be safe against any outside interference." The Grounder probably thought he meant other Grounders and the occasional Generational who wanted to stir up shit. That was the best-case scenario, now.

"Yeah, it's odd," the Grounder answered. "I've done my fair share of playing with the old HUDs. They're pretty secure, and the new ones follow the same protocols, but updated. They should be even harder to compromise. I'm still uncertain why Admin wanted to go back to the old version, but I just do what I'm told."

Perhaps the biomass wasn't only conducting its offensive in full view. Cora quieted a little, and Anderson thought that might be the right answer. Over the past two days, the huge biomass creature had sewed the cleared area with hyphal roots. The ground was covered with tiny moss-like growths, and a few stumpy columns that would likely grow into fungal towers. The science department was eagerly watching the process to understand more about how the biomass grew, while Admin raged and sent nastygrams to anyone they could blame.

He changed the subject. "Any problems at the gates, ah..."

"Corporal Phillipe, sir," the Grounder said. He straightened somehow, while walking. "I've been with the Grounder corps since the very beginning. Minor confrontations, but nothing we couldn't handle."

Anderson nodded along. The Grounders trained by Vagals could be...overly serious at times. It came from them striving to keep up to the augmented bodies of the Vagals, without the implants, the gene therapy from Earth, or any other advantage. They meant well.

"How do you feel about a little exploration, Phillipe? Just you." Anderson suggested. He hefted the folded up powersuit he was holding. The Grounder's eyes lit up.

"I have a suit of my own, sir," he volunteered. "Got it as a hand-me-down ten years ago. Should I get it?"

"Hand-me-down" was the general term for something assigned to the Grounders when there weren't enough Vagals left to use them.

"I think that might be a good idea," Anderson answered. "Meet me in Zeta Radian, near the border with Theta and the wall."

"Yes sir." Phillipe saluted and veered off at a run.

It was a couple hours later when Anderson met up with Phillipe in Zeta Radian, outside the market and near the wall. He got a few stares from Grounders and Generationals, but no one made any threatening moves. It was close enough to the unfinished Theta Radian that not as many people lived here. There were more storage buildings and warehouses. Once Theta was finished—whenever that was—this area would fill in.

Out near the wall, he could see over the radian border to a few of the organically grown structures that predominated Eta and Theta radian. They gave off a subtle feeling of *wrong* to him, as if they would grow into something monstrous. This far out, Theta was largely bare, as the starter seeds had been recalled by Admin Kumarisurajinder after defects started to crop up.

Anderson glanced around carefully enough to see no one was watching. There weren't a lot of people out here anyway. This radian wasn't protected by the stronger materials that made up the walls in Alpha and Beta Radians. He unfolded his suit and inspected it while waiting. It was one of the few things they still had from Earth, though it was old enough to need steady maintenance, mostly in the form of resinplast patches where attacks had damaged the outer shell. There was new wiring as well, using the limited amounts of copper and iron they'd found here.

Phillipe arrived already clad in his powersuit. Not much for subtlety, this one. He must have walked past many Generationals and Grounders on the way. A powersuit wasn't a common sight anymore.

He flipped the visor up as he approached, eyeing Anderson's VaporLite. At least he wasn't one of the stupid ones who used them in emulation. "Ready, sir. What are we planning on doing out here?" Anderson noted that he hadn't asked any questions before volunteering to come along. Some of the young ones had death wishes, but they usually didn't last this long if so.

"First tell me anything strange you've seen out in the larger arcopolis. Admin's had me cooped up in Alpha and Beta for the last several months. There were...concerns about some activities out here."

Phillipe hesitated. It was the first time he'd done anything except immediately answer a question or obey a request.

"Strange, sir? Like, what kind of strange? Anything in particular?"

"Yes. Anything with the Generationals or Grounders. Signals between them? Secret meetings? Odd phrases?"

"Are you suspecting they might be plotting something against Admin, sir?" Phillipe asked. His forehead pinched in worry.

"Not exactly, no," Anderson said, then sighed. "I don't know. I just...you know about the implants, right?" There wasn't widespread knowledge about what they did among Generationals and Grounders in general, but the Grounders training with the Vagals were well informed in case they had to give medical aid to a Vagal.

Phillipe nodded. "I know they give you more stamina and faster healing than the rest of us, and they keep you young like Admin."

"That's part of it," Anderson said. "They also decrease our reaction time, but the way they do that is by helping us make connections in the sensory detail we take in. I've come to rely on Cor...on my implant quite a bit. She's helped me detect threats I didn't even know were there."

"'She,' sir?" Phillipe asked. Of course, he would focus on that.

"Ah, Cora. I've named mine. She's saved my life too many times to count." Anderson waited for the general eyeroll he got from the other Vagals.

Phillipe only nodded. "Seems reasonable. Easier to refer to. But why did you tell me about that?"

"Because Cora has been insisting there's more to this biomass story than there appears. And there's *something* going on with some of the colonists. I just don't know what it is. I think I need to learn some more about the biomass. I thought I knew everything I needed after forty years, but evidently not. I'm going to look around out here and I want you to help. Anything else you've heard before now would be helpful."

Phillipe stared at him for a long time.

"Corporal?" Anderson prompted. He was about to say more when Phillipe spoke.

"I was the one who passed the message on for the pickup."

Anderson blinked at him until the words made sense. "The pickup—like the thing that happened in the market a couple years ago?"

"Then you know about it."

"I *led* that team," Anderson said. "We never got the package. One person dropped it off and someone else picked it up. Do you know what it was?"

"Information from...a friend of mine. They said it was vital to the colony's health, and I believed them."

"That's right around the time the oddities were going on. Who sent the message?" Anderson demanded.

"I'm...not at liberty to say, sir." Phillipe stood up as straight as he could. He was nearly as tall as Anderson, and Anderson was a big man.

"Anything you can tell me will help." He didn't want to make the man break an oath, but he *had* to figure out what was happening.

"They're...not in Alpha any longer," Phillipe volunteered. "Not since..."

"Since Admin moved them out," Anderson finished. "So, it was from a Grounder or Generational. Probably a Grounder if they were in Alpha. And not one who had trained with the Vagals."

Phillipe ducked his head minutely.

"Probably the one who dropped the case off. Didn't get a good look at them. I wonder if they knew at the time. Was that what they were trying to tell us?"

"Tell us what, sir?" Phillipe asked.

Anderson only paused a moment. It would be all over the arcopolis soon, if it wasn't already, and he greatly suspected the people Cora was upset about already knew. "The biomass is sentient," he said.

"Which part? Or do you mean all of it?" Phillipe asked. His eyes narrowed. "Wait, how is that possible? Everyone said it wasn't, even before I was born."

"Things have changed recently. Unclear as yet. Admin didn't drop a chemical weapon on it for no reason."

Phillipe's eyes widened, putting things together. "But then... And they... But it didn't—"

Anderson shook his head.

"And you want to go out in it? We've already attacked it."

"I sincerely doubt it thinks the same way we do, and we have to understand how if we can ever hope to communicate with it," Anderson said. "You saw how fast it reseeded that clearing? That was larger than Theta and Zeta section together. Combined with the odd occurrences around your mystery pickup, I think the biomass is already in the colony. It's *been* in the colony for years."

Phillipe's eyes flicked back and forth as he made connections that Anderson already had.

"It's not interested in conquest," he said.

"I don't think so. It could have eradicated us years ago. Which means it has a different purpose. It's been testing us, figuring out how to kill us—Vagals—and the rest of you colonists. It's watched us build a community, raise children, and grow old and die."

"Not you, sir," Phillipe interjected.

"Right. It likely knows about Vagals and Admin as well."

But Phillipe was twisting left and right, staring at the few buildings out here that had been grown instead of constructed. "It's not supposed to be able to come through the wall around the arcopolis," he said.

"Yes, because of the mycophage on the resinplast."

"The mycophage that didn't work on it."

Anderson considered that for a moment. "I know it's a different formula on the wall, but you're right. We should check on—" He started for the radian wall.

"That's not all, sir," Phillipe said, and Anderson stopped. The Grounder was still staring at the organic houses. "The programmable resinplast they were using for the houses in Eta and Theta? I can't say anything directly, but I think it's linked to that tip I got."

Anderson stared at him. The biomass was in everything. He stared at the buildings around them. Made of biomass, even before it was programmable. The scientists assured them it was completely inert. Except they'd had over a year of technical problems they weren't able to solve. No new programmable seeds had been sent out to Theta. They'd produced the new HUDs at the same time, and those were riddled with errors.

Except they weren't errors, were they? They were specific, targeted changes to vital information. Misdirection and misinformation.

The other faction he'd suspected in the market. It *was* the biomass. It had been inside the city perhaps since they first started building. It had prevented them from going out into it, killing Vagals who ventured outside. It had kept them from learning too much about it. Well, he was going to fix that.

"Come on," he growled, and jerked his helmet on. "We're going to find out what's happening out here."

The biomass had learned about them by living inside their walls. It was time to return the favor. Anderson didn't know if that was a fatal decision, but a Vagal and a Grounder were much less likely to attract attention than a whole squad. He realized Cora had been directing him to this decision for days now, and he only just realized what he'd decided to do.

Phillipe followed him to the radian wall.

* * *

42 years 5 months 16 days after landing

Choi watched the second teal powersuit traipse through Zeta Radian, from a window of the temporary laboratory situated on the edge of Theta. The Vagal who'd carried the first one was discreet at least, but it was the big one with the prosthetic hand who'd tracked them through the market when they made the drop. It was hard to disguise that hand.

The head of the second powersuit turned toward them, the visor open. Choi recoiled. Phillipe's face peered out at them. The last time

Choi had contacted him was over a year ago—after the failed market drop—to ask what had happened. Had Admin finally forced him to give Choi's information? Why had it taken them so long? Or was Phillipe not out here, with another Vagal, in powersuits, to look for Choi?

No, of course not. Phillipe was heading for the wall. Just like the other Grounders and Generationals they'd seen walk out into the biomass. Maybe like Mother Agetha and Aunt Beth had. Now even Vagals and soldiers were doing it.

"Something big is going on," they told Frank, who was asking the biomass questions today. Together, they'd devised a system of equivalences over the last few months and could ask fairly complex questions. Most of it was fed through a deep learning network attached to the main databank out here. It took most of the available space and computing power. If they'd been in Alpha still, they would have had more bandwidth to work with. But even with limited computing power, they could understand some of the answers to their questions.

"You mean past bombing the biomass?" Frank asked. Choi had asked what Answerer thought of the three-kilometer hole Admin had made with their asinine attack. As far as either of them could tell, the response was something like: "An interesting attempt. Not well considered." Choi wasn't sure how a set of equivalences between concepts could sound condescending.

"Phillipe just stomped by in a powersuit, by himself. I saw that big Vagal with the hand about an hour ago."

"Anderson?" Frank asked. Choi was surprised he knew the Vagal's name. "Nice enough fellow. Writes pretty good books."

"He writes books?" Choi asked.

"I think you're familiar with Sona V. Gore." Frank smirked.

"Wait, *that's* who Gore is?" Choi shook their head. "Doesn't matter. Why is he out here alone? Don't Vagals usually travel in packs?"

Frank finished arranging a set of items, then added a number of "V" decision trees and equivalences. Three printers started up in response. They didn't even bother programming in questions half the time. "Maybe we should go ask them."

"Won't they just turn us in to Admin?" Choi asked. "I don't remember the last time I talked to a Vagal."

"They're also on their own—unusual. And this is the first time Vagals or trained Grounders have been seen our here since Admin walled off

Alpha and Beta. Right after they used the mycophage? Not a coincidence."

Choi wasn't good at interactions with people. Frank, they knew. Mother Agetha and Aunt Beth were like family.

"I don't know what I'd ask," they protested.

Frank checked the printers. "Well, then wait five minutes and see what Answerer has to say about it."

Choi followed his gaze. "What did you ask it?"

"I think I asked it why a Vagal and a Vagal-trained Grounder were out at the Zeta wall, but whether the question was understood in context, I can't tell."

Choi joined him at the printers, entering the objects printed and the results into the deep learning network. That took another thirty minutes of computing.

Frank screwed up his face at the answer the network spit out. "Communication with first forms." That was what Answerer called Admins.

"But there aren't any Admins out here," Choi said.

"Maybe it means Anderson will report back to them. With the long-term way it thinks, I wasn't expecting a straight answer anyway." Frank turned to them. "Guess you'll have to ask them yourself."

Choi swallowed. They were a theoretical scientist, not used to going out in the field.

"You know Anderson, though, don't you?" they asked.

"And you have a connection with Phillipe. About the only one of us who does, anymore." Frank tilted his head toward the printers. "Someone's got to keep an eye on this. Go on and tell me what you find out."

Another ten minutes after that, Choi walked through the outskirts of Zeta, head swiveling as they searched for any sign of the two soldiers. They had seen which way they were heading, but that had been most of an hour ago.

When they reached the Zeta wall, they were greeted with a blank expanse of resinplast, looming over their head. There were gates in the wall, but only at certain intervals. The two likely would have headed to the nearest one, if they were going outside. It was the only reason to be wearing powersuits. Choi looked up and down the length of the wall.

They were near the Theta border here, and the wall height dipped down in the newer Radian. The nearest gate was Theta's, if they remembered correctly.

A few minutes of walking, and they crossed the Theta border. The last buildings faded away, and a flash of teal caught their attention. It wasn't a common color in the colony and stood out. They ducked behind one of the last storage units near the Zeta side of the wall and peered out. Why were they still here? They should have been long gone after an hour.

Phillipe and Anderson were both in powersuits now, with the Vagal's mechanical prosthetic un-armored. It wouldn't have fit in the suit, and there seemed to be a special ring around the connection to his arm. A custom job.

They were talking quietly, until Anderson jerked his helmet over his head, swung around to the wall, and disappeared through. Choi had thought the gate was farther out than this. Phillipe hurried after, and Choi ducked out from behind the building. Were they under orders? Why else would a precious Vagal be going out into the biomass? Both would be killed for certain.

Choi had been outside the walls a total of two times in their life, and one of those was the mandatory field trip all kids made. They had gone out with Phillipe, who loved the creepy fungal forest, all made of swinging fronds, and segmented joints, and mushrooms popping out of every surface. Choi had retreated inside as soon as they could.

The only other time was getting samples for a project for Frank, when they went out with one of Frank's elder scientist peers, Femi Sarraf. She was over ninety now, and no longer went on harrowing missions out into the nearby biomass, thank all the stars.

Choi reached where the two had been, hoping to catch up before they got too far out. The wall wasn't nanotanium here, like it was around Alpha and Beta. It was resinplast, maybe even now infected with living hyphae from the biomass. Was the whole colony doomed save Alpha and Beta? How much could the biomass really control when it showed its true capabilities?

They thought back over all the experiments they had run over the years with Frank and the other biological scientists in the arcopolis. Frank had pioneered the resinplast. It had been a rough start, with the biomass breaking through regularly. Then they had developed another masking process for the viral communication vectors the biomass used to communicate with the animal, plant, and fungal cells in its makeup. That had seemed to stop the biomass for years, until Aunt Beth created her mycophage to keep the most virulent biomass replication away from the colony.

That was over ten years ago. Even without the discovery of the biomass' intelligence, it was enough time for it to overcome the viral blockers. Had it done so, and they just didn't know?

Choi placed a hand against the surface of the wall. They didn't see a gate, but the two had passed through. While Zeta Radian was almost full-grown, up to twenty-five meters tall and several meters thick, the wall here was merely head-height. It was supposed to be protection. Was it instead a massive biomass vector, waiting to erupt into the colony?

They shivered, then looked down the length of the wall. Maybe they had misjudged where the others stood. They frowned and kept walking.

Only a little further, and they found a hole in the wall. Not grown, and not a gate, but cut, raggedly. It must have been where Phillipe and Anderson had gone through. Discussing why there was a ragged opening—rather than a gate cut with saws and fitted with steelcrete doors—could certainly have slowed them down a few minutes as they investigated.

Choi trailed a hand down the resinplast—not warm or cold, but the same temperature as the air. It was always slightly disturbing to touch.

They would have liked to examine the edges of the hole as well, but they had to make up time. It was easy to see this had been done quickly, and not with a well-kept tool. It was barely wide enough for them to squeeze through. The two in powersuits must have forced their way through.

Yes. There was a bit of teal paint on a pointed serration in the resinplast.

Choi had been avoiding the next step. Avoiding even looking at the jungle of fungal growth visible from the cutout. They deliberately looked out of the colony. There was no sign of the teal suits.

If they wanted to find Phillipe, they'd have to go out there.

They carefully stepped past the edge of the wall, one foot planted, then another. The land was cleared for fifteen meters or so outside the wall, but then mosslike growth started, transitioning to a jointed patch of hooks growing from the ground, that jangled like metal in a breeze. What even was the evolutionary need for something like that?

Looking at the biomass with the knowledge that it was sentient— some part of it, at least—only strained their awareness of the evolutionary contradictions. It was a thing of chaos, like a child left with crayons and a drawing board, or better yet, a printer and an infinite array of custom shapes. How did that square with the dry, intelligent entity that sent messages to Frank and them?

Choi walked forward hesitantly, coming up to the edge of the moss. There was still no sign of Phillipe and Anderson. Where had they gone?

Another step and they were in the jangling growths. The things brushed against their pant legs, then one crept under their hem, like it was caressing their leg. Choi squirmed, but took another step. Ahead were larger brambles, more growths, and a few smaller fungal towers.

Something moved—probably one of the mobile fungal collections that traveled untethered through the biomass. Choi tensed. They *really* didn't want to meet one. They didn't have a powersuit like the two they were following. Why were they following them anyway? It was insane.

Then the movement resolved into a figure—a human figure, also without a powersuit. As the face came into focus, Choi inhaled, one hand going to their mouth. It couldn't be.

"Mom?"

"Hello Choi," their mother said.

Their alive, whole, healthy-looking mother. They had thought about her so many times over the past six years. They had never hoped to see her again. They'd imagined it so many times, but never like this.

"It told me to wait for you here, but I thought I was mistaken. Yet here you are." She stepped forward, putting one strong hand on their cheek. It was the same hand they remembered growing up, not the cold and shaky hand in the last years before she walked out into the biomass.

Choi closed their eyes at the touch, then opened them again and stepped away. "It told you? Then you know too? But how are you receiving messages, much less decoding them?" They looked over their mother, dressing in old, shabby clothes, but sparkling and full of life beneath. There was something strange beneath her shirt. They could see the outline clearly. Their mother never had large breasts, as she wasn't a cis woman.

Jiow gave a short laugh. "Always one step ahead, aren't you? I should be asking you the same question." She squinted at Choi. "No, you're not a...well, you wouldn't be able to understand it like I could."

"Not a what?" Now Choi was confused. From amazement, to relief, to bafflement, in moments. These weren't the questions they should be asking, at a reunion like this. They hadn't been expecting this kind of emotion today. They weren't used to it.

"I want to be clear here. You mean you know the biomass"—they flung an arm out to encompass the chaos around them—"is sentient? That it has plans and desires and goals?" Now they laughed. "I can't believe *that's* the question I'm asking."

Their mother tilted her head. "It's all connected, in a way, and yes, I'm aware, Choi. I've known for several months now. It's been talking to us."

Choi wanted to follow that point—to drill down to the answer, but there was so much else. They looked closer. There were white veins under their mother's skin. An infection? Probable, if they'd been out here for months. "And you? How are you alive? Where have you been living the last six years? Why didn't you *tell* me? Did you tell Mother Agetha?"

Their mother made a strange motion, her fingers looping past her ear and halfway down her neck. Then her hand twisted, one knuckle moving in a circle. It seemed almost unconscious.

"I've been out here, believe it or not. I...don't remember all of it. It was an odd time, and I would have contacted you, if I could. Please believe me, Choi. I didn't want to leave you alone."

"If you *could*? Did someone prevent you? You're not making sense, mother." Choi could feel the anger swelling up from their stomach. Anger at not understanding.

Jiow shook her head. "It's complicated. I wouldn't say *prevented*, exactly, so much as *not aware*." Her hand rose to the center of her chest, then fell.

Choi had been examining her, seeing all the little physical changes. The strange bumps at joints and chest. It was as if their mother had been reborn, or recrafted. There was no sign of the cancer's effects.

"You're not making sense. I had to detect how the biomass was interfering with the programmable resinplast, then build a communication system from the ground up. Did something else happen out here? Is there a group that made contact before we did?"

Their mother stared off into space for a moment, as if looking for someone. Then she came back. "That's how you made contact! A clever solution. Not the one it chose, but one it's agreed to use. It thinks we're very inventive."

"Mother, you're scaring me," Choi said. They pushed away the growing apprehension. They didn't like assumptions. More often than not, they led to incorrect conclusions. "*How* can you communicate with the biomass?"

"It's hard for me to say." Jiow squirmed, her hand making more gestures seemingly without her control. "I don't mean I don't have the words, but that I literally cannot say some of it. There are still...negotiations that must be made."

"So, you *are* prevented. How?" Choi pressed. They didn't like where this was going at all.

Their mother paused, then seemed to make a decision. Or was given permission. Her hand rose to her chest again, then up to her neck. "It's a transformation, a symbiosis. We've been thinking it couldn't happen, for all the years we were here, when really it just wasn't ready yet to make contact. It hadn't made the...created the...*riders*—" She broke off, eyes twitching as if she were about to start seizing.

Choi caught her as she slumped, afraid she would fall over into the fungus, but the moment was already passing. Their mother shook her head and focused on him. "You see what I mean."

Choi was close enough to see under their mother's shoulder-length hair. To see the growth on her neck. It pulsed in time with the jangling hooks. This close, they could see the raised ridge under her shirt as well, as if a leech crawled on her skin. As soon as she was stable, they stepped away, farther than they had been before.

"What is that on you? Is it what I think? Are you infected? We didn't think it could infect humans." Choi looked off into the distance. "But it co-opted our plants, our animals. Why would we be so arrogant to assume it couldn't do the same to us?"

"*Rider*." Jiow said again. "This isn't what you think. It's nothing like any of us thought. It cured me, is rejuvenating me. Please, come with me, and I can show you how things are out here. Agetha and Beth are here too. Change is coming, whether we like it or not, but out here we can influence what will happen." Their mother extended a hand.

Choi stepped farther back. Both their mothers *and* aunt Beth? This was too much. No wonder Mother Agetha hadn't contacted him. It had gotten to her too.

They had worked with Frank too long—he was the only one Choi could still trust. The two of them knew exactly how the biomass worked—how it borrowed parts from other species to create its own monstrosities. They'd been so blind. Of course, it had done the same with humans. How many of them walked the streets of the arcopolis?

"Are you actually my mother? How can you be?" they asked. Jiow's face grew sad, exactly as her face used to when they'd disappointed her. Or it moved as a well-made facsimile might.

"I promise, I'm the same person you grew up with," Jiow said. She held her hand steady in front of her. They just had to take it. Her face pleaded with them to take it, but her body was a lie.

Choi had mapped too much of the biomass' biology to fall for this ploy. Suddenly Admin's decision of all-out war made more sense. They had to strike fast to keep more of this from happening. Their colony would never be safe if they didn't even have control of their own bodies any longer. Frank's words rang in their ears.

We are only alive because of its curiosity.

They turned and ran back into the arcopolis, ignoring Jiow's cry.

War

42 years 5 months 16 days after landing

Agetha stared at the powersuited Vagals that stood in their midst. They could have been any of the supersoldiers. Both had their visors down. Beth and Phyllis were around the circumference of the clearing, each standing beneath a different fungal tower. Beth had been having glimpses now and then of the network the fungal towers made up. It was an immense information repository.

Others peeked out of the shabby houses set up in their meager village. Juliane was in the middle of the clearing as usual, tending to the seed. He was coming back to himself, but also drifting away. He knew things he shouldn't, even with the connections they shared. His mind suffered at the load, but he'd given them information about how the biomass worked. Every day, the seed's hyphal tendrils stretched farther. The top of it had split, sending out shoots in all directions.

Harie had left written reports of Admin's progression at the house near the Theta wall the past few months. He kept them up to date with how Admin secluded themselves from the rest of the colony, but he'd warned them again and again that they would attract attention, especially after Admin had fired on the biomass. Agetha hadn't paid enough attention. No one came out to Theta Radian, and even less so past the wall. Yet here were two Vagals. She felt Kai collect others, ready to flee.

"What are you doing here?" she finally asked, not acknowledging she was asking the question while standing in the middle of the biomass.

The Vagal in front raised their visor to reveal the pale face of the man who had pulled her husband Daved from a pit—that would eventually claim her husband's life—over forty years ago. Anderson was his name. She should have known from the prosthetic hand, but several Vagals had prosthetics.

"You were in the market that day," he said. "When the biomass decided to interfere in an information exchange. Were you in on it? Are you helping the biomass against Admin?"

Agetha took a step back. She hadn't expected such a direct question and wasn't sure she knew all the answers. She vaguely remembered a confrontation in the market, but she had been sleepy then, barely aware of the urges that had controlled her. Had something been taken? She looked to Juliane. He had been there as well, hadn't he? Cloves and Cinnamon.

"Well?" Anderson prompted. "Were you there? Do you have any explanation for this place? How you're even alive out here?"

She felt Mancin approach from behind and glanced to see if he wanted to take this up, as the de-facto leader here. There was a feeling of a wrinkled face, covered by wrinkled hands, hiding from the sun.

"We're not against anyone," she said. "We're just trying to make a home somewhere where we won't be forced out again."

"But you're in the biomass," the other Vagal said. They hadn't raised their visor, and their voice was mechanized by an anonymization filter. "For how long? It's deadly out here. Everything can kill you."

Now Mancin spoke up. "I've lived in the biomass for over ten years, ever since Admin decided I was too much trouble to live in the colony. It's never harmed me." The wrinkles were back out in the sun.

"It's killed plenty of friends of mine," the visored Vagal said, stepping forward. The other one put a hand on their shoulder. Agetha guessed they weren't a true Vagal. Likely one of the hotshot Grounders who decided to emulate the soldiers. They wouldn't send two of their precious Vagals into the biomass alone. But why not a whole squad? There was something off here.

"You're not the only one who's suffered here, Corporal," Anderson said, and the other Vagal quieted. He turned back to her. "You saw what Admin did a couple days ago?"

Agetha clenched a hand. She could feel the unease through everyone else here. They'd all felt what happened as the biomass was attacked, then shown how ready it was. They'd expected alarm, after the shock of the attack went through their mind. Instead, it was something like amusement. "Yes, we're aware. Admin are fools. We could have told you that would happen. Now they've wasted that method of control, if it ever would have worked."

"That method. Then there are others?" Anderson asked. "There are ways to control the biomass? I need to learn more."

Agetha shook her head, then glanced to Mancin, Beth, Phyllis, and Kai. They were at different places in the clearing, mixed in with other *friends*. Jiow was away at the moment, though not far. She seemed…sad, but Agetha couldn't concentrate fully on her. Beth was weaving her way closer, no doubt attracted by talk of control methods. Her wife had been living that world for decades.

"Not control, no," Beth said as she got closer. "We tried with the resinplast, the mycophage, and with other methods. The biomass will always break through. But look around. There are obviously ways to live *with* it."

Anderson had spun around almost before Beth started talking, as if he knew she would speak. "Living with it assumes some form of communication with it. I'm convinced there are people in the colony already who can do that." He gave a significant look at the assembled *friends*.

"You're not here on behalf of Admin, are you?" Agetha asked. She saw just a hint of shock on Anderson's face before he controlled it. The other one wasn't as smooth, and did a double take toward Anderson, but said nothing.

To his credit, Anderson only paused a beat before answering. "Not directly, no. This is a…personal project for me, but I have the approval of my supervisor." Meaning someone would eventually come looking for him.

"And why do you suspect others can speak with the biomass? How did you decide to come here?" Mancin asked.

Anderson tapped his temple. "You Generationals know how Vagals work, right? You know about our implants?"

Mancin nodded, and so did Agetha. Most Generationals knew, and many Grounders, at least of the first generation.

Anderson continued. "I don't think most of us really use our implants to their full potential. Yes, they're good to keep you alive, but they also help make connections." He glanced around the clearing. "And Cora's been making a lot of connections lately with how the biomass has been acting."

"Cora?" Agetha asked.

"He named it," the other Vagal said.

"So, you have some ideas," Mancin said. "How does that—"

"This isn't a wild hypothesis," Anderson broke in. "I've seen things. Errors in the HUD network, communication vectors in the colony, at the market, between Generationals and Grounders. I just need the last pieces to put it all together." He raised his prosthetic hand, the first knuckle poking out of a fist as he rotated his hand around in the sign for *those who walk.*

Agetha stiffened, as did the other *friends* here. She saw Anderson see them stiffen, and a grin broke out on his face.

"You do recognize it. The vector is here too."

She could feel the others' presence pressing in on her with doubts, fears, and concerns. There were only two Vagals, and they *knew.* She struggled to separate herself from them. Her being was constrained, but she knew how to break out, now. The others might do something rash if she didn't take control.

"Yes, it's here. Though even we didn't know about it until a few months ago."

"Agetha—" Beth hissed, but she waved her wife off. Anderson was smart. She'd seen him enough while the colony was growing to know that. He was doing the calculations in his head even now.

"But some of you have been out here for *years,* like Mancin, and others I could probably name." Kai and Mancin both shot him glares at their trials being passed off without so much as an apology. "How could you not know? If you didn't know..." His eyes widened. "Not communication then. Subservience."

The other Vagal's visor was swinging in confusion between their superior and the rest.

"Not precisely," Agetha said. "It's alien. Completely so in thinking and planning. Until we made contact, there were...blank spots."

"Unpleasant time," Juliane piped up from near the seed. "Though I almost see why, now. We were spared by its unknowing cruelty. Miscommunication. The sense of self is a unique thing." He looked off into the biomass. He was a strange one.

"How?" Anderson asked. His powersuit creaked as he leaned forward. "How does it work?" Agetha hadn't seen a Vagal so interested in learning before. She hadn't had a conversation this long with one either.

"It's likely had our genetic information for some time," Beth said, "just like it's used our plants and animals. Do you know about the bees?" Now Anderson looked confused, and Beth stepped closer to Agetha. "They were infected by the biomass soon after we got here, just like the plant crops and other livestock. But they thrived. They even conquered problems we'd had with them for years in the fleet, because their bodies adjusted. All solved by the biomass. It made minor tweaks to their DNA."

"Bees aren't humans," Anderson said. The other Vagal seemed completely lost, their hands twitching by their sides as if they wanted to do something. Agetha kept an eye on the young hotblood.

"No, they aren't," Beth agreed. "And that's why it took so much longer. We think the man you rescued from the very first cave-in might have been the first subject, her husband." She gestured to Agetha and the second Vagal jerked at the gesture, jumpy. "But then Admin fed it more test subjects, like Mancin, year after year. How could it *not* learn how we worked? We don't have any native defense against it. We never have. It did us a service by not immediately changing us all. Instead, it watched us for decades."

Agetha had known parts of that, but Beth had never put it into such precise words. She'd told Beth about Daved, but now she remembered the lump growing in his chest, so like the one she had now. Her hand rose, not quite making contact.

Beth had learned much in the past months. Agetha had a strange shock of sadness at the thought. While they were being controlled, they thought almost as one. Now they had secrets again, were *able* to have secrets.

"And it's changed you all, like the bees?" Anderson asked.

Mancin stepped closer, along with Kai. "Look at us," he said. "Look very closely."

Agetha saw the moment Anderson understood what the veins of white running under their skin must be. The hard nodules at elbows, knees, and chest. She wondered when they would start growing under her skin and searched for the feeling of revulsion. It was still being suppressed in some way, and Agetha couldn't fully make herself care as she knew she should. There were still miscommunications—lots of them.

Anderson was silent for a long moment, looking between them. *Seeing* them finally as they were, why they were safe out here in the biomass. Any one of them could have walked to the new clearing Admin had made and not suffered any injury. Kai had told them the human shells that patrolled the outskirts of the clearing—the biomass' first subjects—often went far out into the crawling mass, coming back completely unharmed.

"Can you help me talk to it?" he finally asked.

"Have you lost your mind?" the other Vagal shouted, turning to their superior. "You see how it's working against us, turning our people against us. You want to volunteer for *that*?"

"I'm not even certain you *could* make contact with the biomass," Agetha spoke over the other Vagal. "We haven't seen any of your kind out here."

The second Vagal threw their hands up in the air, as if everyone was speaking gibberish. Something about the gesture triggered some memory in Agetha's head and she peered at them. A memory of frustration.

"You can't possibly know where everyone who's gone out into the biomass is," Anderson countered, also ignoring the other Vagal. "We've lost a lot of Vagals over the years. Maybe there's one who managed to find—"

"There isn't. It's never been successfully done," Mancin said. His voice was definitive. "I'm certain."

"You can't possibly be certain," the second Vagal broke in. "The whole planet is biomass. People—or their corpses—could be anywhere."

"They are not. They are in very definite places," Mancin said.

Anderson looked around the clearing. "Then everyone here is accounted for?"

"No, but we know where they are," Agetha said. She eyed the second Vagal, who still hadn't lifted their visor.

"You mean, you know where they are at all times?" Anderson asked. He waited, but no one answered. "Because your reaction times are oddly synchronized. You react almost as if you're all thinking the same thing. All connected."

"And you would still want to be part of this?" Beth asked.

That was the first question that seemed to make Anderson pause, especially as Beth didn't deny his accusation. She wondered if he understood that learning to *talk* to it meant becoming *part* of it.

"I think so. I need answers. I need to *know*. Admin will need to know, eventually," he finally said. Agetha wondered what else had gone into that decision she didn't know about.

"Lieutenant, you can't do this," the second Vagal said.

"I can and I will if I deem it necessary for the protection of the arcopolis, Corporal," Anderson said.

A surety began to rise in Agetha. She'd dealt with that sort of recalcitrance too often.

"And leave me to report that I let another true Vagal be lost on my watch, sir?"

"This isn't your responsibility, Corporal," Anderson growled.

"There's no certainty this would even work," Mancin said. "But if you wish to try..." He strode forward, one hand extended, the white veins layered in patterns on his palm.

The other Vagal jumped in front. "I'm not letting this happen, sir."

"You don't have a choice," Anderson said, trying to push the other powersuited figure away. Mancin was still advancing, unperturbed by the two augmented suits in his way. Agetha felt wrinkled skin warmed in the sun. Confident. This would be a huge step forward in bringing justice to those who had been sent out into the biomass by Admin.

The second Vagal drew a baton from their side holster, raising it to hit Anderson. Every one of his body movements was familiar, though honed by age and training.

Agetha was done with this. She wasn't going to let him control the situation a second time. The first time, when he'd left, she'd been surprised and hurt. Now she was whole.

She stomped forward. "Is that you in there, Phillipe Xenakis?"

The Vagal froze, then rotated toward her as if moved by strings.

"You can't hide from your mother. Not right in front of me."

Anderson's mouth was open in shock. Agetha guessed Cora hadn't told him about this. Mancin was grinning, as were Beth and Phyllis. They'd felt her conviction rise.

She stopped in front of the opaque visor, then reached a finger out and tapped it, right between where Phillipe's eyes should be. "You come out of there."

There was a moment's pause, then the visor slid back. Her son's face had wrinkles now. He was over forty, and she hadn't seen him since he was fifteen and a half. She let her gaze roam over his face.

"You look good, Phillipe."

"Hello mother," he said. "I hadn't planned to—"

"I know that," Agetha said. "Now let Anderson do what he wants, huh? Isn't that what you always accused me of not doing?"

Phillipe's jaw tensed and his eyes hardened, but he stepped back. He looked so much like Daved, when her husband had been concentrating hard. He wasn't the only one who was older and more experienced. She'd been foolish and overcommitted when he was a child. Now—well maybe she was still foolish, but she'd found a rock in Beth, and had more of a family in Harie, Choi, Jiow, and her old contractor crew than she ever had a chance to make with Daved and Phillipe.

Mancin continued forward, as if nothing had ever stopped his advancement. Anderson's eyes were locked on his hand, on the white veins that trailed up his arm to end at the nodule in his elbow joint.

"I haven't done this on purpose before," Mancin said. "None of us have. We weren't as aware then as we are now."

"Troubling times, but maybe a chance for a new sort of beginning. A purposeful one," Juliane put in from near the seed. No one looked at him.

Anderson hesitated for only a moment more, then reached up and took his helmet off. Phillipe tensed at the movement. "A touch at the back of the neck, right? Easy access to the nervous system. I've seen it many times in the colony, but I didn't know what it was then."

"I wasn't joking when I said this has never been successful on a Vagal," Mancin said. "It *has* been attempted."

"But never with knowledge and understanding by all participants," Anderson answered. He shifted, rolling his shoulders, and clacking his prosthetic fingers together. "Cora tells me this is right. I'll become a willing vector. We need someone who can interface between you and the rest of the colony. And I need to understand. Speaking of which, does that mean...it...will agree to this?"

Understanding.

A chill passed through all of those in the clearing who could hear the voice in their head. It was an immediate answer, and Agetha realized there had been no communication from the biomass this whole conversation. There had been the feeling of the other *friends*, but nothing direct.

It had been watching, the whole time. Waiting. If anything, the word pushed through her head had seemed...eager.

Mancin staggered at the communication, his hand drooping before he pulled himself upright again. Anderson eyed him.

"Was that what I think it was?"

"That and...instructions, of a sort," Mancin said. Agetha raised an eyebrow. The biomass had managed to communicate directly to him alone. That was also new. It usually had trouble determining where one person ended, and another began. It was learning quickly, these past few weeks.

"Are you ready?" he asked. Anderson nodded.

Mancin reached out, around the back of Anderson's head as if in a lover's embrace. The touch was not quick, but a solid minute, while both men's eyes closed.

Interest.

Change.

Difference.

Adaptation.

It was chatty today. Agetha hadn't heard so many words together from it at once. Phillipe looked as if he wanted to swat Mancin's hand away, but Agetha locked eyes with him, frowning. He frowned back. Oddly, he seemed more willing to take her direction than when he was a child. Perhaps the effect of age and experience, or training with the Vagals. Maybe that wasn't a bad idea for some of the Grounders.

Mancin opened his eyes first, pulling his hand away and stepping back. Anderson stood still, his eyes moving beneath his eyelids as if in REM sleep.

"What have you done?" Phillipe asked. "Did you change him?"

"Definitely," Mancin said. "But not necessarily in a bad way. We'll all have to wait to see what happens. This is something new, I think. Even to *it*."

Silence stretched for a minute, then two. Anderson stood still, his eyes still flicking back and forth beneath his lids.

"What am I supposed to do?" Phillipe asked, his voice rising. "I can't just go back. I was serious before. Admin will skin me alive if I come back without a true Vagal."

"This will likely take time," Agetha said.

"An hour? A day?"

"It took two weeks for us to get over it," Beth said.

"He's going to stand there for two weeks?" Phillipe's voice rose to almost where it had been when he was a teen.

"Could be. Or maybe he'll grow roots." The feeling of Beth's metal braid ties clacking sounded like laughter in Agetha's mind. She'd heard plenty of stories about Phillipe from Agetha when he was growing up. Phillipe's eyes grew bigger, until he caught the joke.

"Not funny."

"It was, a little," Agetha said.

Anderson's eyes popped open, and he walked to a low seat near Juliane and sat down.

"Sir, how are you?" Phillipe followed him, but Anderson didn't answer. Agetha could see from where she stood that his eyes were glazed. Another connection fuzzed in her mind, not quite there yet. She turned to Mancin.

"You said this had been attempted before now, unsuccessfully. What happened?"

Mancin watched Anderson while he spoke. "I don't remember entirely. This was...before."

Before they were aware of the *riders* in their heads. Before they were *allowed* to be aware.

"What do you remember?"

"There were not many opportunities for direct contact with Vagals or Admin after this had been pioneered." Mancin's hand took in the clearing and all of them. "You know the silent ones that are farther out in the biomass? That was the original result for Generationals and Grounders. Vagals did not live through the process."

Phillipe surged forward. "Then he volunteered for suicide? Who are these 'silent ones'?"

Mancin held a hand out, though Phillipe wasn't pacified. "They are the biomass' early attempts to meld with us, we think. And no, I believe your superior has as much chance of surviving as we did. I found this life after Admin drew themselves and the Vagals back to Alpha and Beta Radians, and began to shut us out. There was a change around that time. Those of us forced out here were no longer attacked and killed by the biomass, but our minds were shut away, until very recently. We have adapted. So has it."

Phillipe stood still for a long moment, staring at Anderson. "I've never been good at waiting."

Agetha carefully kept her mouth shut. Now was not the time. Beth's amusement pushed at her mind.

"But I also can't go back," Phillipe concluded. His gaze shifted to Agetha and she nearly stepped back at the intensity behind his eyes. "This does *not* change any other decisions I've made in the past."

"You're welcome to stay here," she offered.

"Your hospitality is not required," he shot back.

"Jiow is here too," Agetha said. He had always liked his foster mother better than her.

"I...she is? But Choi said..." Something went out of him, and he went to sit beside Anderson, his eyes avoiding hers.

Beth came to her side and hugged Agetha with one arm. "Things are changing faster," she said. With a Vagal in communion with the biomass as they were, there was a chance to bring Admin to a peaceful accord, despite their first attack.

"Let's hope changing for the better," Agetha answered. "For now, we wait."

* * *

42 years 6 months after landing

Choi straightened their jacket for probably the twentieth time. It had taken all of their influence with Admin Kumarisurajinder—*all* of it—to be let back into Alpha for this one meeting, and they'd had to divulge the communication system they'd built with Frank.

"This is not a good idea," Frank grumbled again from their side. He'd argued the whole way, but he'd also been instrumental in getting the science Admin to actually listen to them, and she was the most hands-on of the eight. "You're giving them exactly the power they want. The

Generationals have always been the voice of reason, using their knowledge to build the colony in spite of Admin's ambition."

"And it's not enough anymore," Choi said. "You weren't there. You didn't see her." They'd told Frank about Jiow. And Agetha and Beth, if that hadn't been a lie. They didn't think it was. They'd been so shaken when they returned to the lab in Zeta there was no way they could have avoided sharing everything.

"And you didn't think to snap a picture with your HUD or handheld?" Frank answered. "I wish I could have at least seen her again."

"It's not her," Choi insisted.

"There's no way to conclude that. Are my bees completely different now? No, they act in almost exactly the same manner. Yes, any transformation by the biomass is extremely suspect, but many are simply surface modifications."

"My mother is not a bee, Frank," Choi said.

"I still think this is extreme. No turning back," Frank said. He'd been saying similar vague and gloomy predictions the whole way from Zeta—two of their printers and a supply of raw resinplast carried with them in a case. Choi hoped Answerer recognized these two printers were now separate from the others back at the lab. Printing out only a fraction of an answer wasn't going to go over well with Admin.

The pale, skinny secretary, their hair slicked back, beckoned them forward. "Admin Brighton will meet with you now."

Choi let out a long breath and followed them.

It wasn't just Admin Brighton in the room. It was *all* the Admins. Choi stopped short at the sight, but a strategically placed thumb into their spine from Frank made them continue forward.

Admin Brighton glared at him, looking the same as the first time Choi had seen her, as a child at the opening of Beta Radian. All the Admins did. He was more used to Admin Kumarisurajinder, who they had even spoken to three times before, but it was eerie now Choi looked of an age with most people in the room. Frank, in contrast, looked much older. His gray hair and untidy beard were a stark contrast against the prepped and styled Admins.

"Well?" Admin Brighton asked them. "You've managed to get our attention with your claim of communicating with the biomass. Don't waste our time."

Choi heard Frank swallow before he stepped forward.

"We thank you for seeing us at such short notice, but given the importance of this discovery and recent events, we felt we needed to bring this information to you before it's fully researched and fine-tuned."

He gave a short summary of the discoveries they had made and how the biomass responded while Choi frantically unloaded their case of material and printers, setting them up and initiating the connection with Frank and the borrowed HUD on the administrative network. The Admins insisted Choi and Frank had to leave their new HUD outside of Alpha Radian and use the much-repaired versions that had come from the ships. The network was still faster than out in Zeta. Choi had missed this speed.

After Frank ran down, Brighton pinned him with a look.

"You've referred to 'recent events' several times now. By that, I take it our little experiment is known outside Alpha and Beta Radian?"

Choi looked up. They'd discovered how to talk to some part of the biomass and *this* was what she was asking?

"Yes ma'am," they answered. "I'm afraid it was common knowledge through the colony shortly after you ran your...test." They wouldn't have called it a test. More like flailing.

Brighton's mouth thinned and she typed something into a handheld. Choi saw her secretary stiffen where they were lurking off to the side and type something back.

"It was a very impressive display," they offered, though Frank was shooting daggers at them to shut up.

"It was not impressive," Brighton answered. "It was a shitshow. The biomass had our nuts in a vice from the beginning and we had no idea. Tell me you have some way to get an advantage over it."

They were looking for an advantage? Choi scanned the collected Admins. The thin dignified one and the short round one—Admins Ragab and Kim—seemed like they were possibly more wary about diving into this than the others, but all the Admins were stony faced.

"With all due respect, Admins," Frank said, "there is no advantage at this point. We've been struggling for forty years simply to survive. To think we have any leg up on the biomass now, after we've discovered it's not only world-spanning, but *intelligent*..." He shook his head.

Admin Brighton looked like she was about to jump over the table and strangle Frank. Choi chimed in.

"But even if we don't have an advantage, we at least have a new option: talking. That's what we're here to show you."

All eyes turned to them, and Choi resisted hunching their shoulders.

"Then by all means, do get on with it," said the one with a face like an axeblade—Admin Novikov—in a heavy Russian accent.

"Ah, yes sir," Choi said, and opened the printing application in their HUD. They ported the view to a screen in the table and the interface hovered above it so everyone could follow along. They'd brought some of the "V" equivalences and the more common models they'd printed— the humans, the animals and plants, and symbols of the colony and biomass.

"Basically, we've collected a series of questions and answers about what the intelligence—what we call 'Answerer'—thinks is important," Choi began. They arranged the group of human figures and the symbol for the colony, with the broken leg of the "V" pointing to the colony, to show the favored one was the people.

"What is all this crap?" Admin Xi said, waving a hand at the visuals. "Does it answer questions or not?"

"Ah...it does, Admin." Choi hastily skipped through several paragraphs of explanation in their head. "However, Answerer has little concept of spoken or written language. The best we've been able to do is compare how important it thinks things are compared to other things. By connecting them in phrases, we can communicate ideas."

There was silence for a moment.

"So, when you said you could talk to it, you were lying?" Admin Brighton asked.

"Communication with an alien intelligence must start from basic principles and grow to greater concepts," Frank said. "I did say it wasn't fully researched. Would you have wanted us to wait to show this to you?"

Admin Brighton pursed her lips but waved her hand for them to continue.

"Right." Choi collected themself. "Then the equivalency here is saying that the people in the colony are more important than the colony itself." They gestured at the items on the table. "I'm going to start printing our item that means 'rejection,' meaning this is false, but you'll see the biomass often starts taking over before I'm finished, with a confirmation instead..."

Choi had keyed in the answer, but the printers hadn't started yet. Maybe the biomass was confused about the change in location? They hesitantly started up the print and waited a minute while it completed.

It was the sign for "rejection," just as they'd programmed in.

"I thought you said it would print something different?" Admin Xi asked.

Choi traded a glance with Frank. What was happening? Answerer had eyes everywhere. It knew what they were going to print. Why hadn't it—

Frank's eyes widened at the same time Choi inhaled.

"We're in the Admin complex," they said at the same time.

Choi thought back. Had they used old-style HUDs to communicate with Answerer before? They must have. But the HUDs couldn't be all of it. They looked around the room. The closed, sealed, nanotanium room built from one of the ships of the fleet, meant to insulate against deep space.

They turned back to the assembled Admins. "Apologies. We forgot one key element." They turned to the side of the meeting room, where there was a balcony that looked out over Alpha Radian. They had to hope that was enough exposure.

They threw open the balcony doors. Two seconds later, both printers started at the same time. They both printed the symbol for "confirmation."

Admin Ragab had pushed away from the table and was standing with their back against the wall.

"This means the biomass can see us now? And it couldn't before?"

They had gotten to the answer first of the Admins, but as their words sunk in, the other Admins all started talking at once.

"Close those doors!" Admin Brighton shouted over them all. When Choi didn't move, her secretary pushed them aside and closed the doors firmly.

"You exposed us to it!" Admin Xi shouted. "Anything could have happened!"

Frank shook his head. "Not anything. There are many differences between what Answerer can see and what the biomass can act on."

"Communication can't proceed without Answerer being able to see what the setup is," Choi added. "It seems to communicate largely visually."

The Admins gradually all sat back down. There was a lot of typing on handhelds going on, and looks back and forth between them. Admin Xi banged a hand on the table at one point.

"Continue, with the doors open," Admin Brighton said finally. She didn't look pleased.

"Thank you, ma'am," Choi said. They crossed to the door, but paused before they opened it. "This is actually an excellent test. We'll keep the doors open just long enough to show you how it communicates, but close it afterward so we can discuss the results in private."

Now Admin Brighton looked thoughtful. "I see."

Choi worked with Frank over the next hour to show how Answerer confirmed or denied equivalencies, and worked through a little bit of the database they'd put together to answer questions. The Admins darted glances through the open balcony doors the whole time. Choi assumed they'd be sealed shut and the ship-legacy, vacuum-rated air conditioners run full blast soon after they left to clear out any...spores? Bits of fungus? Something else? They still didn't know the method of communication.

"Now you understand, what questions do you want to ask Answerer? You'll have to phrase them in a manner similar to the ones we've already asked."

"Ask if it will let us survive," Admin Brighton said immediately. Choi wondered if the Admins had discussed the question while they had displayed the printer's capabilities.

"We can do that," Frank said. It wasn't a question he or Choi had asked directly. Choi hoped it wouldn't make Answerer change tactics suddenly.

They set up a list of equivalencies—using the biomass, the colony, the human inhabitants, and the concepts of time and survival—in a complex formula, spread across a table.

Choi ran a final set of confirmation prints to make certain Answerer understood the setup, then asked the question.

One of the printers started.

Admin Xi leaned forward. "What's it doing?"

"Sometimes the answer is a straightforward confirmation or rejection," Choi answered. "That's the way we've modeled this question."

Answerer did not print a confirmation or a rejection.

"This also happens sometimes," Frank said calmly, though Choi could see he was adjusting his shirt and the back was soaked with sweat. "Answerer will print a new object if its reply is more complex."

The finished object was a human figure. Choi frowned, and compared it to the models of the four human forms the biomass had identified in the colony—Admin, Vagal, Generational, and Grounder.

"Why do you have calipers?" Admin Ragab asked, looking interested.

"Answerer is oddly exact for such a chaotic entity," Frank said. "When it prints the model for a Generational"—he held up one figure— "it's the same every time, to the millimeter. It's actually how we determined that it had classified our society."

"Which one did it print?" Admin Brighton asked. "Which one is the key to our survival here?"

Choi finished measuring.

"It's...none of them. It's a new human figure."

* * *

42 years 6 months 3 days after landing

Anderson awoke. He was sitting near the node of potential in the clearing under the fungal towers. His powersuit was gone, and he was dressed in unfamiliar clothing.

Phillipe shot to his feet nearby.

"He's up for real this time!" the Grounder shouted.

No, "awoke" was the wrong word. He remembered flashes from over the past...day? Days? Weeks? How long had it been? He felt...different. One hand drifted up to his chest unconsciously, then back down to his lap.

The feeling of dirt-stained fingers grew in his perception, as did that of a wrinkled face in the sunshine, metal beads clacking together, cooking soup, cloves and cinnamon, and a wind, frolicking in the sun. He knew what they meant, and he didn't at the same time. Cora wasn't pumping anything through his system, which is what he would have expected with erroneous sensory data floating through his head.

"Sir, can you respond to me?" Phillipe asked. Anderson told him that of course he could respond.

Except he didn't.

"Sir, can you speak now? Let me know you're fully awake this time rather than wandering around like a zombie. I managed to contact Captain Noce and tell them you weren't dead, but they want answers as soon as you're up."

Anderson focused on moving his mouth. It was as if that was a new part of his body, unfamiliar. He worked his right hand. The motors were stiff. They hadn't been serviced in the last few days. He got to his feet.

"I....can....speak." His voice was hoarse, and his hand rose again to feel his throat. "Water."

"Here. It hits everyone differently." Hands in Dirt pushed a resinplast mug of water into his prosthetic hand and he drank all of it in seconds.

No not Hands in Dirt. Why did he think that? The Generational was named Agetha Xenakis, if he remembered correctly. And she'd said Phillipe was her son, right before...

"Do you remember anything of the past two weeks, sir?" Phillipe asked. "Can we go back to Alpha now?"

"Give him a moment to get his bearings, Phillipe," Agetha chided.

Anderson saw the Grounder bristle, then control himself. If they'd been stuck here for two weeks together...

"I...wasn't asleep," he offered. There was something off. Something missing, and he couldn't place it.

"You've been operating in a semi-autonomous state," Clacking Braids said from his other side. No. Doctor Beth Harley was her name. "It's unusual. We tend to see forgetfulness and repetitive motion, but full cognitive suppression is a completely different symptom. It certainly tried out a different tack with you."

More information from before the break was coming back to him. He'd needed information and asked to talk to the biomass. He'd known there would be a change, something like what the others had gone through, but he hadn't expected two weeks to pass in what amounted to a coma.

"Did it work?" he asked Agetha.

She crossed her arms. "I don't know—you tell me. But I can feel you now. You're like...a block of nanotanium, given mobility."

"Feel—you mean..." He reached out and grasped the dirty hands and the clacking braids, gathered them up. His perception widened.

Beth and Agetha both straightened, Beth making a gesture over one ear and down her neck.

"How did you do that?" Beth asked.

"I'm not sure what I did," Anderson said, then blinked. "Cora." That was what was missing. There was no reaction to events. He felt blind.

"Your implant?" Agetha asked, then she cocked her head. "There is something different about your feeling. Like there's another layer I can't quite..."

Desire?

Anderson glanced between the others. They hadn't reacted to a voiceless word echoing in their head.

Desire.

Improve.

Communication.

"Do you hear that?" he asked, breaking into whatever Agetha had been saying.

"Is it talking to you?" Beth asked.

Anderson nodded. "I think so." He did desire communication. He felt like he was missing another limb with Cora gone.

Connection.

Anderson's knees buckled and he sat back down on the bench. He *felt* everything. Those sensations around him were just the beginning. He touched one of the immense fungal towers with new senses and watched the ferny branches waver in response. There were thirty-two humans in this camp, but there were more out in the biomass. Some were surprisingly far away from the city, nearly to the area of new growth that the first forms—Admin—had created, but they felt hollow and unresponsive. There were more in the arcopolis, all third and fourth—no, Generational and Grounder, mostly in Theta and Zeta Radians.

And the *life*. All around. It was the same life—the same entity—but expressed in variety and function like he couldn't believe.

Improvement.

Structure.

Existing.

Anderson nodded along with the thoughts. There was much more meaning, in deeper layers, but he didn't have the capacity to parse it yet. The speech wasn't all in a line like humans thought. It was folded, and rippled, and layered, spreading out fractally to convey complex intentions.

His eyes fell on the node in the center. Cloves and Cinnamon was sitting next to it, keeping it fed with nutrients and information, but the Grounder's eyes were on Anderson.

There was so much potential contained in that little pod.

Phillipe snapped fingers in front of Anderson's face, and he jumped. Cora would have alerted him, before. In hindsight, there *had* still been an alert, but buried in so many other sensations.

"Sir, do you think you can go back to Alpha?"

He got the sense Phillipe had asked him that several times.

"No. Not yet. I need to be out here for longer," he said. "You can go back if you want. You could have gone back before now."

"Sir, I can't possibly go back and tell them I left a Vagal out in the biomass," Phillipe objected. A beat. "Plus, I've had a chance to catch up with Mother Jiow and...and Mother Agetha."

Anderson programmed an identification hash and sent it to Phillipe's suit computer. "Here. Give that to Captain Noce when you get back. That will give them the answers they need for now. Tell them I'm looking into what we last spoke about, and that I'll provide updates if possible. They will provide any documentation you need to avoid trouble."

"Oh, I...I see," Phillipe said. He still seemed reluctant to leave.

Improved communication.

"Yes, it is. I look forward to talking with you further," Anderson said. The others stared at him.

"It's learning," he said. "I think it might have taken over Cora and put her to a new use. I think it learned something more about us in the exchange."

Agetha closed her eyes for a moment, and he could almost sense the thread of connection between Hands in Dirt and the biomass, like someone whispering in the next room.

"You're right," Agetha said. "It's different. It's saying more."

Anderson turned back to the node. That was the most important part.

Cloves and Cinnamon moved aside as he approached it, as easy as not stepping on your own feet when walking. It had had another two weeks to grow since he was last really aware of what was going on. There were hyphae stretching across the clearing, almost to the fungal towers at the edge, though many were hidden underground. When they fully connected, then growth would accelerate exponentially. The towers were so full of life! How had he ever thought they were anything but tiny cities to the biomass?

"The time is getting close," Cloves and Cinnamon said, and Anderson nodded along. He didn't know exactly what the node would do, but they would find out soon. "Full integration will take many of us to nurture."

Replication of innovation.

But whose innovation? Was the biomass speaking of the colonists? Multiple meanings danced out of his comprehension, tied up in those simple words.

Children bring advancement.

The Children, that was them. That was how the biomass thought of them.

Hands in Dirt and Clacking Braids were approaching. Frolicking Wind, the one that was the Grounder's second mother, wasn't far away. He could feel everyone around him as if they were constantly broadcasting their position. As if they were a well-trained squad. He was already closer with them than he had been with any of his teammates over the last forty years. Now he'd started to filter the vast amount of information Cora, or the biomass, or both, were giving him, there was so much more to know.

"Do you know what it is?" Agetha asked, looking to the node. It was the height of his knees, the top twisting and opening in strange patterns.

"Not yet," he said. Perhaps it was time for a little prodding.

Can you understand me? he asked Cora, or where Cora would be if the implant had been unchanged.

Understanding. Decoding.

He hoped that was an affirmative.

What is this seed? He looked down at the lump of resinplast embedded into the ground, just in case the biomass was taking clues from his body language as well. He thought it likely.

Replication of innovation.

That's what it had said before. At least it was consistent. He repeated the phrase to Agetha and Beth.

"Which innovation? Whose?" Beth asked. Anderson shook his head.

"Asking."

Elaborate. He assumed simpler communication might be better.

New growth. Hybrid. Residence. Adjunct.

"You look like it wasn't very clear," Agetha said. "I can feel some of what it's saying to you, but much of it is closed off. I think it might have learned about individuality from you. Before, it had trouble talking to just one person."

"It's very clear in some senses, but not in others," Anderson answered. "This node is growing, that's clear, but the biomass seems to think it's a new place to live, maybe? Or a way for us to communicate more effectively? Hard to tell with this level of communication."

"You have more than we'd had, to this point," Beth said.

Gathering.

Friends.

Riders.

Anderson cocked his head. Those words had different meanings, he suspected.

"What would 'gathering friends and riders' mean to you," he asked Agetha. She traded glances with Beth, and both of them paled.

"Is that what it's doing?" Beth asked. "Those are words we used when we couldn't speak directly about it without having a break in consciousness. Where did it pick them up?"

"Maybe from me?" Anderson suggested. "I think it learned a lot from Cora."

"Think of its capabilities," Beth said. "We've only scratched the surface of communicating with it, but now we know this world-spanning, intelligent fungus has plans that involve us."

"Does replication mean it's trying to mimic what we've done here?" Agetha asked.

Anderson nodded. That felt right. "Replication. Yes. It's trying to think how we do. It's had so much trouble before now because we're...small." He shook his head. "No, that's not the right word. And 'limited' sounds condescending. I think it's truly interested in us, but past that, its intentions are too complicated to understand. It's thinking on a global scale."

Beth looked around the clearing. "Then this place is where it's concentrating its efforts to talk with us. A place where we can come to exchange ideas."

Agetha inhaled. "I think it's building us a new city."

* * *

42 years 6 months 10 days after landing

"Are they here?" Jane asked Christiaan. It was the middle of the night, and she yawned. She had fallen into a set schedule over the years and didn't like to vary it. After the nervous little Grounder and their Generational elder had left, she'd started planning immediately.

She remembered the Generational. He'd even presented findings to her before, but he'd been so much younger then. Had so much time really passed?

"Admin Ragab will be first, as you requested, Jane," Christiaan said. They checked their handheld, now neutered of any connection to a network, for the time being. "In another thirty seconds."

It had been a game of cloak and dagger or passing notes in school. Jane wasn't sure which was more appropriate. They'd had to find *paper* first. *Real* paper, not resinplast. There were still a couple of boxes left from the fleet Christiaan had found in a closet. Her secretary/lover proved their worth once again, leaving folded notes in appropriate pockets, concealed with soothing gestures, for the appropriate person to find at a later time. Where had they first honed their techniques? Jane knew there were prestigious and secretive schools in Christiaan's past, before they became her secretary. She would have to ask someday. Carefully.

There was a quiet knock on the door. Three taps, then one. They were back to clubhouse passwords to get in.

And she wasn't in her office, either. She was in a little-used side room that had once been a botanical bay on the UGS St. Christopher. Christiaan opened the door a crack, then wider to admit Ahman's lanky frame, closing it quickly behind them.

"You got my note," Jane said.

"I did," Ahman said. They looked pale. "I thought it was a joke at first, but after that display..." They shook their head. "I can't stay long. Rebekah's condition is getting worse by the day. She gets confused if I'm not there."

Ahman's spouse, a Generational, now much older relative to Ahman. They knew what they had gotten into when they married her, and Jane wasn't about to get into that domestic situation.

She nodded. "I'll be quick then. I want to set up an untraceable communication. Just you and me." Ahman's eyes flicked to Christiaan. "And Christiaan, of course. They will act as liaison. We must have complete confidence the biomass will not overhear our discussions, and they will not be recorded anywhere. That's why I asked you not to bring any electronics." Jane paused. She should have led with that. "You didn't, did you?"

Ahman flattened a hand. "I assumed that might be the case, from the handwritten note."

They set up callsigns and drop locations, and Jane let Ahman know about the store of paper. It was only to be used for information that had to be out of their heads or hands. There would be no storage on any devices, the only communication directly from one Admin's mouth to another's.

Two hours later—enough time to assure Ahman was situated back with their spouse, tending to their health—there was another knock, this one two taps, then three.

Christiaan let Rajani in.

"You got my note," Jane began.

"I assume you want a system out of the influence of the biomass," Rajani said. "I've got ideas already. Who's in?"

"Just you and me," Jane answered. "And Christiaan, of course. They will act as liaison."

Rajani had excellent ideas—ways to combat a xenobiology that was still not well understood after forty years—just as Ahman had strategic insights neither Jane nor Christiaan had thought of.

Two hours after Rajani left, Wenqing's knock of one, then two announced he had also found Christiaan's note. After reassuring him that it was only the three of them collaborating, Jane grilled him for military strategy, unencumbered by the opinions of the other Admins. There were a few tricks the old general had that might make a dent even in the biomass' sprawling presence. Plus, he volunteered a few chemical compounds he'd been keeping up his sleeve.

An hour after Dmitri had been scheduled to appear, Jane got ready to go back to her bed.

"Three out of four isn't bad," she said. "Either Dmitri didn't find the note, which I sincerely doubt, or the former spy decided to do some sneaking on his own."

"I'll keep a special eye on him, Jane," Christiaan said.

"I know you will. We're up against a bigger opponent than I ever imagined. Making the other Admins fall in line was just a warmup. This biomass thinks showing off its power will cow me? It's made its first mistake."

"It is a world-spanning organism, Jane," Christiaan said. "There's no way to destroy it."

Jane grinned at them, showing off her teeth. "War is fought on many fronts, as you should know. The biomass' mistake wasn't showing that it was intelligent. It was showing that it wants to *talk*."

"You're going to talk it to death?" Christiaan asked.

"No. I'm going to talk it into *serving* us." Jane grabbed their lapel. "Now, let's get back to our rooms. I need a good fuck, and then I'm sleeping in tomorrow."

Christiaan followed her out, an eager smile on their face.

* * *

42 years 6 months 3 weeks after landing

Developments were proceeding quickly and satisfactorily. Multiple communication methods had borne fruit with the Children. Each new interaction created new possibilities, and it was projected that ease of information transition might even grow exponentially in coming solar rotations. Adapting to the Children's restricted data transmission was difficult, but not impossible.

While the communication by image creation was not as efficient, it might prove more effective for transmission in a wider area. There were confusing separations among the Children, even past the six forms, and the evidence that multiple communication streams had been developed independently proposed a lack of internal consistency, though those meanings could be layered for simultaneous treatment.

Higher-functioning nodes had been processing every interaction and had supplied suspected correct meanings to the Children. Much nuance was lost because of the lack of interconnectivity, though efforts to improve the Children's reception has been largely successful. Using the third form—the evolutionary dead-end of the Children—for practice and perfection of interface had led to other benefits as well: first allowing the fourth form to be connected, and now a single instance of the second form, where previous attempts had been met with failure, both of the instance and of the growing connections. It was no wonder the second form had been resistant to previous attempts. They contained an encrypted secondary level of interpretation that would be a boon to further communication.

The attempt to create a second Ring of Death had fortunately been intercepted so that the appropriate area could be targeted for reseeding as soon as possible. The motives of the first form were still unclear. It had been attempted to explain the need for full subsummation as a vector of communication, though that plea may have failed. Fortunately, other vectors had presented themselves soon after. The first forms were fortunately limited in number, and though they seemed not to have the secondary processing the second forms did, they had other biological protections and secrets.

The instance of the second form deserved more direct attention. The interface growth within the instance was similar to others that had been discovered previously, though this network seemed more fully integrated with the instance. Were the Children learning as well? The interface seemed perfectly adapted to receive the appropriate signals, with only a little augmentation, though it was largely crafted of dead matter.

An entire group of higher-functioning nodes was processing ways to replicate the interface in the forms that did not already use them. Though there were likely reasons to restrict the interface to only the protective form, restriction was only useful in some aspects. Redundancy was just as useful, especially when multiple communication aspects had been identified.

From simple physical connections, to mobile nodes, to subsummation of aspects, and now to direct communications, knowledge of the Children was growing. There was new vocabulary now. Concepts and processes that had not been encountered before. *Friends. Riders.*

Originally, the Children had been considered little more than aspects of the larger whole, as was expected, but these Children held more. It was theorized, only in the latest few solar rotations, that each entity had unique processes not contained in any other entity, allowing quick innovation and recombination, though paired with poor transmission methods.

There was so much to learn from the Children. And so much to teach them. Once the error of the second Ring of Death had been corrected, it was hoped the first form would lead sensibly, driving centuries of interaction that could be tapped for the creation of new forms and concepts.

Truly this was a time of change.

End of the Biomass Conflux, Part II
Stay tuned for the conclusion, *The Spores of Wrath*, coming soon!

ACKNOWLEDGEMENTS

This book really gets to the heart of the story I wanted to write for this trilogy. It's about change, and new beginnings, and transition of form. As with all my books, parts of what I'm interested in at the time leak through, and you can see that here with beekeeping and the machine learning elements used to communicate with the biomass.

The heart of the trilogy is also here, in the form of the market drop in chapter four. This was a writing exercise I went through about ten years ago with one of my fellow authors, Robin C.M, Duncan. You can see a similar market drop happen in his book, *The Mandroid Murders*. No writing happens in a vacuum!

I seem to have fallen into a certain naming convention for this series, which started as a joke, but then came to actually mean something. I pick my titles and chapter names with care, and they usually have a couple meanings if you look deep enough. I loved the juxtaposition of reaching out to what's close to a deity-level consciousness (even if it's just a Small God), with the simple translation of trying to talk to someone who thinks differently.

Thanks as always to wife Heather. We're approaching twenty years of marriage and I'd do it all again. She works her butt off copy-editing for Space Wizard.

Thanks also to the READ group and what's becoming my in-house editing, design, art direction, review, and merch team! Seri, Robin, Sara, Natalie, Katie, Kelly, and Reese: you're all awesome.

Finally, thank you to everyone who backed the Space Wizard Science Fantasy Year 1 Kickstarter! This trilogy will span Year 1 and Year 2, and I hope for there to be many more!

ABOUT THE AUTHOR

William C. Tracy writes and publishes queer science fiction and fantasy through his indie press Space Wizard Science Fantasy (spacewizardsciencefantasy.com).

His largest work is the Dissolutionverse: a space opera with music-based magic, including ten books and an RPG. He also has a standalone epic fantasy with seasonal fruit-based magic through a LGBTQ+ small press.

William is a North Carolina native and a lifelong fan of science fiction and fantasy. He has a master's in mechanical engineering and has both designed and operated heavy construction machinery. He has also trained in Wado-Ryu karate since 2003 and runs his own dojo in Raleigh NC. He is an avid video and board gamer, a beekeeper, a reader, and of course, a writer.

You can get a free Dissolutionverse novelette by signing up for William's mailing list at http://williamctracy.com

Follow him on Twitter at https://twitter.com/wctracy or on Mastodon at https://wandering.shop/@wctracy for writing updates, cat and bee pictures, and thoughts on martial arts.

Please take a moment to review this book at your favorite retailer's website, Goodreads, or simply tell your friends!